The
Search
For
Mister Lloyd

Griff Rowland

The right of Griff Rowland to be identified as the
Author of the Work has been asserted by him in accordance
with the Copyright, Designs and Patents Act 1988.

Copyright © Griff Rowland 2015

First published in Great Britain in 2015

Published by
Candy Jar Books
Mackintosh House, 136 Newport Road
Cardiff, CF24 1DJ
www.candyjarbooks.co.uk

A catalogue record of this book is available
from the British Library

ISBN: 978-0-9931191-7-0

Printed and bound in the UK by
CPI Anthony Rowe, Chippenham, Wiltshire, UK

i Gwynn a Beryl

CHAPTER ONE

Graceland, Bangor

Hello. Hi. I don't suppose you've seen Mister Lloyd? No. Course not. Silly me. Blue-bar wings? Green ring on his foot? No? OK. Thanks anyway. Excuse me. Hi. Sorry to disturb an' all that. My pigeon's gone missing. Seen him waddling about? Answers to the name of Mister Lloyd. Light grey feathers, dark underbelly. Racing type. Green ring, right foot. No? Yes? What? You think so? In which direction? Oh. Thank you, thank you so much.

I wish it began like this, but it doesn't.

Graceland was where he was kept. I'm standing there now, looking at the view from the loft and admiring the still water of the Menai Strait. Its perfect stillness, mirroring the trees that billow and burst onto the far bank, is deceptive; a delicate balance reached as two opposing tides collide. I think it is a little like me on that day when he never showed up, my stomach heaving and lurching but no one able to tell.

The sun had reached the horizon and, squinting through the spider-webbed window, I traced the silken lines up to the reddening sky. A small dot blossomed into a huge chequered banner: Taid's racing pigeons waving, heading home, weaving themselves triumphantly through the air and landing to their own applause while my grandfather cheered

1

and banged on the biscuit tin. The call of home. All had made it, except Mister Lloyd.

'I'm afraid we're out of time, Mostyn bach,' said Taid, his harsh words sounding so gentle as the last clang of the biscuit tin fell silent in Graceland. 'Best cut our losses, there's a good lad.'

Even now I still like to sit here in Taid's pigeon loft, looking out through the spider's webs – my grandfather and I tried never to spoil them: *'All that work.'* We live on the mainland between the bridge and the pier, overlooking this fine view. Ahead of us Menai Woods and the strait itself; beyond, the island and the so-called Millionaire's Row – white marine residences jutting through the trees. We are not so wealthy, of course, but, facing west, as Taid would remind us daily, we had sunsets for which there was no price; each day the gift of a new canvas, the same view but always a different light.

The picture that evening was bleak. I'd been on the planet eleven years at this point and this was knock number two, the first being when Dad had left much in the same way three years earlier. Vanished. You see, Mister Lloyd had been a gift from Taid when Dad went – displacement therapy they call it – a very generous gift considering the thousands his bloodline was tipped to fetch at auction. From the moment I slipped the identity ring on his tiny leg when he was just ten days old, I was hooked. I suppose because my father had also disappeared, I was somehow placing all my hopes on Mister Lloyd.

'Don't frighten him,' Taid warned. 'Otherwise you won't be friends for life.'

Quite a few years have passed since my tale took place,

this 'bloody-minded' search for Mister Lloyd. Bloody-minded was Mam's term for it. I can see why now, but at that age it was the only way. I wanted him home! My own homecoming a few years later saw me on a single-carriage train speeding along the north Wales coast. It struck me then I should tell my story as the lofty outline of Bangor flashed like a magic lantern through the leaves in the bright evening sun. The pink haze gave home a curiously grand appearance. Not quite like arriving in Manhattan, you understand, but when we pulled into Bangor station, where Mam was waiting with open arms, you had the impression of somewhere bigger.

I had been inter-railing from one city to the next with Lowri, Gareth and Tim – you'll meet them soon. I took in all the sights as per the itinerary, but I quietly carried out my own survey with a third eye, my pigeon eye, clocking the winged citizens of Europe. I checked for strays with their telltale green rings in the feral crowds, looking for the Mister Lloyds of this world, as I had done in London that year, and longing for a reunion. In snatched moments I had conjured memories and hurriedly, secretly, jotted down reminders in the travel journal my mother had bought me, together with the poster she'd stapled and folded to the inside, and a trigger to it all, the pin-prick to where the search began.

Kitchen table, a few years earlier. Home, Bangor

Missing. Lost. We sat in silence overlooking that same view, albeit from lower down the bank than Graceland and the scene double-framed through the glass hatch and the patio door. The lilac tree needs cutting, I remember thinking, its white flowers long rusted and obscuring the last of the day's sun. It was a July when Mister Lloyd vanished, during his first international race. One he was meant to win. Like the others he set off from Belgium but four long days had gone by and no sign. I stared at the blank piece of paper, a would-be poster and my feeble attempt to bring him back. The words stopped short, waiting for a decision at the tip of the pen. Mam cut in.

'Mostyn, missing or lost, does it matter? Surely it's more important you get on with it?'

Taid, being the silver surfer he was even then, had registered the numbered ring on reportstraysonline.com. This would have been the Sunday, according to his records, a small Letts diary which has proved useful for dates and timeline here. But now it was a Thursday and no email had come through. I can't have been much company.

'Just try a few out!' Mam shouted, and seeing more blank sheets fan out, I wrote the first part of the story. Not a literary tour-de-force, perhaps, but I like to think of it as a pivotal piece of writing, nonetheless. Here's a copy:

LOST

Light Grey and Dark Grey Blue-Bar Racing Pigeon.

Purple head. Green ring on right foot. Breed: Flying Tippler

(GB07J43777)

Answers to the name of Mister Lloyd (in English or Welsh)
if found please call Mostyn Price on 01248542865
Or Log on to Report Strays Online

www.reportstraysonline.com/misterlloyd

It needed a photo, of course, not that scribble above, but I held up the piece of paper for a closer inspection, scrutinizing it as an outsider, a passerby. You see, I'd rubbished missing posters in Hampstead, a posh part of London where we stayed one summer, not because I had no sympathy, but because I didn't see the point. And telling good folk you had lost a bird so often called a 'rat with wings' was tantamount to checking yourself into a loony bin.

'This'll make me a laughing stock.' Mam walked to the sink. 'Who, I ask you, is going to tell Mister Lloyd apart from all the millions of pigeons out there? Laughing. Stock.'

Mam didn't answer at first. She had her back to me but I could tell she was looking up at the darkening bank before she resumed the back-and-forth polishing of the new mixer tap handyman Maldwyn had installed earlier that day. 'Well, it might be a bit pie in the sky.'

The pain in the back of my throat was making my eyes water.

'Oh, that's it. You all think I'm mad! What is the point in you making me write this?'

The polishing stopped. 'Because, young man,' she said with her J-Cloth brandished in my direction, 'I'd like you to do something, if only for you to get it out of your system!'

'Oh ay, and I suppose you'd like me to snap out of it!' My fist landed on the unfinished piece of paper and swiped it aside. It flew off the table – we both watched – landing with quiet dignity on the quarry tiles.

'Snap Out of It': our family motto, the very utterance of which brought about some unintended truce. Mam walked over to the kitchen table, pointedly stepping over my outburst, and sat down, staring. We did this now and again, the two of us looking out for a spasm, a quiver, maybe a tightening of the lip, anything that suggested the other was about to buckle. Mam won.

'Hallelujah. It's nice to see a smile back on your face.'

I nodded.

'Look, I know *you* probably think that no one's going to be able to tell him apart, but there are others like you and Taid who might.'

It was a reasoned argument but not much comfort when I considered Mister Lloyd could have been anywhere between Bangor High Street and Belgium. My stomach simmered. All I knew for certain was that life wasn't going to be easy for Mam with me like this.

I considered my options. A mission to Belgium was unlikely, loath as I was to accept this. Yet sitting and waiting, with only a parish-style poster and an unresponsive online appeal, hardly felt like progress. For the last three years, through word and deed, I had devoted my love and affection to that bird, forging trust through his training, believing, like Taid, such reverence essential for a really outstanding performance. We had a connection but it had not been enough and I had failed. I looked down and caught sight of the white sheet of paper lying on the floor. I turned my gaze back up. 'I can't give up, Mam.'

'I know, Mostyn bach,' she said, throwing a coaster in the fruit bowl. 'There's not a day goes by—' She flicked open a Sunday supplement and gave out a small laugh. 'There was a time when not an hour went by.'

Three years earlier I too had lived through the hell. But at least I'd had Mister Lloyd to keep me going. True, Mam had me to get her through but deep down I knew it unlikely I'd ever grasp the enormity of her loss, nor she mine. All we could do was try to understand. We didn't always succeed.

'Does it get better?'

'You just get better at it,' she suggested, purposelessly cradling pens in the curve of the magazine. 'Listen, cariad, it's not as if Mister Lloyd is a missing person.'

I didn't say anything.

'Just *try* and carry on. For me,' she pleaded, her soft cheek docked in the palm of her hand and pushing the folds of her skin. I saw Nain in her, her own mother. 'Go to school, sit this week out. It might make the waiting – well, less agonizing. Before you know it, it'll be the summer holidays and then—'

'We've got to go and find him!'

'Not without some clue as to where he is! I'm done with wild goose chases.'

'And I'm done with vanishing tricks.'

'Right.' Mam got up and walked to the door, gently side-stepping my pathetic effort. 'When you said Mister Lloyd was your Racing Pigeon—'

'Yes, racing – not some feral—'

'Don't you mean *is*, Mostyn bach?' she cut in, before walking into the dark of the hallway.

'Is,' I echoed. Of course! Hurriedly I retrieved the poster and wiped it clean with my sleeve. There it was, my little flyer and, yes, it definitely needed a picture. I opened Mam's laptop in the dining room, called up the web and scrolled down Favourites. Keen to print off the same photograph as we had used for the online bulletin, one of Taid's and the most handsome of my Flying Tippler, I signed in to Report

Strays Online with my username, The Winged Athlete, and password. We had specified in the site's settings that we were to be notified of any progress by email, but I was glad of any excuse. There it was: my page and said image.

Naturally I'd hoped to find good news greeting me but I had put on a face that was ready for bad. I clicked on Mister Lloyd's page, scanned the main bulk; all seemed in order. I scrolled down to the visitor counter and saw it was up to ninety-seven. I was impressed. A browse to the right showed me nine users had recommended the page to other sites and four had liked it with a thumbs-up, but there was still no news. Ping! A new window burst onto the screen, making me sit back. Someone had left me a Track, someone going by the name Misterlloydfanclub.

Mister Lloyd didn't have a fan club. Up to this point I'd believed I was his only fan. Who was it claiming his name? This being cyber-world, it could be genuine concern or a cruel prank. My eyes darted to the door then up to the ceiling, Mam pottering upstairs, ruling herself out. Looking back to the screen, I swallowed hard and clicked on the profile. Blank image and no info. Nothing except a green dot telling me they were online. What a fool – my image bandied to a screen elsewhere and users laughing at my world. Dry mouthed, I clicked on Send Message and had just begun to type *Hello there* when the page refreshed itself and the green dot turned red.

'Drat,' I cussed at the screen. 'I was sending you a message!'

Misterlloydfanclub had gone offline. My fingers tapped nervously at the mouse.

Someone was watching my progress.

II

Trafalgar Square, London

Come quickly, fly with me. We will do the introductions in due course but for now let's fly in to see him, take a closer look. There, do you see? Oh, he must be so dizzy with all those lights, squatting on his perch. Yes, it's definitely Mister Lloyd plumped on that ledge. His appearance does suggest to the casual passer-by that he is comfortable in his new home. An expert eye, one such as Mos— *Mos...tyn*, am I right? Yes, an expert eye such as Mostyn's, for example, would see beyond this veil. Look how bewildered Mister Lloyd is, thin and worn out. He fears the trauma of the journey that brought him here has eroded his sense of home. This is the worst aspect of the domestic pigeon going missing; I have seen it countless times. No, don't worry, we won't frighten him. We can't frighten him. We are invisible to him and we are here to observe only but I promise I will translate as much as I can; after all, I am an interpreter – of sorts. Yes, yes, introductions later and, yes, we will go back to that point where he began his journey. I'll take you there; it is my job, you see, but for now we are in London, Trafalgar Square, in fact, for this is the strange world where he has landed.

It's noisy, isn't it? Nothing we can do, I'm afraid. And no, it's not cold as such, but it is draughty where he is perched. No roof, no box, no seeds and no Mostyn. (I'm getting the hang of his name now.) Anyway, look at Mister Lloyd; how the memory of Graceland must pound him on that Portland stone ledge as he contemplates his new fate as the Accidental Quitter. Dorian called him that – you will meet him – his new so-called friend. Dorian is also a pigeon, a feral one, and I've decided on that name for him. I'm rather pleased with it! But, yes, back to Mister Lloyd, who is wondering how he ended up here and whether this is his life from now on. Dorian has no answer, of course; he just told him he was a quitter and scarpered straight for some chips; he was late for an appointment down in Soho or some such place. Soho is a meaningless name to Mister Lloyd, of course, but I am the go-between for you – the translator – to give you an idea of where they are and how they're feeling. I can tell you life in the capital is proving hard for Mister Lloyd. Let's face it, we all have feelings, don't we?

He looks down at the hustling humans. This is what you are to him but there is one amongst you who is different, much more dear. Mostyn. He's looking for Mostyn. Peculiar name, isn't it? Very north Wales, but that's why I've brought you here to see him: to connect. They are connected. I'm not sure if we can bring them together, mind. That is up to Mister Lloyd and Mostyn. It is their determination that, we hope, will do that, and we cannot interfere in the minds and the will of others.

We are here to observe. All we can do is follow Mister Lloyd until we know he is somewhere safe. But be warned; once that is the case, my job here will be done and I will have to fly off to the next pigeon fancier that calls on me. At that point you will need to put your trust in fate.

They're obsessives, you know, these fanciers.

CHAPTER THREE

Graceland, Bangor

The King of Rock and Roll saw to it that Taid's Pigeondom was named as it was. Elvis and Taid were fellow fanciers and Taid had insisted it be called Graceland. Well known amongst the North Wales Pigeon Fanciers and Homing Club and many associations beyond, it often featured in *Racing Pigeon Weekly*. It was what was deemed in the trade as a 'winning loft'. Of course, dull things had been said about it, articles sheathed in envy. 'The Cobbled Coop' ran one headline, describing it as a crooked, wooden-clad hotchpotch of a complex and the vision of a mad eccentric; others, more enlightened, thought it an architectural gem. Elvis, I knew, would have approved of this small but impressive collection of towers and walkways, nesting boxes, box perches and—

— *Wowee! Is that a shipping container attached, Mostyn?*

— *On the money, Elvis. It also doubles up as Taid's house, would you believe?*

— *My-my* —

As I showed Elvis around I realised it had always been a land of grace for me. So too for Taid, who had moved up here to the top of the garden when Nain died, giving me and Mam free rein of the house below.—

Limited to groups of six, Thursdays and Saturdays <u>only</u>,

13

fellow fanciers flocked to have the Guided Tour, on condition they kept its location under wraps. I often wondered whether the pigeon-like topiary hedge heralding the back entrance at the top road wasn't a bit of a giveaway to the would-be thief. Indeed, I half-wished Mister Lloyd *had* been stolen; it would have been an explanation at least. Perhaps Misterlloydfanclub or whoever it was would know of his whereabouts, may even have taken him hostage and would soon be demanding a ransom. After all, such breeds went for thousands. All sorts of fears crossed my mind as I ran up the path for that evening's tour. I crept into Graceland and found Taid giving his usual performance.

'Let me indicate the sheer amount of draught excluders dotted around this, the interior of the main loft.' I quote him here verbatim, so often had I heard him and witnessed his extravagant gesturing with his walking stick, useful on such tours to point things out or call in the stragglers still absorbing the loft's exterior. 'As you know, pigeons can withstand high and low temperatures. They need plenty of fresh air but,' he said with a foreboding resonance only me, Mam and the cooing residents understood, 'they cannot endure draughts. Nor should they. Kindly close the door behind you, there's a good chap.'

Too late. The draught brought about a small fit of sneezing in Taid. Thirteen. Short. Sneezes. Quick. Succession. To. Be. Precise. *I do beg your pardon.* A rummage around worn Savile Row pockets. *Help me here, boy. You know, Christmas gift. Nain. The Liberty ones.* Damia – too late. I ushered in the last of the party and, shutting the door behind me, found a set of Nain's pigeon print handkerchieves in the usual place, tucked in the holster that

14

hung from the coat hook. I handed one to him, noticing the embossed initials for the first time: R.G.J. Ronald Gwynn Jenkins.

'I do beg your pardon. Now, let's get on with the show,' he said, recovering his command. Until he retired Taid was Professor of Zoology at the University and as a hobby had kept racing pigeons, spurred, we had no doubt, by Charles Darwin's research into the domestic variety when writing *On the Origin of Species*. I had heard it from several sources that Professor Jenkins, as he had been known, had cut quite a dash during his lectures. I could see what they meant. 'All of life,' he would tell his hushed Graceland audience in a sort of clipped tone, his local lilt left on the indented seat-pad of his old wingback chair, 'All of life is here in front of you.'

To an extent, he was right.

'A good dovecote should face south,' he continued, this time placing the handkerchief securely in his shirt pocket. 'This loft, built with my own fair hands, is a particularly good example, making full use of the sun. Now, I appreciate some of you prefer to call it a coop.' He peered over his glasses and smiled. 'A mere case of "You Say Potato".'

This granted the party a momentary chuckle but Taid moved on, fully aware that some were here for good advice, not merely a good nose around.

'Now, let me introduce you to my feathered friends,' he said, turning briefly away from his audience and pointing at the various perches dotted around the loft, lightly tapping some of the shelves and single nests. 'My breed is the Flying Tippler. Always stick to the same breed. Here I have allowed two square feet per bird and in each enclosure I house eight pairs maximum. I'd strongly recommend not going beyond that. Now, through this gangway,' he announced, pointing his visitors to the door at the other end of the loft, 'we shall make our way to the hospital, or as some would call it, the isolation cage; essential if you suspect any of your flock is sick or has picked up a disease during the course of a race—'

There was an uncharacteristic hesitancy in his voice.

'One or two will inevitably take that bit longer to find their way home,' he continued emphatically. 'It is a matter of precaution that they are placed within this isolation cage.'

'That is,' chipped in one helpful visitor, 'if they are able to find their way home.'

I heard some chuckle and thought, what would Elvis say?

'Here,' piped another. 'I read in an article that you usually opted for the 'kill all diseased' appr—'

'I think you'll find,' Taid cut in, his expression hardened, 'I was also quoted as saying that there are *two* schools of thought.'

— *Don't think twice, kid. It's all right.*

'Onwards,' he said hurriedly, goading me to lead them through.

I shook my head apologetically. Taid didn't persist and I watched them all shuffle behind him, along the gangway in a butterfly chase of words, scribbling on note pads, underlining facts. 'Hospital.' 'Downwind.' 'From Main Loft.'

'Mind the red plastic bath,' I could hear him warn. It was Mister Lloyd's own.

And so, as the inquisitive voices trailed off, I was left alone in Graceland. Here was Mister Lloyd's home and I could still smell his presence. There were his initials, engraved on a small brass plaque beneath his compartment. Next to his, Earl and Lady Grey's (Ma' n Pa); to the right was Anne of Grey Gables (M.Ll's tipped to be girlfriend and the perfect match for a world-class offspring); up above, Idwal Slab and Greysta (Slow Developer and Trouble Maker, respectively); and two rows down, Grey's Anatomy (the pin-up and the main competition for Anne of Grey Gables' attention). They had all flown home after that fateful race.

I shut my eyes and listened to the rhythmic cooing surrounding me, ticking over like the purr of an engine, Taid's words ringing from the passenger seat, me at the steering wheel learning how to drive.

'Mostyn! A successful racing pigeon – check the eye sign – needs the will to come home.'

The will to come home, I repeated.

'That's good, now Graceland needs to be a Temple of Peace – mind his gullet.'

Temple of Peace.

'Where was I? Yes, each feathered creature should be happy with his loft and master.'

Happy with his loft and master.

It had not been like taking over a small family business. I don't think it was intended that I be fully trained in all aspects of Pigeon Fancying and breeding the same calibre of winners as Taid: racers with a lust for speed and a precise homing instinct envied throughout north Wales. I was more of an accidental fancier. Absorbing all Taid's techniques I'd learned to examine for diseases, the spring of a pair of tweezers being especially useful to wedge open a beak and take a swab inside and out. I monitored the moult process, his eye sign, the down of his plumage, all in the name of inspection at first but over time it became an affectionate ritual. I loved his waxy blue-bar wings, so typical of the Flying Tippler with his rainbow-like neck feathers, changing grey to purple – 'Do you see? Hold him this way' – green – 'Now that way' – blue. Iridescent was what Taid called it. And so, in the three years it took me to train Mister Lloyd, we'd got quite used to each other. We had an understanding, as I liked to call it.

I must have been lost in this world of happier days for, when I next looked around, the visitors had left. I stepped out of the main loft in search of Taid and walked along the gangway, past the aviary, and rushed down the steps to the shipping container Elvis had so loved. Darwin HQ is what we named it, a corrugated steel box Taid had converted into a secret den with cut-out windows and a flue stack reaching high into the sky ('I don't want to hear birds coughing all night'). Its rusty, tarnished-red exterior suggested nothing of the cosiness that was to be found inside.

Taid was knelt on a kilim saddle bag floor cushion and closing the stove door when I entered. Even in early July he liked to light the fire in his bedsit warren full of books, medicines and a year's supply of Royal Honey and Nazaline Drops.

'Don't suppose there's any news,' I enquired, trying to sound casual.

'Go see for yourself.'

I slipped behind the desk in the designated 'study' and switched on Taid's link to the outside world. He hauled himself up, still nursing his knee.

'Taid,' I said, hearing the computer whoop itself into action. 'If Graceland is meant to be a temple of peace, then it must have been me that did something wrong.'

'Well, if your connection with Mister Lloyd is as telepathic as you make out, then you know that's not true.'

'Yes, but if this is meant to be a happy loft, Mister Lloyd must have had issues,' I said, logging on to my settings. I stared at the hard drive as it tried to find me, gurgling annoyingly at leisure. 'So where is he?'

'How many times? This is a risky business. Any number of things could have gone wrong. Lord knows I've stopped counting.'

'So how do you cope with so many casualties?'

He didn't answer. I took my eyes off the indecisive screen and turned to see my grandfather rearranging the seat pad of his wing chair.

'I think you have to accept that Mister Lloyd was chased, more than likely killed by a Falcon,' said Taid as he finally settled into his seat with the day's newspapers. 'The twenty-one day rule is there for a reason.'

In the browser I scrolled Favourites and clicked Report Strays Online. I typed my username. 'What do you mean the twenty-one day rule?'

'The association's rule of thumb is this: if there's a no-show after twenty-one days, consider your bird well and truly a goner.'

I left Taid to his paper and turned to the computer, counting back to the moment Mister Lloyd should have been back. We were on day four. No way was he dead. I knew it. It was not too late, but quite how or where I would find him I had no idea. I scanned the home page. More thumbs-up and recommendations, but no news. Then I looked at the top bar and saw the number one floating above Recently Viewed. It could only be him: Misterlloydfanclub. Hurriedly I looked over to Taid. He was still reading. I opened Messages.

'Hi there,' I typed. 'I like the name.' I tried to think of something witty to write but thought it best not to mention stalking. Instead I invited him in. 'I'm in Members Chat, want to join?' I pressed return and a window appeared telling me my message had been sent. I stared at the screen. No reply. Had I made this up? I checked I was online, looked under the desk and nudged Taid's broadband connection with the toes of my trainers. When I resurfaced a chat invitation box had appeared. I clicked accept and typed in a greeting.

TheWingedAthlete: Hi
Misterlloydfanclub: U ok?
TheWingedAthlete: Gd ta. [Softly, softly, catchee monkey] U?
Misterlloydfanclub: GD. Soz 2 hear of UR loss.
TheWingedAthlete: Aw. 10Q [means 'thank you']. I have a question 4U. Y U called Misterlloydfanclub? I mean, glad 2 hear, but y? LOL

The pencil icon at the bottom of the box told me Misterlloydfanclub was typing, but his message took a long time to appear. Whether he was writing or just thinking what to say, I waited. Up it came.

> **Misterlloydfanclub:** New 2 site, cudnt think v 1.
> **TheWingedAthlete:** Aw. U lost a racing pigeon 2?
> **Misterlloydfanclub:** No, bt I'd hate it 2 happen 2 me. Found this site by accident. It'z cool.
> **TheWingedAthlete:** 10X. That's kind. It's a strange feeling 2 have something disappear from ur life. Anyway, I'm Mostyn. What's UR name?

I waited for an answer, the nervous silence broken by ruffling newspaper. 'Quick, tell me your name!' I wanted to shout before it was too late. With the mouse cursor hovering over the Minimise button, I turned and saw Taid wrestling with the folds and trying to flatten the business section into a readable page. I turned to the screen and a message landed. When I read it I felt like I'd had an eleven year old's equivalent of coronary heart failure.

> **Misterlloydfanclub:** Just call me Elvis.

Elvis? I looked above the monitor where I had just imagined him. No one. To my side, Taid was peering over his bifocals. At that age, I was still learning about déjà vu, coincidences and getting used to my overactive mind but nobody could know I already had an Elvis in my life. He was just an imaginary friend I turned to when, really, I was just talking to myself; not that I did it in front of anyone else, you understand – they might think me barmy – but for anyone out there who does the same, you'll know that when you talk to yourself you see eye to eye with 'the other' and can happily chat on many a subject. Having Elvis turning up on Report Strays Online; was a different matter.

Misterlloydfanclub: Hey where u got 2?
TheWingedAthlete: Soz
Misterlloydfanclub has quit chat.
[*Damn it*. An automated reply.]

I didn't know what to think. Hurriedly I highlighted the dialogue and right-clicked copy. I went into Word, opened a new document and pasted in the dialogue. I'm still amazed I did this – that it occurred to me I should play safe and keep any incriminating evidence on file. I called it 'TSFML1', filed it under Mostyn's Documents and hurriedly closed down all open applications.

'Everything OK, dear boy?' Taid had lowered his newspaper. Obituaries, I now saw.

'Yes,' I replied blankly, focusing on the date at the top of the page. July 7. My watch said the same. I already felt I was going mad but now my head felt it was about to explode. I went over the events I knew had taken place, all the way back to the previous Saturday, the day Mister Lloyd left Graceland for Belgium. There hadn't even been a proper goodbye.

Mam was waiting with a mug of tea at the top of the driveway. From up in Graceland I watched The Beast, a lorry festooned with chrome bars and multiple spotlights, as it reversed loudly up the drive, headed more towards the hedge than the garage it was aiming for. The Belgium race was the main event in the North Wales Pigeon Fanciers and Homing Club calendar. Mister Lloyd and his crew were being picked up and transported there by Maldwyn, a self-styled handyman who had moved back home to Bangor after a ten-year stint in Dubai. This and That was not really a career choice but Mam had been pleased with her new mixer tap and, judging by the sheen on his lorry, this geezer certainly got by all right.

The loud roar echoed round the crate by my feet. Some of the elders jumped and flapped, yet Mister Lloyd remained passive in my grasp. I had taken him out of his basket, bathed him in the red plastic bath and dried him with a hairdryer. I was about to place him in the special transporter crate with the others when I first caught sight of Maldwyn, jumping out of his cabin, defeated at only halfway up the drive. He was a tall, supposedly good-looking man with salt-and-pepper hair and pool-blue eyes, knocking on a bit, say forty, in jeans and a white T-shirt that revealed a shawl of tattoos. I would have called his appearance gruff but I have since been assured that some women find this look 'hot'. Either way, he was definitely sweating.

'Drove this beast all the way from Dubai, you know, ay,' he said to Mam without as much as a hello. A lot of tattoos, I thought, and a Bangor 'ay' accent. Despite all those years away Maldwyn knew where he belonged. He set about throwing open the shutters on the side of the lorry, the whoosh of its rolling slats revealing dozens of similar crates neatly stacked on top of each other in a grille-like formation. 'Custom-built, you know, this. Had practically every club in the whole United Arab Emirates wanting to buy it off me, ay.'

'You should have taken the top road, Maldwyn bach. Much easier,' said Mam, following him round to the back of the lorry. 'You know, past the topiary.'

'Damia, yes. Forgot about that, ay. Still getting used to the place again,' he said with a nervous laugh. 'Oh well, here now.'

Mam stood silent.

Maldwyn checked himself up and down. 'Forgive the rig out, by the way. I know Eddie Stobart used to do the shirt and tie thing, but I can't be— '

'Cuppa?'

'I'm not stopping, Mrs Price, if it's all the same,' he replied, leaping on to the deck to shift a few crates in a desperate bid to make room. 'Loads to do.'

Even from my position up the back garden, I could tell she was disappointed. 'Oh, I know. Meinwen's been on the phone already asking whether you were on your way. I said you hadn't even got here yet.'

'Traffic, Mrs P. Appallin' in Bangor now, yeah?'

'Ofnadwy. Maldwyn?'

'Yes?'

'I'm still Paloma, you know.'

'Yes, yes, of course,' he said, corrected. 'Right, where am I going to put these buggers? Iesu, you know Gwil's got another three crates for me apparently. Hoping to make up for last year's disappointment, no doubt. How am I going to fit them all on?' He jumped off, looked at Mam and smiled bashfully. Not only was I putting my trust in this chap to collect and drive my feathered competitor all those hundreds of miles, but it was he who was to release them all at the other end in Leuven, Belgium. The race and their fate were in his hands. Nervous fanciers like me dotted all over north Wales were depending on this man to do his job, eager to spot their pigeons approaching from the horizon, grab the race band and time-stamp it with the clock. Game over.

'They're waiting for you round the back,' she said, breaking the now awkward silence.

He ran up the garden steps, two, maybe three at a time and threw a wave at Taid, who was scuttling from Graceland to Darwin HQ.

'Howaya, Professor?'

'Maldwyn,' greeted Taid in a way that suggested 'Hello, glad you're here, *now shift!*'

From then on it was somewhat botched. Taid and he exchanged a few words. I placed Mister Lloyd in the crate with the others, clumsily in hindsight. I threw in his blanket, something familiar, then Maldwyn's large hand came into the frame.

'Alright?' he said as if we'd known each other all our lives. He shut the crate and, picking it up with both arms, made his way towards The Beast. Not a good start.

'Hang on,' I called out. 'I haven't even said goodbye!'

Maldwyn turned and began to walk backwards. 'Oh sorry, mate, where's me manners, ay? Well, so long!' he shouted, passing it off with a parting nod and a trip over Mister Lloyd's red plastic bath. He nearly fell to the ground, crate in hand.

'Watch it!'

Equal coos of outrage poured out of the crate. I ran over but, as I neared, rumours of a false alarm were already spreading amongst the Graceland lot.

Maldwyn leaned in close. 'Tell me the professor didn't see that.'

'Never mind the professor,' I expostulated *sotto voce*. 'What about Mister Lloyd? They're not even on the lorry yet and—'

'All right,' he said as he set off once more, 'don't get your knickers in a twist!'

I didn't say anything and began to follow.

'Listen now, yeah, these guys have won wars for us,' he continued. 'I guess they'll survive a tumble with Maldwyn, ay? Anyway, looks like you trained him good and proper, from what I remember.' We had reached the garage roof. 'Two hundred miles from Oxfordshire, wasn't it? First race an' all. No mean feat, that.'

Whether it was small talk, backtracking, or a genuine compliment, I couldn't help but smile.

'This should be a doddle,' he added with a wink.

I shied away and caught sight of his tattoos: all of them rock doves and pigeons.

Taid knocked on the window, tapped his watch and made a 'call me' sign.

'Will do, Professor! Right, got to go.'

I began to guide him down the steps. 'So, the trick,' I explained, 'is to release them so that they are hungry enough to want to come home as fast as they can—'

'But not so hungry that they are starving,' Maldwyn cut in as we got to the bottom step. 'You don't say.'

'Correct. Otherwise, they'd have no strength—' I

stopped, realising he would, of course, know all this. I was about to apologise when I saw his attention had now turned to the kitchen window, where Mam was reaching for one of her special mugs from the shelves by the sink. The one I'd bought her. He beamed. She beamed. He gave a small wave. As did she.

Oh, please. No boyfriends. We'd said.

'Maldwyn?' I said. 'Meinwen and Gwil are waiting, remember?' I marched on, pulling out a bag of mixed seeds from my pocket, and decided to dole out further instructions. This Maldwyn needed focus. 'Now, I give them small seeds with their food. This wheat barley and oats combo should be as plump as possible; peas and beans uniform in size; corn or maize, again, should be of a good colour. Not peanuts. Mister Lloyd's not ready for peanuts and bad ones can ruin *everything*. Garlic is allowed; thins the blood and—' I had got to the back of The Beast and was gazing in wonder at the prison-like interior, all decked out with cell upon cell of precious lives, all in this chap's hands.

'Tell you what, I'll skip their feed before the race and give them a good drink,' said Maldwyn, putting the crate to rest on the deck. 'Even got pressed garlic in the drinker, ay. See it there?'

His pointed finger directed me to a tangled hose tied to the cabin wall and, next to it, the latest drinker to have hit the market. I had seen it advertised in Racing Pigeon Weekly.

'You will be careful with them, won't you?'

'Jeez,' exclaimed Maldwyn, his arms folded and leaning back on the lorry. 'Good job you were at school last time. Could have been curtains for you and me and we haven't

27

even got off the starting block.'

Curtains? Starting block? This man spoke in riddles.

'Listen, mate, they don't call me Maldwyn "The Liberator" Jones for nothing, ay,' he piped in an American twang. 'Now pass us them seeds.'

I laughed and handed him the pack. 'The Liberator? You're not serious?' he winked and, with his left arm acting as a pole vault, jumped on the back of the lorry and squatted down by the crate. 'Say toodlepip to your mate, sunshine. I'm late and I'll get it in the neck from the club if I don't get a move on, let alone Meinwen and Gwil.'

With not quite the ceremony I'd imagined, Maldwyn lifted the crate and shoved it in its slot.

'Wait!'

We both looked round. It was Mam dashing towards us.

'Seeing as you're short on time, Maldwyn bach, it's a To Go tea!' She was holding out a travel mug, somewhat out of breath. 'Milk and two sugars, if I'm not mistaken.'

He pulled down the last of the shutters, revealing the large logo emblazoned on the lorry's side: 'Maldwyn Jones – Distance No Object'. I thought of Mister Lloyd.

'Now, I'll want that plastic beaker back, Mal, if you don't mind. Sentimental reasons.'

He looked at the travel mug. '*Contigo al Fin del Mundo,*' it read. Time being of the essence, he didn't ask. 'I'll look after it. See ya, Mostyn.'

'Hwyl, Mister Lloyd bach,' I whispered under my breath, trying to imagine the chorus of a thousand pigeons gently cooing to the rhythmic rattle of the crates, trundling hundreds of miles along the motorway. 'I'll be waiting.'

Maldwyn climbed into the cabin, Mam grabbing the door and swinging it shut. Ignition on, my legs taking the blast of soot from its exhaust, off the lorry sped – to Belgium, via Meinwen and Gwil's.

It was a clear, warm and balmy night, not quite dark, but a blue-purple colour that became lighter as it neared the horizon, the same gradual change of colour undergone by the throat, breast and belly of my most cherished feathered friend. Mam was downstairs in the kitchen, directly below my bedroom. The sound of the dishwasher wafted upwards through an open window, while over the garden fence, through black leaves and branches, you could see the higgledy-piggledy outline of Graceland, its two orange-lit windows winking at me in the light breeze. Part of me wanted to go downstairs to see if Elvis was online, but I knew Mam was doing one of her translations that night and the laptop would be out of bounds. I settled on the old-fashioned and flicked through the atlas, hurriedly at first, till Taid's words rustled through the trees, reminding me to 'respect the printed page'. I was retracing Mister Lloyd's path in my head, trying to make sense of it all. A message by someone going by the name of Elvis had been chilling enough; now I needed answers. Elvis was my missing link but only Maldwyn knew what had happened to Mister Lloyd on that day. He had given his account, sure enough, but what if *he* was Elvis? No, silly thought. I flicked over another page and found Belgium.

Belgium, I began to think. Until recently racing pigeons had been a national sport. Belgium. *Think!* Chocolate. Tintin. Detective. Belgium. Belgium. Hercule Poirot.

Detective. Agatha Christie. Miss Marple. Miss Mar – I was coming to the end of an Agatha Christie, *The 4.50 from Paddington,* from Nain's pocket crime collection and, although not left to me, I'm sure when I told her I loved the covers, it was noted. Nain, always smart till the end, had not fashioned herself on Ms Christie's heroine but she did say 'I see' rather a lot. Anyway, since she'd died, the books were neatly stacked on my bedside shelf. And now they'd given me an idea. It went something like this:

Miss Marple is an elderly lady imagining things, and in *The 4.50 from Paddington* she explains to the Inspector how she came to solve the crime, what brought her to her conclusion and, crucially, to the murderer. She said the solution was all in Mark Twain, an author I had heard of, who wrote about the "boy who found the horse. He just imagined where he would go if he were a horse and he went there, and there was the horse."

Not a solution, maybe, but it was what I needed. My own imagination. I was the boy who would find his racing pigeon. I'd traced the route, pictured the scene. Now all that was left was to be reunited. My imagination would bring us together. I know it's better not to question but my two worlds were to collide in a spectacular way.

IV

Railway Depot, Leuven

Ah, good, you're here. Firstly, welcome to the Kingdom of Belgium and all that, but we need to hurry! Follow me. So glad you could make it, and just in time too. Right, gather round. I've brought you here to what they call the liberation site. As you can see from the train carriages to your left, it is in fact an old railway depot. But let us make our way past those carriages and towards the lorries and the cars and row upon row of tiered baskets – *so many* – and let's quickly climb on board The Beast, as I believe it is called. Come on, hurry along. Up we go. There's plenty of room and, look, there he is: one, two, three columns in and third, fourth level up. Our Mister Lloyd!

He is pacing, bobbing his head back and forth, still in the same crate as when he set off from Bangor but here he and his fellow passengers are a long way away from home. They do not know how far; they haven't worked it out yet. All they know for sure is the climate here is a touch warmer and the humans drive their cars on the right. It is confusing, I know, but that won't put Mister Lloyd off course as he follows the roads home. That won't be the reason he landed in London either. No,

31

he will follow the sun, use the magnetite crystals in his tiny brain, recall the smells of Graceland, resource all his faculties to bring him home and into the hands of Mostyn Price! Oh, how he hopes as he waddles around the wire mesh!

Now cover your ears! I forgot to warn you, I do apologise, but that loud metallic thunder is the lorry's shutters rolling upwards. And what a draught; it's so strong it's almost a gust! And look how it blows the pigeons' feathers on end and themselves to the back of the crate. Mister Lloyd and the others hobble frantically to the edge of the new light and peer through the mesh, drawn to the warm breeeze and eager for a closer look at the vista beyond. Ahead is that expanse of railway carriages we saw earlier, stacked baskets and row upon row of parked-up lorries. Some, like this one we're in now, have their shutters wide open, full to the brim with crates. Humans murmur as they mill and inspect. Of course, Mister Lloyd cannot tell you what is being said but you and I would know these are mostly Flemish, French and English tongues with a bit of Dutch, Italian and German voices floating here and there.

Daylight has flooded the crate and the startled cluster of waxy feathers huddles together. Look how Mister Lloyd's green hackle, glossy in the new light, turns purple as he takes in the grey heads and red eyes darting about, twitching the mesh with their beaks.

'It's time.'

To the trained ear this is the call of Earl Grey. I am translating for you now. Yes, he does sound calm but that same trained ear can trace some tremor in this coo and he has more than a passing similarity to Mister Lloyd. You see, not only is he the senior member of this crate, he is also Mister Lloyd's father and, this being the young squab's first flight over water, it is understandable things are a little frayed.

'But where are we, Earl G?' This is he, our Mister Lloyd.

'Not sure,' his pa replies. 'Although I'm sensing we've been here before, wouldn't you say, Lady G?'

We want to shout 'Belgium!', but to them it means nothing. Only home has any real meaning and the race is imminent.

'He's getting the hose.' This is Lady Grey, wife and mother. Her mind is on other things.

'Lady G?'

'I'm mesh-twitching!' (I'm translating on the spot here, but you get the drift.) Lady Grey is admiring the sight of Maldwyn Jones, the driver of The Beast – it must be him, his name is on the side of the lorry – wrestling with the hosepipe which has tied itself in a spaghetti-like knot at the back of the lorry. Although Maldwyn is cursing the 'blessed thing', Lady Grey knows the familiar sight signals the drink before the leap.

'Tell me, have we been here before, Lady G?'

'Yes, dear.' Her loud coo silences the crate. 'Have you not seen Priscilla on that 'camion' over there?'

Earl Grey looks blankly at her.

'You were caught blowing your crop with her last year, Earls darling.'

33

Oh dear. Now this is embarrassing. Earl Grey had been following this French bird with his puffed out throat, a sure sign of his advances, and he does not like to be reminded of such infidelities. But never mind, move on we must. This is mere distraction and we have more urgent things to consider. Look how he paces. Graceland can't come soon enough for the trainee but the poor blighter is finding it bothersome to calculate his way home. A large human face appears on the other side of the mesh. Mister Lloyd recoils but soon sees it is Maldwyn emptying a bag of seeds into the feeder before he vanishes once more.

'Is that it?' This time the coo comes from the mouth of Grey's Anatomy. 'There's hardly enough to go around.' (But look how he tucks in, nonetheless.)

'Then hold back!' Mister Lloyd exclaims with the up-and-down of his wings and to the applause of the others.

Grey's Anatomy stops, looks around and cusses. He gulps the last few seeds in his bill before waddling over to Anne of Grey Gables, who is cooing softly next to Lady Grey.

'He's untangled the hose,' she remarks. 'Drink, anyone?'

'I'll have a large one, thanks,' pipes Earl Grey.

'You're going to need it,' says Lady Grey. 'It's a long way home.'

The buckles of the crate ring loose! This is it! See how Mister Lloyd's feathers change colour. It is a pulse shooting through his blood in a rush of excitement. He

34

will be picturing Mostyn – 'did you say blue eyes, freckles and a funny cow's lick?' – back in Graceland by his T3, clockwatching, rattling the biscuit tin and calling out, eager to remove his rubber ring. *'Stop the clock!'* The words ricochet around the crate as Mister Lloyd recalls snuggling in Mostwyn's clasp. In his head he is there, home and out of danger but, sadly, we already know that this won't be his fate.

The mesh gates open.

'See you on the other side,' says Earl Grey, his parting coo drowning in the racket. Look at them, the whole depot and each basket and crate spilling thousands of racers skyward. Heart pounding, Mister Lloyd watches Earl Grey disappear into the distance. With an elegant take-off Lady Grey follows a fully braced Idwal Slab. Daunted, Mister Lloyd steps forward and hovers on the threshold. Grey's Anatomy barges past, Anne of Grey Gables swiftly in tow, and our friend is sent off his purchase. He lands back at the gate but sees he has been left alone to face the terrifying freedom of life beyond the crate. His hackles rise, his tail fans out and he looks towards the chaotic sky. 'Home,' he coos and off he flies.

CHAPTER FIVE

Bedroom, Bangor

TheWingedAthlete: Hi. It's m
TheWingedAthlete: *e [bloody typo]

Shaky typing, more like. I had woken up in the night, crept downstairs and fetched the laptop. I knew I'd be in trouble but I wanted to go online. Truth was, it felt weird, dangerous even. Chatting to friends online was the everyday – MySpace, as it was then, and MSN were the norm; Facebook was new and at the time more for the oldies – but not knowing this 'fan club', let alone how I would get to know their real identity, was too much of a temptation and it made me nervous. In fact, I was in a quandary. If I told Mam or Taid, it was a sure-fire way to get this person blocked and I would never find out who it was that seemed so convinced Mister Lloyd was still alive. It would have to be my secret, I decided, and went straight into chat.

He was there.

Misterlloydfanclub: Soz. Had 2 dash earlier.
NAAC.
[Not Always At Computer.]
TheWingedAthlete: No biggy!
[This was a lie. It was! I started typing again

> but virtual Elvis beat me to it.]
> **Misterlloydfanclub:** So Winged Athlete.
> What's occurin'?

Any notion this might be the ghost of the real Elvis ended there. Only the Welsh would say 'what's occurin''. Elvis himself had died on August 16th, 1977. Mam could vouch for this because she'd been on holiday, staying in a house that overlooked the Museum of Welsh Life in Cardiff, when she'd heard the news on the radio. She said you always remember where you were when legends die. She was eight and having a bath.

> **Misterlloydfanclub:** U still there?
> [I sat up in bed.]
> **TheWingedAthlete:** I couldn't sleep.
> [This was true.]
> **Misterlloydfanclub:** Me neither. ☹
> WAN2TLK? Hold on in there. He's not
> dead.
> **TheWingedAthlete:** LOL u say this but not
> every1 feels same.
> **Misterlloydfanclub:** It's lonely isn't it?
> **TheWingedAthlete:** Wot U mean?
> **Misterlloydfanclub:** Believing in urself.
> **TheWingedAthlete:** Yes. So, who r u
> really?

The pencil icon, which indicated whoever was on the other end was typing, stopped scribbling. I was convinced this person knew me. I looked through the window, saw the

Darwin HQ lights were off and ruled out it being Taid. Mam was also asleep; I had checked when I passed her room. Then it hit me that it might be Dad, trying to reach out, make up for the past. He knew about Mister Lloyd; the bird had hatched before he left and this would account for how he'd known his name. But if it was Dad, what would I say to him?

The pencil icon came to life once more.

Misterlloydfanclub: LOL! I told u. Elvis! Duz it matter? I'm just sorry 4 wot u bin thru. Rooting 4 u Rn't I? U R sad. WANNA HAPPY ENDING!

[I could see my hands were shaking so I thought it best to sign off.]

Misterlloydfanclub: No, w8!

TheWingedAthlete: Y? This feels weird.

Misterlloydfanclub: LOL. not stalking u. On me life. Chatting will help. Ok so from where he fly from?

[Was this a trap? Oh, what the heck.]

TheWingedAthlete: Leuven.

Misterlloydfanclub: IC. Where, a square, a café?

TheWingedAthlete: Liberation site off the E40, old railway depot. U 4 real?

Misterlloydfanclub: No. LOL. I want 2 kno about ur bird. NE probs when they set off?

[Feeling strangely pleased by the attention, I typed some more.]

TheWingedAthlete: There was an admin

---

error but Maldwyn said conditions good. no rain, wind or fog. shud've been a straight run 2 Dunkirk.

Misterlloydfanclub: An' he's stuck there?

TheWingedAthlete: *shrugs shoulders*. Look I shud go. Sleepy now.

Misterlloydfanclub: W8. Who is Maldwyn?

TheWingedAthlete: Who RU? Do u know me?

Misterlloydfanclub: gLOL! Ok again. Leuven? Maldwyn took him to Leuven? Man? Woman?

TheWingedAthlete: Male. He's a liberator.

Misterlloydfanclub: What's that? Sets things free?

TheWingedAthlete: LOL. U cud say that. So is it U?

Misterlloydfanclub: ??? U think I'm Maldwyn? Nooooooo! Soz. It's Elvis! NEway. Go2Go. Keep ur I's peeled 4 ne signs of hope. Chat soon. TTFN.

TheWingedAthlete: TTFN?

Misterlloydfanclub: Ta ta for nw. Here if u need me. Always.

Up it came again: ***Misterlloydfanclub*** *has quit chat.* The cyber voice. My only comfort. Gone. Spooked and disappointed, I too quit and, lowering the laptop gently onto the carpet, I tried to get to sleep. Tomorrow I would confront The Liberator.

VI

Mid-air, Leuven

'**S**un. Right, where's the sun?' It is how Mister Lloyd begins The Drill to get him home. Keep your wits about you. We're up in the sky now – sorry about the noise and for hurrying you – but we need to be watching the flying athlete dart through the airborne scrum. Thousands like him are shooting in all directions, desperate to untangle the confusion, so do keep up, if you please, otherwise we'll miss the action.

'Steady! Watch where you're going, will you?'

No wonder Mister Lloyd forgets his manners at this point. He's clearly got other things on his mind.

'Where's the bloody sun?'

He seeks the help of Earl and Lady Grey but they have vanished in a haze of feathers. He calls out for Idwal Slab. He does not answer. Oh, please cope, Mister Lloyd, cope!

He flies away from the chaos but he's not found the way home yet. Ah, yes, he has found a quieter patch of the sky. Hopefully here he can work out a route. 'Come on!' we hear him chide himself but we'll need to get a bit closer if we want to hear the rest. Quickly now.

'You've done this before. Go through the routine. Sun.

Where's the sun? Right, it's coming from… the sun rises in the east. Good, we're getting somewhere. You want to be heading northwest. Come on, where's your brain telling you is north?'

Mister Lloyd scans the Earth's magnetic field and hovers. He is waiting for his magnetite crystals to detect the correct force that will guide him home. He knows the bands are strongest at the poles and hopefully he is now feeling the pull of the north because he is turning in that direction. With the moon at a hundred and eighty degree angle to the sun he has concluded that Graceland is most definitely in a north-westerly direction. There he goes, look, whooshing past the dwindling swarm in an anticlockwise direction and veering on a straight run south of Ghent at fifty miles an hour. We need to follow fast.

In the distance he sees the grey-bronze lustre of Anne of Grey Gables, travelling alone. Buoyed by a sense of achievement, Mister Lloyd soon reaches the beauty. With her show-stopping tricks and – when the sun catches the sheen of her feathers – the looks to match, Mister Lloyd has long been dazzled by her elegance. Is this his chance? Yes, I bring you romance too!

'Well, hello there!' Yes, that's him pulling up to her side, the last coo trailing off.

'Oh, hi,' she answers coolly. Has he overplayed this greeting? She performs a backward somersault and loops underneath Mister Lloyd, appearing deftly on his right. 'Bracing, isn't it?' She is so funny.

They're weaving in and out of each other. It seems

fun but Mister Lloyd is no acrobat and can't compete with her corkscrew spin, an old Roller trick which requires five full turns at top speed without dropping altitude. Now it is Mister Lloyd's turn. He makes a good start but – careful Mister Lloyd! If only he could hear us! He has dropped altitude by several feet in a matter of seconds and it takes him several more to re-ascend. Up he comes and phew!

Oh dear. His wing biffs hers.

'Boundaries, Mister Lloyd. Boundaries!'

Our friend tries to claw back some dignity by uttering a sorry sounding coo. Did you hear that? It sounded something like, *So, how come you never talk to me at Graceland?* It is clear by his nervous tone that this question has been on his mind for a while.

Oh no! The look she gives him is blank but, hang on, the red iris of her eye suggests she is about to reply. Could this be it, the blossoming of something? Sadly not yet. For, look, she seems distracted. Her attention is drawn to an ominous disturbance ahead. Mister Lloyd turns his one-hundred-and-eighty-degree eyesight in the same direction and sees flocked thousands suspended in mid air; it seems the entire homeward-bound participants of the North Wales Pigeon Fanciers and Homing Club and all the other British associations taking part have hit the airborne equivalent of a brick wall.

They cut short their tomfoolery, as they must, and accelerate towards their gang. But, oh no, what is this? Look out everyone! As if from nowhere a huge bird hurtles across their path.

'What was that?' Mister Lloyd is reeling from the shock, as are we.

'Peregrine falcon. Do not befriend. I repeat. Do not befriend,' she warns. 'They're out to get us. That's why they're in such a tizzy over there.' She flies on to join the crowd and Mister Lloyd follows.

They are stuck, trapped in Dunkirk. This is where the North Sea meets the English Channel. Rain, wind and fog loom on the horizon. Behind the flight falcons guard their only escape. The elegance of a happy homebound flock has given way to a deafening grey Catherine wheel and the making of an uneasy atmosphere, but we must stick by, watch from the wings, if you'll pardon the pun. Anne of Grey Gables flies closely by Mister Lloyd's side as they search for the Graceland battalion.

'Everyone looks the same, somehow.' Mister Lloyd says, his eyes darting all around.

'Found them,' coos Anne at last. She swoops up to the family, taking Mister Lloyd with her.

'Where the hell have you been, Anne?' coos Earl Grey. 'We've looked everywhere!'

'We were fooling about.' It sounds pathetic and Anne of Grey Gables utters an abashed coo. 'Sorry.'

'I didn't see any of you lot hang around for me when we set off,' retorts Mister Lloyd.

'We thought we'd lost you! Oh, never mind, you're here now. I don't suppose you had trouble with those You-Know-Who's back there, did you?'

'No,' they both coo. Only we know they are lying but saying yes would have set off an even bigger alarm and tempers are already frayed as it is.

'That's good.' Earl Grey sounds calmer. 'You know, it's funny, we can travel miles and miles, over an untold amount of hostile territories, mountains, forests, deserts and cities, yet when it comes to a vast expanse of water, I mean, look at us! The Menai is a breeze in comparison.' (Again, this is not what they call it, but this is to what they are referring.)

'Did you have a nice time?' Lady Grey wants to change the subject we see. She has clocked the recent developments between Mister Lloyd and Anne of Grey Gables.

He is about to answer when Grey's Anatomy swoops in. 'No pit stop, no chance of a drink and the weather's closing in; no wonder this lot's in a faff. We need the shortest route home. These falcons sniff out the young ones. It'll be each to their own, you'll see.'

'You'd certainly know about that,' chips in Idwal Slab, his roving eye, too, landing on Anne of Grey Gables.

Mister Lloyd edges himself closer to the beauteous hen.

'We've no option but to travel direct,' spouts Earl Grey. 'We'll be all right. There's nothing to it. I once flew over the Atlantic, you know, many moons ago.'

'All very well with your heroic Atlantic trip, but we're all going to die here!' Grey's Anatomy has also forgotten his manners. 'How, oh great one, are we going to travel direct?'

'I've been to the Smithsonian,' begins Earl Grey. 'In—'

'Washington, yes,' cuts in Lady Grey. 'We've heard it all before, Earls.'

I'll paraphrase the rest of her version for you: it had not been as easy a journey as had been made out, he too had come across bad weather, he'd hitched a ride on the Liverpool-bound Queen Mary with a loud American flock who thought they were on their way home to Florida. They all ended up in sunny Rhyl.

'Funny how life—,' Mister Lloyd muses but he is stopped mid-flow. What is this? Has he spotted something? It could only be that mosaic of tarnished-red shipping containers on board that large vessel making its way out to sea. It must be Graceland calling!

'Gentlemen! Might I suggest we take the ship that's leaving port right now?'

Eureka!' exclaims Idwal Slab.

Mister Lloyd looks pleased.

'If we take this ride we can wait till the rain has passed. You never know, in a short distance the sun could be shining and bingo! We're back on course. Home!'

'You have saved us!' coos Anne of Grey Gables in rapture.

Mister Lloyd begins preening away at his feathers.

'Well done, dear boy,' adds Earl Grey.

'You're welcome!' Mister Lloyd watches them fly towards the containers, not knowing that he has secured the path home for everyone apart from himself.

CHAPTER SEVEN

Bedroom, Bangor

'*There'll be bluebirds over the white cliffs of Dover,*' I sang, eyes shut and in a fug under the duvet. I was dreaming of pigeons now. '*Just you wait and see.*'

Oh, the wait! My eyes opened to a downy darkness.

'Mostyn!'

Mam was shouting through the floorboards, her tone decidedly harsh. If I didn't stir there would follow a loud bang of the kitchen ceiling with one of Taid's walking sticks. Soon after that, a wet flannel. Over my face.

'Alright! I'm coming!' I protested.

'Have you got the laptop up there?'

I tossed the duvet aside and leaned over the edge of the bed. Idiot. There it was lying next to the poster along with a notebook and pencil. I had meant to put it back.

'Sorry,' I ventured, rolling back onto the mattress.

Beneath me something crashed on the table – a plate or a mug, the dragging of a chair against the quarry tiles and now, heavy footsteps. Her speech began at the top of the stairs. I leapt out of bed.

'*Oiga carino*! You know full well I don't like you taking that thing away from its usual place.' Without even a knock she barged in. 'Not that I mind you using it,' she added, scanning the room for "that thing", 'but not up here.'

'It is meant to be portable,' I said, handing it to her.

'Yes, but it's not yours to take. You always mess the settings. This is my lifeline, Mostyn!' (A bit dramatic, I thought.) 'Deadlines, remember! Was working on it late last night, thought of a few changes in bed, got to it first thing —' She took a deep breath. 'Well, I thought we'd been burgled. Did you get up in the middle of the night or something?'

I held up the poster and her tight expression began to soften.

'Couldn't sleep?'

I nodded. It was partly true. Mam came to sit on the side of the bed.

'Oh, I'm sorry. The printer broke last night, which is really why I'm cross. You know me. Whenever such things go wrong it drives me mad.'

I looked at the poster. The poster that was going to tell a tiny bit of the world I had lost my pigeon, the poster which – then it dawned on me: how was I going to print my poster now? The printer was broken! What about Taid's? Dash it. Too old. Too slow. (His printer, I meant.) Flamin' heck.

'What's the matter?'

'I need more than one copy! I need that printer!'

You see, I'd banked on not going to school that morning. I'd sat my exams; next week was the end of term and until then we were tarrying, playing games. In my mind it was a waste of valuable search time. But now that Mam's printer was finito, I had no choice.

'You'll have to do some photocopying in school,' said Mam coolly, making to go. 'Speaking of which, get a wiggle on, young man, you're going to be late.'

Let me tell you a little bit more about my mother. She is, I suppose, quite attractive, and definitely just a bit feisty, as you may have gathered – not unlike Bangor's version of Penelope Cruz. She laughs it off whenever I say so but deep down I know she's pleased with this comparison. Nain, Mam's Mam, liked to say she was a descendant of some shipwrecked Spanish merchants who had been washed up on the coast near Barmouth after an ill-fated voyage along the Irish Sea back in sixteen whatever-it-was. Lots of dark-haired north Walians claimed the same. As for our family, we went along with it, for Nain mostly, but I suppose it did make sense. Taid and Nain agreed on calling her Paloma; it means dove in Spanish and although as a household we spoke both Welsh and English, she herself had embraced her mythological heritage and learnt the lingo. She has a good ear for language: Bangor brought out the Bangor in her; London, when we made trips there, brought out the Londoner in her; as for her Spanish, well, she speaks it like a rattling castanet, slipping up only on occasion between the Welsh 'cariad', meaning 'love', and '*carino*' in Spanish. Same thing, she claims. Which is true. These days she works from home, translating art books into English for a famous gallery in Madrid, as well as the odd article for a few fashion journals. And it all began on a little laptop – her lifeline, she liked to remind me. Oh, and in her spare time she likes to watch Pedro Almodóvar films and *Coronation Street*. Gutsy women, she says.

I felt the bang of Taid's walking stick against the ceiling below me as I began my morning routine. I slipped on my trousers, assigning the bedroom for worrying about Mister Lloyd and the poster, and the bathroom for Elvis and my blessèd cow's lick. At the kitchen table I gave way to Idwal Slab's victory in the race.

'I mean, he wasn't even seeded by the club,' I wailed, part jokingly. 'Now, that's humiliating!'

Mam was browsing the Family Notices in the Menai Mail and not looking up. 'Cariad, life isn't fair. Full stop.'

A gentle knock. With the back door open, he must have heard us.

'Not interrupting anything, am I?'

Mam shot up and out of sight. The Liberator had landed, to-go plastic beaker in hand.

'Morning, Maldwyn,' Mam shouted from behind the hanging cupboards. I averted my gaze and focused on a plate of toast. *Is it him?* I knew Maldwyn was not technically at fault for Mister Lloyd going missing but I found blame in everyone. Maybe it was his guilty conscience that prompted this strange online campaign of hope. Maybe he was compensating for my loss. But the kitchen was not the place to ask. Through the corner of my eye, top right, an apron quickly landed in a heap in front of the Rayburn. No doubt there was a quick check in the mirror before she made her appearance from behind the units.

'It's this beaker, Mrs Price.' If Mam fashioned herself on Penelope Cruz, here was her Antonio Banderas hovering on the threshold and looking rather nervous. 'I did get your message, ay. Sorry. 'S been in the cabin all along.'

I turned to watch him as he handed it to her. Carefully.

'I could've kicked meself.' He glanced over his shoulder and saw me skulking about with a piece of toast. 'Sentimental value an' all.'

'There was no rush really but all's well that ends well,

Mal bach.' She gave it the once over. 'You needn't have washed it.'

'How's the tap?' he ventured.

'Gleaming, Mal bach.'

As far as Maldwyn was concerned Paloma Price was definitely worth the whistle and had been since school. A teenage crush he had never forgotten from the moment he saw her enthroned as Miss Bangor 1987, on a float in the Carnival and led by her own army of majorettes. It looked like he was still in that moment, watching from the crowd, when I stood up, toast in hand, poster in the other. I looked at my watch and made my way towards them, leaving any thought of confronting Elvis behind. 'Mam?'

'Sorry, I'm blocking you in, aren't I?'

''Fraid so. Did you bring the lorry?' Mam enquired.

'Damia, no. Did you want stuff taking to the skip? I've only got The Mid-Life Crisis with me, Mrs P—' He stopped, rolled his eyes. 'I mean, Paloma.'

Mam smiled.

Oh puh-leeze. I made my way past them and into the yard.

'Even better, Mal,' she said and pointed at me. 'This one's late for school. Won't take long, seeing as you *are* blocking us in. Fresh brew waiting for you when you get back.'

With my back to them I closed my eyes and took a deep breath. Was it him?

'Right, then,' he said, stealing himself away. 'Let's be having you.'

'Oh, and Maldwyn,' added Mam. 'Don't suppose you're any good with printers?'

'I can certainly have a look, ay.'

'You're a life saver. Now hurry, Mal bach.'

I had heard that a mid-life crisis was something that happened to some people when they had got to a certain age, usually when it crept up on them that time was running out. My own, I had decided at that very moment, would manifest itself in an Aston Martin, a trophy for what I'd hoped would be a well-spent first half. The outcome now differs as each year passes, of course, but Maldwyn's came in the form of a mustard yellow MGF two-seater and, wondering whether this was a legacy of doing 'this and that' in Dubai, I slid down the passenger seat in the hope that no one would spot me.

'No more news about Mister Lloyd, I take it?' he felt prompted to ask, just as we took the turn that led into Deiniol High, sandwiched as it was between the port and the mountains. Not much had been said up till this point. I hadn't known where to begin.

'You can drop me off here.'

'I was going to take you to the main entrance. 'S nearer, ay.'

'Not allowed, sorry.'

Maldwyn duly pulled up to a side gate as directed. 'Right, well, here you go then.'

'Thanks,' I blurted, having trouble finding the handle in the leatherette door panel.

'Pull the yellow lever thing,' said Maldwyn helpfully. 'It's a Special Edition. Only three hundred made.'

'I can see why,' I added, about to go.

'I lost one of my pigeons,' he said when I was halfway out.

I slid back into the seat.

'I mean, we're talking years ago now, ay.'

The school bell went but all sense of time and fear had evaporated.

'Shut up! What happened?'

Maldwyn surveyed his cockpit. Dust fled his touch when he wiped the facia, as if it too knew what he was about to tell me was reckless. The audacity of hope, as Barack Obama would coin a few years later. 'He came home. Took three weeks, mind.'

I looked at him. 'Are you taking the piss?'

Maldwyn laughed. 'You'd better hop it. Last call, mate. I'll tell you later.'

Was it him? I swallowed hard and cast him some bait, almost under my breath. 'Elvis?'

'What's Elvis got to do with it?'

'Is it you?'

Maldwyn splurted a laugh. 'Well, I may be a legend, but beg y'pardon? What are you on about?'

'Nothing,' I said, realising my mistake. 'Laters!' As I got out of the car I was beaming, none the wiser as to who Elvis was but strangely full of hope. I slammed the door, unaware that, somewhere up above, Lowri, Gar and Tim were banging on the classroom window. I watched The Mid-Life Crisis perform a three-point turn, its yellow paint glowing, almost blinding me in the morning sun. Then the enhanced exhaust kicked in and faded into the distance. 'That car's got to go,' I remember thinking and ran to class.

It's not that I loathed school. I just hated Lynton Chivers. Let me tell you why: bell goes, we walk between classes;

Lynton shouts, 'Oi!' I roll my eyes; he says, 'Pigeon Nancy!' I carry on walking. Corridor trip-up, Lynton grabs and pulls jumper. I say, 'Gerroff!' then try to think of something funny. He says I 'fancy pigeons', they all start laughing. Big deal. Him: 'Weirdo.' Me: 'Eff Off.' Him: 'Weirdo.' Me: Eff *off.* Him: 'Perv.' Me: '*Eff. Off.*' Him: 'Nancy.' Head gets knocked against wall, Lynton and gang walk off. Typical drill. All very dull.

Today I was late. Staying focused on my photocopying mission, I took the gym entrance, slipping past the sports changing rooms, empty at this time. It was also the furthest point from the head teacher, Mr Griffiths' office. If timed well I could slip past the biology lab at the bottom of the stairs and disappear amongst the trickling mob that was beginning to make its way down to assembly. I got to the top floor, passing closed doors and the muffled calling out of names in alphabetical order. I gained speed, catching the letter P at the furthest end of the corridor. With the skill of a cracksman I turned the door handle.

'Price, Mostyn!' Self-Help Ms Hughes called out, her eyes fixed down at the register.

'Present, Miss.'

When her eyes lifted from the page, I'd thrown my bag onto the nearest desk and slipped next to—

My heart sank, head collapsed onto bag.

'Howaya pigi' da'dcy.'

I thought, *please, not here*. Not in front of Ms Hughes's class. Hang on, what did he say? I turned my head to its side and looked at Lynton. 'Did you say "Dancing"?'

He darted a quick check in Ms Hughes's direction then pressed his elbow into my neck. 'Shut your gob, you dumbo.

I got a cold.'

My neck cricked as he let go. I tried not to look in pain and hauled myself up when I saw a hand appear between us, giving Lynton a clip round the ear-hole and me a tap on my shoulder. It was Lowri, sat with Gar and Tim. 'Here, give him this,' she whispered, rummaging in her bag and winking at the other two. She held out her fist and dropped a small tincture bottle into my hand, not unlike Mister Lloyd's Nazaline drops. 'Seeing as he's got a cold.'

'Morning to you an' all,' I said and examined the bottle. I didn't recognise it but, too late, Lynton snatched it off me.

'What is it?'

A nudge from Lowri. 'He's to sniff it up his nose. Quickly.'

I turned back to Lynton. 'It should clear you up.'

He looked at me, then turned his gaze to Lowri and began to unscrew the cap.

'Assembly!' announced Ms Hughes.

'Right, let's scarper,' said Lowri, grabbing my bag and dragging me to the door before the rest of the class had got to their feet. 'We're going front row. Far away from him!'

Mr Griffiths liked to hold us hostage by his use of the dramatic pause and a bobbing head. His theme for the day was Friendship. I tried to look captivated but my mind was drifting onto photocopying. Not knowing where to begin, let alone how many I needed, I looked around, tallying up a random figure, but was distracted by an ashen-looking Lynton being escorted out of the hall. I elbowed Lowri hard. 'Oi! What the heck did you give Lynton? He's just been carted off! White as a sheet.'

Lowri peered over my shoulder then leant into my ear.

'Hand sanitizer.'

'What?'

'Well, I think so,' said Lowri. 'Smelt like it. Makes you all queasy.'

I could hardly believe what I was hearing. 'You mean you don't know what it is?'

Gar leaned round and tugged at my elbow. 'She found it in her brother's bedroom,' he told me helpfully, Tim giggling behind.

'Oh, brilliant, Lowri. Now I'm really in it.'

'Ah, nonsense! He snatched it off you. Willing participant. He'll live.'

'So,' she said, clutching my arm as we finally scurried out of the hall, 'your seagull showed up yet?'

'Not quite, no, Lowri. But thanks for asking.' She meant well, I suppose.

'Any news from the seagull website thingummy?'

'Nada,' I replied.

'Tell you what,' she said, clutching me in even tighter, 'I'll email Crimewatch, see if they can do a reconstruction.'

With her skinny jeans, unruly black hair and heavy eyeliner, Lowri's rebelliousness stretched to unlimited cheek and a hurried roughing of outfit when she got to school each morning. Her parents, pleased with her eagerness to arrive early, and so immaculately dressed, never found out. I didn't know if it was a crush I had on her, or if it was love.

As official gang spokesperson, Lowri wasn't one to beat around the bush, but skirt around the issue of her and me we did. Trouble was, we were best friends. She told me about girls – who was in, who was out – while I doled out advice on boys. Painful at times; neither she nor I could give anything away, me not thinking she'd be interested and probably too shy to ask anyway. Fear of rejection, perhaps, and so we both settled on being friends.

'Anyway, what was that yellow jalopy we saw you in earlier?' she asked. 'I couldn't bear to look at it, it was so ugly. Do we need to talk about this, Mostyn?'

I turned around and saw Gar and Tim smirking. 'You didn't!'

'So, whose car was it then?' asked Lowri.

I looked at all three. 'Maldwyn's. A friend of Taid.'

'Try again.'

'OK. Mam knows him too. He's fixing her printer. That's all.'

'Fixing the printer, is it? Very convenient, I'm sure. In that case, we definitely need to talk about Maldwyn,' She squinted at me. 'You work on that car, babe.'

Sweet, unforgiving Lowri. She nudged me on and I walked ahead till I felt another arm reaching over my shoulder. Self-Help Ms Hughes.

'Poor boy. You're hurting forward-slash grieving, aren't you?' she analysed, her voice switched to life-coach mode. With earnest eyes, relishing other people's pain was her life's purpose. 'You know, when I lost my pet cat four months ago, I oscillated between rage and sorrow. But I found yoga, meditation and keeping myself busy helped, as and when and so forth.'

Elvis? It couldn't be. Truth was, anyone who was being nice to me was now a suspect. But my suspicions could wait; I'd just realised my photocopying challenge was going to be a cinch. 'We're coming to the end of term, miss,' I pointed out. 'There's not that much to take my mind off things.'

''Tis true, Mostyn,'tis true. When are you next with me?'

'After double French, miss.'

'Well, I'm sure we can find something. Let's see—'

'Any photocopying, miss?'

'Right, where am I vis-à-vis photocopies? Ah, yes. Mock exam paper copied for Year 4! Remind me to give you the department's account number and paper. You know the school policy on paper accountability.'

'Yeah, yeah. "Mr Griffiths takes a stern view..."' Damia! I had forgotten the matter of paper accountability. I gave out a heavy sigh. Self-Help Ms Hughes grabbed my arm.

'Is it the hurting? Maybe you could do with some chakra clearing.'

I smiled politely. 'So, how long did it take you to find your cat, miss?'

'I didn't, dear boy. Never came back.' She patted me on the shoulder. 'But as Sonia tells Uncle Vanya at the curtainly end of Chekhov's eponymous play, "we shall rest!" And, like her, I too have found peace.'

She nodded stoically and I watched her walk away, leaving me motionless in the flowing, throbbing corridor. She had ruled herself out as Elvis there and then. I would skip *Uncle Vanya* but decided to look up oscillating and, possibly, chakra clearing.

The photocopier room was situated by the headteacher's office but you had to call by reception for the key. I handed the chit to Judith.

'I'd better check it's working,' she said. 'I've had to call out the repairman twice this week and with all these reports to do... Let me check. Stay where you are.'

My eyes darted around, searching for more paper. I clocked the green bin behind the desk chair: used A4 paper. Then I heard loud banging noises and even louder cursing from next door: Judith kicking the photocopier. I was about to pounce on the recycling bin when she walked back in.

'It's working.' she announced, quite breathless and dishevelled. 'Go 'head, boy.'

'Umm, I'm just going to do a few test pages on some old paper if that's OK,' I said, my right cheek in a spasm and passing it off as a smile. 'I wouldn't want it to break down on me and waste the department's paper.'

'Good idea!' she said, pointing at the green bin. 'Take whatever you need.'

Thirty sheets churned out happily while I smoothed out the frayed edges of my loot, realigning them as a neat pile in the A4 drawer. Exam papers sorted, I unfolded the poster, placed it upside down on the scanner. I had counted forty-three sheets in all and pressed the amount on the small screen. The machine obliged and out they came.

Job done, the bell went. I gathered up all the copies and scarpered out of the door.

Holding both sets in one hand, with only my forefinger to separate the legit and the loot, I ran along the corridor. Facing the oncoming horde like a scrumhalf taking possession of the ball, I ducked and dived through the playtime rush hour. Straight into Lynton's path. He looked fully recovered from his funny turn and in rude health. I felt the thrust of a fist hard on my chest and a hand grabbing my sweater, tearing the neckline.

'Don't you EVER dare make fun of me EVER again, d'ya hear?'

'I never!'

'What was that poof juice you gave me?'

'You snatched it off me! Anyway, it was just a hand sanitizer!'

'Don't lie, Pigeon Nancy!' Lynton pulled me in close. I wanted to retch. 'I don't like you cos you're a pigeon perv. Your pigeons spread germs. Just like this,' he said and spat in my face, a show for an increasing circle of spectators. I tore myself from his grip and, still clutching the photocopies, wiped the spittle with my sleeve, involuntarily revealing what I held in my hand.

Lynton snatched them from me. 'What have we got here then?'

I wanted to pull them back off him. I tried but he held them high. He was tall for his age and I had to jump to even try and reach. The spectacle was beginning to draw the attention of eager scrap-seekers. I gave one last jump and grabbed them off him.

'Nothing! Get lost!' I shouted to a few cheers. I tried to stuff the posters into my pocket but it was too small. One of Lynton's mob came in from behind, grabbed my wrist and wrenched them out of my hand.

'Can't be nothing,' said Lynton, taking the posters from his assistant and rifling through my work. He then started to chuck them on the floor one by one, much to the amusement of the fair-weather crowd. 'Lynton! Lynton! Lynton,' was all I could hear.

'Oh look, pictures of your poncy pigeon,' he roared, holding up one for all to see. He took hold of the last dozen or so and started to rip them in half.

Torn pieces flew into the air. In slow motion fragments of hope and hard graft floated downwards like feathers. Something inside me snapped and I lunged, punching Lynton in the face with all my strength. He doubled up in pain but then quickly charged towards me, thrusting my head against the wall. I felt the full impact. He pushed me further up, lifting me off the ground. What followed happened very quickly. Maybe he stepped on one of the fallen pieces of paper; maybe the hand sanitizer hit him all over again. Whatever happened, his foot slipped backwards, causing his right leg to buckle and his chin to land on my knee. We all heard his teeth snap together. He fell to the floor and, seeing Lowri's jaw wide open, I gave him a kick in the stomach. But then, scuffling between the chanting crowds, feebly at first, the linen-clad Mr Griffiths grabbed Lynton, then me, and steered us straight into his office.

I wished I had stayed in bed.

CHAPTER EIGHT

Headteacher's office, Bangor

'But NOTHING! I have it on good authority that you hit him first. People saw you. I have witnesses.' Mr Griffiths turned away to look out onto a view of the old port and Beaumaris beyond.

'But, Sir! HE tore my…' I stopped. It was no use telling him about the poster. I took a deep breath and began again. 'I was sent by Ms Hughes to do some photocopying. The bell went and I was running back with the copies.'

'Liar,' Lynton added. 'Ms Hughes isn't lookin' for a lost pigeon, is she?'

Mr Griffiths turned from his reflection. 'Go on, Price.'

'I know I shouldn't have run, sir, but I was trying to get back to Ms Hughes's classroom and he just grabbed me. Look!'

Mr Griffiths seemed unimpressed by my torn jumper. 'Why did you grab him, Lynton?'

'He gave me some nasal oil thing this morning. Told me to sniff it up my nose. Said it would clear me up.'

'I never! That was—' *No, don't bring Lowri into it.* 'That's what I was told, sir.'

'What did the label say?' Mr Griffiths cut in. 'You should always read the label.'

'There was no label, sir,' said Lynton. 'But it made me

61

feel sick and I didn't like it.'

'You grabbed it off me. I didn't know it would make you feel sick,' I protested. Mr Griffiths was looking away so I carried on. 'And even if I did, I wouldn't have given it you deliberately!' This was true. *Oh, just fess up,* I thought, *let's get out of here.* 'Look, I'm sorry and I'm an idiot.'

I hoped we could leave it there but Lynton persisted.

'He's weird, sir.'

The headteacher rubbed his eyes before deciding he needed to sit down. He placed his elbows on the desk. 'Weird?'

'He keeps pigeons, sir!'

Mr Griffiths sat back and began to rock his head gently from side to side. 'Pigeons,' he repeated dreamily, his eyes half closed. 'My grandfather kept pigeons. He claimed it saved his marriage.' His eyes opened wide. 'Are you saying my grandfather was weird?'

Lynton froze. 'No, sir, but—'

'But what, then?'

'Pigeons, sir! They're dis-gust-ing!'

'Disgusting is someone spitting in your face,' I snapped.

The headteacher leaned forward. 'Lynton, may I just remind you that being different is not a reason for picking on anyone. It's cowardly, do you understand?'

Lynton mumbled something.

'I can't quite hear you, Lynton.'

'Sorry, sir.'

Mr Griffiths sighed. 'Don't apologise to me. Apologise to him, you idiot!'

Lynton looked away. 'Sorry.'

'Mostyn?' said Mr Griffiths expectantly.

I took a deep breath. 'Sorry for hitting you.'

'So, what am I going to do with you?' Mr Griffiths rose to his feet and surveyed the view. 'What do you think I should do, Mostyn, eh? Lynton, any suggestions?'

We both shrugged our shoulders.

'Well, I'll tell you,' announced Mr Griffiths. 'A week today, last day of term, we'll hold a debate. The whole school's invited. The subject shall be Pigeon: Friend or Foe. You both have strong views, indeed are experts in your field. So, you two: for and against.'

I think I heard Lynton gasp but I couldn't be sure.

'Oh, and a no-show is not an option.' And with that, the headteacher headed to the door and I felt the gust as he swung it open. 'It will be excellent. Dismissed.'

Boys' toilets. I waited for hot water, washed my face and looked back at me in the mirror. I started to smile. I couldn't help it, didn't understand it somehow, but I was grinning as I pat-dried my face. Then I knew. I had waited almost a year to deliver that punch. I went back to the water and splashed some more. *Oh, Mister Lloyd, why did you have to go?* I stepped out into the ghostly noise of an empty school corridor and approached the stairs, in search of my bag. Grabbing hold of the handrail, I contemplated the climb ahead.

Through the glass pane, Self-Help Ms Hughes was pacing up and down the classroom with an open book. *Uncle Vanya*, I imagined. I knocked; she looked to the door, excused herself momentarily from her beloved listeners, who readily agreed, and walked to the door.

'I've come to get my bag, miss,' I murmured.

Ms Hughes beckoned me in. She grabbed an envelope as I retrieved my bag, and walked me back out again.

'I'm sorry about the photocopies, miss.'

'Don't worry,' she said, 'your friend Lowri picked them up. She has her good points. *They* were unharmed, not like your— You left the original face down on the photocopier.'

I opened the envelope and pulled out sheet upon sheet of brand new Mister Lloyd posters.

Elvis, was it you?

'I went down to the photocopying room to see what had happened. Thought fifty should be enough.' She tapped her nose before pointing at the copies. 'Only, thing is, there's a mark on the original, I'm afraid. Here.'

I looked down. A tea ring and a crumb of toast. My flawed masterpiece. 'No worries. Diolch, Ms Hughes.'

We were now by a tree outside the old Woollies, where Boots is these days, Gar standing astride the flowerbed and Lowri balancing herself on his shoulders. She needed a better reach of the trunk. I slid the inaugural sheet into a plastic pocket, Tim by my side, drawing pins at the ready. It all had a touch of ceremony, I thought proudly, handing Lowri the very first poster.

'So he's a pigeon now, is he? Whoa!' she said, trying to regain her balance. 'Careful, Gar!'

'Always was, Lowri.'

'Well, break it to me like that, why don't you. Careful! Anyway,' she continued, balance regained and thrusting a pin into the wood, 'what makes you think, yea, that your pidge will be found on Bangor High Street? If he got this far, wouldn't he want to be in the palatial surroundings of

Graceland?'

'Gee, thanks.'

'Just saying. I mean, why fly all the way home, get so near and live it rough down the road? OK, Mister Lloyd's got all the shopping opportunities he needs here but, no offence, like, isn't this a bit hopeless?'

I didn't let on but she had a point.

'Come off it, Lows. Think of it more as progress,' piped up Gareth. 'Isn't that right, Mozzie?'

I nodded.

As did Tim. 'What if it was your Little Nell. Wouldn't you be doing all you could to try and find her? Dog, pigeon. What's the difference?'

She smiled briefly and began to straighten the poster. Up there on Gar's shoulder she cut a lonely figure. She had told me she had her eye on Tim and I hadn't the heart to tell her that his was on Gar. Maybe she knew this; maybe she was trying me out. It made me think: when I find Mister Lloyd I would confess all I felt and be done with it. I pictured that moment, her laughing in my face.

'You are joking me!' she screamed, bringing me back to outside Woollies. 'Have you seen this?'

I jumped on the bench for a closer look.

'She's only gone and given you marks for your spelling. It says here "six out of ten, see me." Cheek!'

I craned my neck. 'Where?'

'Only kidding!' she said, slipping off Gar's shoulders and onto the flowerbed in a heap of laughter. I think it must have brought the colour back to my ashen face, if only for a moment. My phone went off and I reached into my pocket – an incoming text message from Taid, his selfie flashing urgently on the small screen.

'Hurry home dear boy. Sum ML1 news. CUL8R'

IX

Oh dear, it's as we suspected. It did not take long before Mister Lloyd felt weak – he still does – and you can see he is fast losing his bearings. Below him the few houses, roads and cars give way to trains, vans, buses, lorries. Traffic everywhere and people too, walking the streets like the ants he would have once watched in the garden of Graceland. And ahead on the horizon he sees a cluster of tall buildings, the likes of which he's not come across before. Though weak and in desperate need of rest, we can only hope Mister Lloyd does not give up. He mustn't give up, because Mostyn is waiting.

'Can't stop now,' he tells himself. Oh, this resolve is much to our relief, wouldn't you say? A train speeds along on a track beneath him. With any luck he will be thinking of the *Beagle* and, yes, in a snap decision – quick, let's go with him – he shoots down and lands on one of its carriages. Hold on tight, it's going at quite a speed but at least he is safe. For now.

Unbeknown to Mister Lloyd this is the 08.58 from Brussels to London we are travelling on – and without tickets! It is coming towards the end of its journey but,

67

alas, Mister Lloyd is nowhere near the end of his. And we can see he is in pain, hungry and in need of water. He knows he is lost. Let's hope he doesn't feel too sorry for himself. He has every right to feel sorry for himself, of course – who could blame him? – but the danger is that such self-pity could slow down his resolve to find home. He is inspecting the gash in his abdomen; blood oozes from the wound, even though, luckily, travelling at fifty miles an hour through the cold air has quickened the clotting process. He bends his head down to try and clean himself up with his beak but as he does he sees two large claws land on the same carriage. *No, it can't be*, he tells himself, looking up again. The train is approaching a tunnel and, as the darkness nears, Mister Lloyd shoots vertical – we must follow! – leaving the Falcon stranded on the roof of the carriage, first class we now see from this new angle. And there he goes, disappearing into the black hole.

With the You-Know-Who off his back, or so he thinks, Mister Lloyd continues in the direction of the city. He tries to work out his way home but cannot attune his magnetite crystals to the North or South Pole bands. Mister Lloyd is tired and weak and his sense of home is blighted further by an array of strong electromagnetic fields. He is totally unaware he is following the train's route through the tunnel! The 08.58 from Brussels reappears and, oh no, there it is again! Up shoots the bird of prey, coming straight at him. There isn't much time, Mister Lloyd! Go! Go! Go! He ducks under the You-Know-Who and shoots off, drawn – he doesn't know why – to a series of masts dotted around the city. It looks like they are navigating his route, guiding him by some dizzying signal. To wherever. This city, this London, is drawing him in.

On he flies through one such metallic mast structure but the falcon, in this instance, is not so clever. Behind him Mister Lloyd hears the squawk of the distressed bird He is still alive but has become hopelessly entangled. This device that seemed to throw Mister Lloyd off-course is leading him to safety! He flies for his life; we must follow, above and in-between tall towers, domes and concrete blocks. He flies until his lungs ache, until his wing muscles can work no more, until he falls from the sky.

CHAPTER TEN

Darwin HQ, Bangor.

I kicked open the container door, a technique only known to the few. 'What's happened?' I asked, out of breath and barely able to speak. I had run all the way up Love Lane, cutting straight to Graceland via the top drive.

'Hey, calm down,' said Taid. He was casually doling out Royal Jelly capsules into the pill organiser he had received by post that morning, the back pages of the Sunday supplements being his only retail weakness.

'Tell me!' I was astonished by his lack of urgency. 'Hurry home, you said.'

'Well, he's been spotted but not found, "as such",' said Taid, miming speech marks before finishing his administering and making his way to the computer.

'Where? What does that mean, "not found"? Who spotted him? Come on, Taid, get with the programme!'

'Looks like he fell out of the sky in London.' The silver surfer lifted his bifocals and hit Print.

My eyes shot down to the telex-like machine as it considered its response. It croaked like a pheasant, randomly and stupidly. I gave up and dashed to the screen. I felt my throat tighten.

From: Simon Blake [simon@systems-fidelity.com]
Sent: 08 July 2005 18.24
To: info@reportstraysonline/mostynprice
Subect: Mister Lloyd Sighting!

Good day!

Not wishing to get your hopes up or anything, but I thought I'd get in touch as I have just seen your pigeon! I haven't found it, as such, but I did see it and thought you ought to know! I work as a Systems Emotions Analyst in an office at Tower 42 in London – the building formerly known as the NatWest tower, you may recall. Anyway, I was up on the roof having a cheeky fag – not meant to be there obviously, but that's another story! (I am going to give up after the holidays!) I was standing there when over on the ledge I saw what looked like a bird lying on the edge! He didn't look too good, to be honest. Had a gash, barely conscious if you ask me – I'm sorry about this!

'Sorry? He's injured! Why can't this guy come to the point?'

'I quite agree,' said Taid, closing the pill organiser lid. 'Should we ever trust a man who has an overenthusiastic penchant for the exclamation mark?'

The pheasant gave a final croak. I turned to the printer, snatching the completed copy and continued reading.

On further inspection I saw he had a ring band and I made a note of it on the Gooseberry (my wife's term for it! She is HIL-AR-IOUS) and when I'd finished the fag I went down to the office to Google what I should do with a lost pigeon. I found you guys and went to look for a box but by the time I came back up, he was gone! It had begun to rain by then, so I don't know what happened! It's a mystery! Don't know if this helps, but anyway I thought I'd let you know, in case you were wondering where he had got to. I'd say he's definitely in the Greater London vicinity.

Best!
Simon Blake
IT Systems Analyst

I think I sat down at this point, my mind a whirl. The Greater London Vicinity. That could be anywhere. I turned to the computer and went to Favourites. I was looking for my 'friend'.

'Is this Simon Blake chap a member of Report Strays Online, Taid?'

'I don't think so,' he said looking over, 'he just emailed the link. Why?'

'Nothing.' I looked over my shoulder, saw that Taid was unpacking a delivery of Nazaline drops and took the cursor over to the username search box. I typed Misterlloydfanclub but it told me Elvis was offline. I clicked Back and took hold of the printed email once more. Stumped, I looked at Taid.

'So what do we do?'

'Not much we can do, Mostyn bach. Apart from the fact he might be dead or alive in London, we're none the wiser.'

I wiped my eyes a little. They had got a little blurred.

'I'm sorry, my boy. I don't want to raise your hopes. Racing pigeons is full of uncertainties. It's hard, but you have to accept that we've lost Mister Lloyd.' He paused. 'Acceptance is something we all have to learn.'

'I won't accept it, Taid. I won't. I won't,' I remember shouting, mouth dry. Kicking the door to Darwin HQ wide open, I ran to the house, hard copy of the email clenched in my hand. 'I'll search for him in London, if need be!'

'Have you been to see Taid?'

I was entering the kitchen. 'Yup.' It was abrupt, I know. I threw my bag on the table along with Simon Blake's message and made my way to the sink, helping myself to some water.

Mam turned from the stove. 'It's a bit inconclusive, isn't it?'

'What is?'

'The email.' She sounded uneasy, to be fair, and held up the piece of paper. 'Taid told me.'

'It certainly is.' I snatched it off her, making my way through the hall to the stairs.

'Wait a minute! What happened to your sweater?'

For a good while now I had managed to keep the delicate subject of Lynton Chivers from my mother. Life, I found, was easier this way, but that afternoon at the top of the landing I had been well and truly rumbled. 'Not now, Mam. Please!'

'Aren't you going to say anything?' she called out.

I pretended not to hear and slammed my bedroom door shut.

With the vigour of the unclean I threw off my uniform and got changed. Tracky bottoms, frayed hoody, check shirt. More like myself, I trod over the discarded debris and sat on the bed, catching sight of the posters jutting out of my bag. Keep my mind occupied, Self-Help Ms Hughes had suggested. I grabbed a pen and began to write a list on the back of Simon Blakes's email. Stupid Simon Blake.

TRIP TO LONDON.

CONTACT LONDON CLUBS.

VETS, CITY OF LONDON.

CRIMEWATCH

UPDATE ONLINE.

BULLETIN BOARD.

TALK TO MALDWYN. HOW HIS CAME HOME?

MALDWYN = ELVIS???

EMAIL SIMON BLAKE!!!!!!!!!!!!!!!!!!!!!!

SAY SORRY TO TAID.

MISTER LLOYD DEAD????

RUBBISH.

HOPELESS.

WHERE THE HELL IS DAD?

PATHETIC.

I HATE LYNTON CHIVERS.

I kicked my bag and took a swipe at the posters. Taking to the walls, I pulled off pictures, centrefolds and pin-ups, many of them covering the evidence of a previous incident. Why should I care? I asked myself. He was only a pound of flesh. I fell in a heap on the bed, staring at the walls now decorated with a constellation of oily dots, remnants of tacking gum, where cars and bands had recently promised much more. I tried to look into the future, like Nain had done with her tealeaves, but no sign emerged. I was looking at a dust-blackened cobweb that hung inside the ceiling pendant when a faint knock on the door broke the silence: Mam.

'Hello? Just to say that tea's ready,' she announced, edging the door open – enough to catch whatever she needed to see.

When I sat down, Mam turned off the radio. I knew this opener: always a signal for a chat. I looked down at my plate. Cumberland sausage and mashed potato. Canny, I remember thinking. Canny that she should have chosen a favourite. She slid into the seat opposite me while I sloshed Worcestershire sauce on my plate, waiting for her words.

'Look, I want to tell you something.'

I began humming to the joy of food.

'I'm sure that whatever happened today was not your fault, Mostyn bach, but – well – are you in any trouble?' She caught my eye and I saw that her beauty had taken on a stoic air. I was ready for this: *Uncle Vanya* – 'We Shall Rest' all over again. Looking back I can see she must have been desperate to rid me of my misery, to get the old Mostyn back. I had released glimmers of my old self since the loss of Dad, glimmers that gave way to brighter periods, but losing Mister Lloyd meant we were back to snatched moments and many of them botched. 'Is someone bullying you?'

'What?' I had been holding the knife and fork with an extra tense grip but now they landed on the plate. 'No!'

'Fine.' Mam looked down at her plate and began to move some food. The screeching of fork on plate wore on the silence. 'Well, that's that, then.'

I should have left it there. Yet the thought that my Mam could know of my being bullied, that she should know of my daily hell brought about some panic. 'It's not me,' I blurted, too ashamed. 'I'm not the one being bullied.'

Mam looked up. 'So what happened to the sweater?'

Oh God! This was a total mess. *Quick, think!* I swallowed hard, keen to mop up more than just the sauce. 'This lad. No-one you know' – *quick, anyone!* – 'anyway, he's been giving Gareth a hard time, calling him all sorts of names.'

Cowardly, I know, but how could I explain the shame?

'Taunted him for a few months now,' I continued. 'Teachers ignore it, of course. Anyway, he tripped him up during break and banged his head against the wall. I went in there to help, as you do, obviously, and he just grabbed my sweater. End of. I'm sorry.'

'Don't be sorry. It's only a sweater, Mostyn bach. Good God, doesn't matter about that.'

I smiled and picked up the knife and fork.

'Poor Gar,' said Mam after a while. 'You know, I read an article in one of those *Give Me a Break!* magazines the girls pass around in the hairdressers. It said three things about bullying, not necessarily in this order: first, suffering in silence, one of the worst things you can do.' She had put her knife and fork down by this point and was counting with her fingers. 'Second, fighting back can get you into even more trouble, and three, most important, it's never your fault. Tell *him* it'd be good for him to get things off his chest.'

I began to regret my line of tactic. 'An Error Carried Forward' was what Dr Rees, my maths teacher, would say – a mistake by any other name.

'Do you think he's got someone to talk to?' she asked. Looking back I can see what she was doing. 'It's flamenco tonight. I'm seeing his mam for a glass of cava after class. I'll have a chat.'

'No! Don't do that, please, Mam,' I protested.

'Do what?'

'Well, I said to Gar I wouldn't say anything. Wouldn't want to embarrass him.' The tide inside me was rising but I was trying to remain perfectly still.

'Don't you worry, Mostyn bach. I'll be very discreet, but there's no way anyone should suffer in silence, is there? Tell me, does Gareth think this is what he deserves in life?'

I looked down at my plate and began twisting the fork in the mashed potato.

'I want you to know that, if such a thing were to happen to you, you can come and talk to me. It's not what you'd deserve,' added Mam and, in hindsight, it did sound as if she might know more than she was letting on. 'Look, you've been upset these last few days with Mister Lloyd disappearing an' all that, but I don't see much joy in those eyes when it comes to school, full stop.'

'Well, you're wrong there, for a start,' I snapped. I see this now as panic. 'I don't care about Mister Lloyd anymore.

It's only a stupid bird that got lost, forgot its way home or, for all I know, couldn't be bothered. It's probably dead, so why should I care?'

'What nonsense is this? You can't have stopped caring about Mister Lloyd overnight?'

'Why not? You did!'

'What do you mean? Just because I don't think your whole life should be validated by a single bird, doesn't mean I don't care.'

'That's not what I meant.'

'Sorry, Mostyn, I don't quite follow.'

She was following all right, but in her eyes I should be man enough to spit it out. Oh, how I regret this!

'You stopped caring when Dad left. You said you loved him but that didn't stop him leaving, and then when he did you gave up! You obviously can't have loved him enough, otherwise he wouldn't have gone. And look at you now.'

'Now?'

The telephone rang but it didn't stop me.

'Now that Bangor "ay" lad is sniffing around.' This still haunts me now. It was unrehearsed but it came from somewhere.

Mam's eyes welled up. 'Right,' she said, rising to her feet. 'Well, thank you for that. Is that why you think Mister Lloyd went? Not enough love?'

I couldn't answer; I couldn't even hold her gaze. I looked away, the ringing telephone piercing through the entire house.

'Well, you tell Gareth,' she said, writing as if with a heavy pencil, 'and in however which way you wish to word it' – why was she pointing at me? – 'His life may be hell for him now, but paradise will come later if he sets his mind to it.'

She opened the kitchen door and went to the phone.

I stared at the age-worn plate, counting its scratches and the rutted inroads I had made into the mashed potato. I felt hot and soon lost focus. 'Family hold back' was the saying. We hadn't that night. I heard Mam pick up the phone.

'Hello,' she said, clearing her throat. 'Paloma Price.'

A beat.

'Oh, Joy! It's you. Excuse me. I've got a frog in my throat. No, no, you're alright. We've just finished supper.'

Joy Rathbone. From London.

XI

Tower 42, City of London

He's opening his eyes! Mister Lloyd is opening his eyes! OK, he looks confused as he stirs but don't we all when we wake up? And then there is the strange sensation in his leg. What is this? Is it someone taking hold of his ring? After the peregrine falcon he is naturally wary but this is less threatening. Gentler, somehow. Mister Lloyd moves his head and finds it is a human in male form. He whiffs a bit – smoke perhaps. Mister Lloyd's first reflex would be to recoil from the unfamiliar human form but so traumatized he must be after his chase that fear and exhaustion have frozen him to the spot. He feels drops of rain land on his feathers, as must the human on his shirt. At least we assume this is the case, for he is now running for shelter and Mister Lloyd is once more left alone and hopefully, this time, out of danger.

The rain is here, not drops now but lines and lines of it, and without weather boards to protect him from the elements, what is Mister Lloyd to do? I have seen it so many times in cases such as this. These lines of rain look like the dowels in the sputnik traps he faced every morning from the comfort of Graceland but, sadly, they are not them and he is not there. He curls into a ball and looks around from his perch on the edge of the building. Whoa, watch out, Mister Lloyd, it's a long way down! But why does he not set off in a vertical fashion, as he did, and so well, back in Leuven? Find home, Mister Lloyd, we want to shout, but we must remember he is weak and in shock and, besides, he cannot hear us. And without wishing to alarm you, this lack of energy suggests all his homing faculties are shutting down. He doesn't set off.

All around him more buildings and windows and nothing familiar, except what looks from here like a giant headless pigeon. Don't worry, Mister Lloyd, we want to tell him, this is the Gherkin! It's another famous landmark, we'd like to add, but even if we could, would it make him feel better at this point? Up above there are only clouds and when he looks left or to his right all he has is a sea of geometric shapes. He knows he is far from home and, more worryingly, clueless as to his whereabouts. But look, he still wants to fly away, we know he does; watch as he throws all his strength into getting on his feet. Trouble is, in so doing he is becoming aware of a numb feeling in his legs. Oh, please be careful, Mister Lloyd! His feet lie perilously close to the edge of the building and, stretching his wings to compensate – oh, this is a mistake – his tail wing fans open, bringing about a sharp pain in his abdomen. It is dizzying and with that Mister Lloyd loses his balance and falls forty-two floors.

CHAPTER TWELVE

Darwin HQ, Bangor

Having cleared the table and filled the dishwasher, I determined from the conversation she was having with Joy Rathbone, old best friend from college, that Mam was in it for the long haul. I'd hoped to wipe the slate clean. Lord knows I'd made enough enemies for one day but, clearly, what with their raucous laughter coming from the next room, my apology would have to wait. I went to look for Taid. I needed his help. To cap it all, there was the debate.

I called out for him as I approached Darwin HQ. The lights were on but there was no answer. I edged the door open to find the fire lit and Charles Darwin gyrating to a disco beat, screen-saving for Taid. It sent me to a different childhood.

Return to sender, Elvis piped knowingly from the stereo. I pictured him standing, admiring Taid's book collection that lined the walls of the entire shipping container.

–*Are these all about the pigeon world?*

–*Sure are. Insulation and Inspiration, Taid says.*

'Taid?' I called again. Was he in Graceland? I walked past an immersed Elvis but, feeling overwhelmed by the reading I had ahead of me, I made Charles Darwin disappear and logged on to my account.

Misterlloydfanclub: Bin w8ing 4 U. Get da Kofi on.

TheWingedAthlete: Not stayin 4 long,

Misterlloydfanclub: I C there's bin a sighting.

[I wasn't sure how to respond to this]

TheWingedAthlete: Hw d u know?

Misterlloydfanclub: GLOL [Genuine Laugh Out Loud] IC ur Upd8 on bull board. Username – ProfJenks. Know him p'raps? LOL C'n in da London massif?

[Taid must have updated the site after my hasty exit. I double-checked and clicked on the bulletin board. There it was with a special message to the London clubs. Elvis was right.]

TheWingedAthlete: I C. LOL! Yes. London. Can u believe?

Misterlloydfanclub: All roads lead to London, Mostyn.

[This took me by surprise, so I thought it was time to knock this Misterlloydfanclub on the head.]

TheWingedAthlete: Not being funny, right, but is this u Maldwyn?

Misterlloydfanclub: ??? Who he?? The liberator?

[Not that I felt scared, but it suddenly struck me that while I was trying to corner Maldwyn, it could also be Dad. And if it wasn't Dad, could it be Ms Hughes? She'd be

> frog-marching me straight to counselling. No
> thanks, I thought, and kept it neutral.]
> **TheWingedAthlete:** Y u says London?
> **Misterlloydfanclub:** LOL. Only sayin, if
> that's where he is, may-b u shud go.
> [If only. Elvis was saying everything I wanted
> to hear.]
> **TheWingedAthlete:** Who RU? Do u know
> me?
> **Misterlloydfanclub:** GLOL! I'd like to get to
> know U. So where were we, Leuven? Who
> took him to Leuven?
> **TheWingedAthlete:** Maldwyn, u no this!
> **Misterlloydfanclub:** Dude, the liberator!!
> **TheWingedAthlete:** So is it u?
> **Misterlloydfanclub:** ?? Me? Noooo. Soz.
> It's Elvis! Got2Go. Chat soon.
> [Then up it came again.]
> **Misterlloydfanclub** has quit chat.

I stared at the screen, highlighted and copied the
dialogue, no nearer to finding out who my friend was. My
fingers quivered above the mouse in between clicking all the
clicks. Strange thing was, I didn't feel in any danger. That's
the trouble when you live online. Up till then no threat had
been made; in fact, it was all rather encouraging: a lone
voice telling me to carry on. Whoever it was, they wanted
me to go to London. A risky pursuit, I knew, but one that
could result in finding Mister Lloyd. I put the computer on
sleep mode and, closing the door behind me this time, I
made my way to Graceland.

At the foot of the steps I heard someone singing. Not Elvis but Taid and definitely coming from the loft. I climbed the steps and knocked once on the door.

No answer. I knocked again, but still no response. I slowly pushed it open and saw him there, his back to me. It was Taid cleaning out the loft with a broom and listening to his iPod.

'*Waft her, angels through the sky,*' he sang, launching into a crescendo, completely unaware of my arrival. With Earl Grey and the gang safely penned next door, Taid was giving the loft a once over. '*Far above yon—*'

It would startle him, I knew, but there was no other way. I cleared my throat. 'Hellooooooo!'

He jumped, turned and banged his head on a wooden perch. 'Iesu mawr, you frightened the life out of me.'

'I didn't try to!'

'You didn't try not to either. Any sensible boy would have knocked!'

'I did!'

'And you left the door of Darwin HQ wide open earlier.'

'I know, I'm sorry. You're shouting, by the way.'

'Am I?' Taid pulled an earpiece out. 'Well, with good reason!' he added, putting the broom to one side. He looped the headphones and slotted the iPod into a pouch in his utility holster, one more of his many magazine purchases. Another was a nylon scrubbing brush which he now produced. 'Clean lofts, keeps 'em happy and full of vigour.'

I thought of my bedroom and its mess. 'I've come for some advice, Taid.'

'Oh, really?' he quipped and took to his next task, this time Mister Lloyd's box. 'How about helping me with this?

That's good advice. Not to mention technically your job.'

Did I imagine it? 'What are you doing?' I wanted Elvis.

'What does it look like I'm doing? I'm disinfecting Mister Lloyd's nest.'

'But he's not dead.'

'He might not be. As you know, high body temperature plus fast circulation equals superfast healing. He could be living the life of riley for all we know. But it doesn't necessarily mean he's coming back.' Taid raised both eyebrows.

How could he say such a thing? As much as I'd professed to not caring about my 'stupid' racing pigeon earlier, I knew deep down I couldn't just switch my feelings on and off like a light. Life would be easier, admittedly, but it didn't happen that way.

'Look, Grey's Anatomy and Anne of Grey Gables seem to be getting on well,' he explained. 'I need the compartment to fit them a new nest box.'

'Yikes. We haven't even buried him yet!'

Without hesitation Taid gave the box a thorough scrub, his tongue firm and curled against his lip. Sweat began to stream bead-like down his chin. He stopped. 'Can I just say one thing?'

'I think you're going to anyway, aren't you?'

'I'll let you into a secret.' He held out the scrubbing brush like his glasses earlier that day. 'Even the best fanciers endure bad luck, my boy. You just buck up and bounce back. Hard to believe, I know, even for someone as perfect as your Taid, but it takes a lot of patience. This is a cruel business.'

I nodded.

'You can't just start at the top, it's just not possible. You've got to watch your birds well to produce winners like these. Learn from mistakes, understand and accept and try, try, try again. Now, it's not all doom and gloom – there's an awful lot of pleasure to be had along the way – but the trick is, young man: never give up.'

'Like it or lump it?'

'Look, I'll do you a deal,' said Taid still holding the scrubbing brush. 'Even if Mister Lloyd does come back, we'd have to confine the poor critter to the hospital for a few weeks. I don't want him passing on any insects or a disease to those lovely things. Agreed?'

'I thought you preferred the "Kill All Diseased" option.'

'Iesu – there are two schools of thought!'

'Patience,' I reminded him.

'My point is we couldn't put him back here anyway, do you see? So, if he comes back, I promise we'll build him a new compartment – find him a mate. But if he doesn't, then I also promise to help you try again. You might not want to agree now but at least you know you've got another chance.'

I looked around the empty loft, the penned birds next door cooing eagerly for their clean surroundings, happy and full of vigour. 'All of life, eh?'

Taid smiled. 'If you feel up to it, you can have any of Anne of GG and Grey's young squabs as your own and we can start afresh.' He held out the scrubbing brush in my direction and, with a wink, gently kicked the pedestal into position. 'Deal?'

I took the brush and stared at it. Hard.

Why had Mister Lloyd not come back?

Taid handed me a dust mask. I thrust back my sleeves and climbed the pedestal.

This was his home!

I stared into the empty space of Mr Lloyd's cage. With some reluctance I began brushing. Slowly and gently at first, until I was overtaken by a compulsion to clean.

I mean, who were these critters that were about to take Mister Lloyd's place?

I scrubbed with all my energy – scrubbed and scrubbed. Vigour! Get into the corners!

They had no business.

I brushed and cleansed.

And Taid, why was he being so callous?

I buffed and cleansed, my knuckles chafing against the wood. Nobody, but nobody saw things how I did. They were all conspiring against me, wishing Mister Lloyd gone. Rage. Brush. Scrub. Cleanse.

Who was this Maldwyn anyway? Trying to get his foot under the table as if the past didn't matter.

Then I remembered. I lifted the mask and sneezed out the dust, coughing until it was out. This is exactly what Mam did when Dad left. She went a bit mad. I scooped out the corner with my nail. One day the house had been cleared when I came back from school. I saw her in the bay window and knew something was different. Told me Bangor High Street's charity shops had done well that week. She laughed. I didn't. I scrubbed and scrubbed. Then the garden caught fire. She had been burning Dad's things and it spread next door. Taid tried to hose it down at first but it became a job for the fire brigade. They nearly lost Graceland and there had been an almighty row. Then they took her away for a rest. We went to visit, Taid and I. That's when I bought her the travel mug. Saw it in a pound shop, a European reject from Spain with Spanish writing. I thought it would cheer her up and she looked pleased. 'With You to The End of the World' is what Mam said it meant. I removed the mask and blew out the last of the dust.

'You see, you've got a knack for it,' said Taid when I climbed down.

I froze. 'What have I got a knack for exactly? Picking total losers?'

'Snap out of it,' he said, leaning in to inspect my work. 'I meant the cleaning.'

I wiped the sweat and the dust off my face and gave out a small laugh. 'You're just saying that to get me to do all of them.'

'Well, there's a lot to be gained from purging the soul,' proffered Taid, his head almost wedged in the compartment. He pulled himself out. 'Does it feel any better?'

I supposed it did but I didn't want to let on. I extended my hand to help him down. 'I think I was a bit mean to Mam at tea time,' I confessed, guiding Taid off the stool.

'Oh, really?' he said, sounding more concerned about his inability to slot the scrubbing brush back into its rightful pouch.

'Yes. I got into trouble at school. She's worried I'm upset and I told her I didn't care about Mister Lloyd.'

Taid looked up at this point. 'I see. Go on.'

'And then I said she didn't care about Dad now Maldwyn was on the scene.'

'No doubt it'll blow over. We all say things we don't mean when we're upset,' he added, going back to his holster and giving the brush a final thrust. 'Hang on. Did you say she's seeing Maldwyn?'

I hesitated, worried I had not only upset her but had now dropped her in it. Taid's eyes lit up.

I nodded nonetheless. 'I mean, it's not strictly true. On the cards, so to speak.'

'No way!' said Taid, unable to conceal his excitement. 'No way!'

'Yes way,' I said, decidedly bemused.

'Well, that is terrific news!'

Taid started to collect his tools.

'You really think so?'

'Yes,' he said emphatically.

Clean lofts, I thought.

'We all deserve a chance to find happiness. What do you think this is?' Taid added, pointing at Graceland like an air steward pointing at the emergency exit. 'This was the only thing that kept me going when your Nain died.'

Did I shrug here? Not sure.

'Look, it's not because Mam's forgotten your father, far from it, but don't you think she deserves a second chance?'

I didn't say anything.

'Anyway,' said Taid, changing the subject. 'Didn't Maldwyn's pigeon come back? Have you asked him about it?'

'Chance'd be a fine thing.'

'Good enough for you now, is he?'

I couldn't quite make out his point but his words stayed with me.

'Now what did you want to ask me?'

'Well,' I began. 'Let's just say I need some lecturing tips.'

'I see,' said Taid. 'Well, let's just say my big thing is enunciation. Right, we're done in here.' He handed me the broom and his tools before opening the door to let the two of us out. I switched off the Graceland light and we left the wooden loft in the peachy glow of the sun setting over the Menai Strait.

'By the way, who taught you this cheek of yours?'

'No idea, Taid.'

It took a good hour before I was fully briefed on how the library worked but by the end of it I felt suitably bullish. True, I might have to skim through *On the Origin of Species* but small matter, I thought, as I left Darwin HQ to face the music. It was dark when I began my walk, the obscure path dimly illuminated by the house. The on-off sequence of light boxes signalled that my mother was on her way out. It was *Close Encounters* Bangor style and she was definitely fussing. From bedroom – off – to bathroom – on; flush lavatory, bathroom off; landing stairs on; back to bathroom – off. Landing on; to hall, to cloak room – on; coat on, cloakroom off; to hall, to kitchen – *always* on. Always, bless her, switching her feelings on and off like I professed I couldn't. Maybe she was just better at coping.

Mam threw her coat onto the back of a chair, beating me to it by seconds. She was wearing her victorious orange dress. It was her millennium outfit, the one she wore the night we joked we'd never survive. She was rummaging in her handbag as I walked in, and spoke without looking up.

'Oh, there you are,' she said, bringing out her lipstick. 'I was beginning to wonder where you'd got to.'

'I was helping Taid.'

Mam ambled from the table to the mirror above the key rack and began to apply a deep rouge. 'Listen,' she said distractedly, 'I can't stop. I'm off out with Gar's mum. We're skipping flamenco. We need cava.'

At least that's what I thought I heard, her speech mumbled through her tightly pressed lips.

'Please don't say anything.'

'We'll see.'

We'll see? 'Please. Mam!'

She checked herself sideways, left, right, up and down. 'I said don't be silly, didn't I?' She reached for her coat and flung it over her arm, catching sight of me looking suitably abashed, I hoped.

'I didn't mean to be so horrible, sorry.'

'Now's not the time to talk things over,' she said, straightening her dress. 'Anyway, thank you for clearing up.'

I was about to say 'don't mention it' when I heard the sound of an excitable *Dukes-of-Hazzard*-style car horn. It was The Mid-Life Crisis waiting.

Mam, resplendent in her millennium dress, stood frozen on her spot.

'So, going for a drink with Gar's mum, are we?'

She turned her head to the mirror and considered her profile once more. 'I told him to text.'

Second chance, I thought, taking in a deep breath. 'You sure that orange dress isn't going to clash with his yellow open-top?'

Mam looked at me goggle-eyed. 'Why do you think I said nine thirty?'

''Cause it'd be dark?'

'Bang on.' She laughed. I wondered if she'd forgiven me for my earlier outburst, or if her good humour was on account of Maldwyn. 'Right, got to go. In a rush!' She barged her way to the door. I was about to close it when she pushed it back open. 'By the way, that was Joy on the phone earlier. She's keen on a house swap again this year, convinced we're heading for a double-dip recession. They've offered their house in London for two weeks. Said I'd offer them a house by the sea in return.'

She pulled the door shut, leaving my astonished expression reflected in the glass. 'And tidy up those posters, young man,' she called out from the other side, 'there's a job to be done!'

'Have fun!' I shouted back, hoping I sounded sincere, my gaze following her past the begonias in the window box.

TheWingedAthlete: UL NEVER GUESS!
Misterlloydfanclub: Whassup? Hit me.

Bedroom tidy, posters re-tacked (well, the ones worth saving) and I'd already begun a list of everything I needed for the London trip. I was downstairs at the laptop, wanting to share the news. Misterlloydfanclub was waiting. It couldn't be Maldwyn; he was supposed to be with Mam. Unless this was their idea of a date: the two of them, cava in hand, giggling away as they typed.

I was being silly, I told myself, and carried on.

TheWingedAthlete: We r goin 2 Lndn.
Misterlloydfanclub: Brilliant! Who's we?
TheWingedAthlete: Me and Mam

Misterlloydfanclub: What about ProfJenks? Is he ur dad BTW?

[This could still be a trick: Dad, less likely Maldwyn, hopefully not Ms Hughes and, please no, not a burglar. Tread carefully.]

TheWingedAthlete: ProfJenks is my grandfather. He NEVER leaves pigeons so just us 2.

Misterlloydfanclub: IC. Gr8 news. When u goin?

TheWingedAthlete: Tomoz I hope.

Misterlloydfanclub: Tomoz? But wot abt-

TheWingedAthlete: Wot about wot? The debate?

[I waited for a reply. It was a long time coming.]

Misterlloydfanclub: Debate? Wassat? LOL. Skool!

TheWingedAthlete: WTF? Debate about Pigeons. NE Way, London more imp. It's @ end of term. BTW. Wot's it 2 u?

Misterlloydfanclub: Nada. Bit sudden. Is that wot ur mum says?

TheWingedAthlete: No. She wnet out.

Misterlloydfanclub: Who's she gon out wid?

[Whether it was Dad, Ms Hughes, Maldwyn or a burglar, I wasn't sure how to respond.]

TheWingedAthlete: MYOB [Mind your own business]

Misterlloydfanclub: LOL Her boyf?

TheWingedAthlete: LOL.

Misterlloydfanclub: Y?

TheWingedAthlete: Bit weird, tha's all.

[I wanted to take this back but it was too late. I'd practically announced her relationship status into the ether-world.]

Misterlloydfanclub: Y Not? Might be nice for UR Mam 2 hav a nu fella.

[I didn't say anything.]

Misterlloydfanclub: So, is it that bird man? The one who sets things free?

[I looked at the Block User button, saw Misterlloydfanclub. There was no image, no information whatsoever. I was talking to a blank profile. What was I thinking?]

Misterlloydfanclub: U still there? LOL u started packing or sumthin? Ok gd luck looking 4 UR bird. Rooting 4 u.

TheWingedAthlete: 10Q. GTG. Mam's back. Chat soon.

She wasn't. I just wanted to pack.

XIII

The City of London, London

The skyline takes on the colour of the darkest grey feather, and a million walking feet echo through its streets. This is the soundscape of London – noisy, isn't it? Traffic, tooting, sirens, underground trains and planes flying up above. It gives way now and again to the rumble of a thunderstorm, which threatens to overwhelm our early July evening. And, of course, it is rush hour; people are leaving their offices, always eager to take the first means of transport home. Look how they rush! Buses stop, start; alarm bells warn of closing doors; umbrellas are bursting open to a chorus of car doors slamming. Look out! Engines roar to overtake; footsteps hurry, some tap dancing over puddles for orange-lit black cabs, others disappearing down stairways like water down a plughole. But don't go down there with them, please! Come quick! I'll show you another shelter. Oh, the pelting rain!

Mister Lloyd stirs. That's it, out of the wet and under the lid of this wheelie bin with me! Apologies and all that, but we have to see what has happened to our bird. There, look, wedged between piles of what must feel like luxurious cushions, he tries to stretch out his claws, sandwiched as he is amongst the plastic bags. He can feel them, at least, but whether he is on his back, his front, upside down or even the right way up, it is easy to be confused in such darkness. However, we must be grateful that the bite into his abdomen has narrowly missed the oil gland above the rump; that could have been fatal, and so too his fall from the parapet of one of London's most famous high-rise buildings. How lucky that he landed here seconds before the owner shut the lid! Floating in and out of delirium in the softness of his surroundings, he looks strangely contented. We can imagine he is conjuring images of home. There he is, back in the gentle care of his trusted friend Mostyn: splashing in that lovely bath; pecking a Royal Jelly capsule, in the hopper back in Graceland, such a daily treat; a sip or two from the abundant drinkers, water on tap and plenty of it. So much water to drink, so much water to... so much water, so much, so... Mister Lloyd has gone again, but only for him to wake a moment later with a start. That pelting rain!

Wet, greasy, slippery bin bags! Oh, and forgive the smell. This is certainly not what Mr Lloyd was born to, nor you for that matter, I hope. Cover your noses if you must. He fidgets, disgusted, even though he knows they cushioned his fall from that high building – yes, it is coming back to him now. He is familiar with wheelie bins, has patted about in a few outside Graceland – but none as smelly as this, surely? We can only hope Mister Lloyd isn't actually thinking he is already home. He stops his fretting to take stock but bags are all around him, squeezing and pressing, while up above, against the closed lid, the rain pounds. Surely it must add to his unease. No, he is not home. At least he knows that, which is something. But he has to get out. Now. This very minute! Mister Lloyd begins to push and pummel. Suffocation sets in as the weight of seemingly dozens of slimy bin bags press tightly on him. He pecks, kicks, jabs and heaves but such movements are only making matters worse, Mister Lloyd! He dislodges rubbish – for a second thinks he is winning. But the bags collapse on top of him.

'I can't breathe!' he coos. It is useless. We can hear him, but can't help him.

He nudges forward with his bill – what is that? – suddenly a deafening sound rings out. It is as loud as a gunshot. Had circumstances been different, the blast would have sent him flying, but in this instance Mister Lloyd discovers he can fill his lungs again. Aha! His beak has pierced an air pocket in one of the bags. This happy accident will be a welcome respite for the worn creature, however temporary, for he remains a prisoner and still very much in the dark. This hell seems endless, the past almost without meaning and he is far, far away from Mostyn Price!

His thoughts turn to food. All around him an overpowering stench. The bag's contents are full of food. Desperate times call for desperate measures, as they say. His tastes, refined up till now, matter little. Mister Lloyd sniffs his way into boxes, bags and paper napkins. Filling his beak, he gorges, devours and wolfs lettuce, beans, white bread, gherkins, burger meat, fries and tomato sauce down his hungry gullet. It brings about a rush of blood to the head as his sugar levels begin to crank up once more.

Now he needs water. 'Right, what does one have to do to get a drink round here?' His coos aren't addressed to anyone in particular but it's a good sign – he's mending. With renewed energy he follows his nose. It brings him to some liquid left over at the bottom of a paper cup. Desperate for hydration, he yanks at the rim with his beak, dislodges and edges it gingerly towards him. He reaches down to the bottom and drinks the liquid by suction, glugging it so hard he barely draws breath. Embedded as he is in slimy, wet, greasy rubbish, it is the first time in a while he has felt this good. 'Happy days,' we can hear him coo but his reprieve is hijacked when his attention is drawn upwards by a waft of cool air. The beat of the rain has ceased and – was he seeing things, or is that really a corner of watery moon? Someone – he can hear a human voice – has opened the lid and is rifling through its contents.

'One man's rubbish is another man's treasure,' we hear that human say. Despite his fright, Mister Lloyd can sense his fellow scavenger is in the same predicament. This wheelie bin is also *his* lifeline and his fate. It was the reason why the lid was open when he fell from the sky and shut when he landed. His whole life must have flashed before his eyes for the second time in one day!

Mister Lloyd tries to remain calm as he listens to the

human rummage deeper. We too must remain quiet. Is this Mister Lloyd's chance to make a dash for freedom? He darts – *please watch out!* – all around him, here and there, looking for a way out.

'Aargh! Rats!' shouts the man. No, please don't panic. The man is simply confused; he does not know what it is making the disturbance. He slams down the lid, plunging Mister Lloyd back into the dark.

CHAPTER FOURTEEN

Home, Bangor

L ondon beckoned. Call it a hunch, call it gut instinct, call it what you like, but Simon Blake's email and Joy Rathbone's phone call had strengthened my conviction that Mister Lloyd was out there. True, his sighting had brought about mixed emotions but ultimately it had only fuelled my determination to find him. Knowing that I, Mostyn Price, was going to London, changed everything; the end of term and Mr Griffiths' school debate could go and whistle. Or so I thought.

Saturday morning: it had been a full week since I'd last seen Mister Lloyd. According to Taid we'd have only fourteen days left for my search; otherwise I'd have to accept he was a goner. We needed to get to London. I shot up, sitting bolt upright, and shooed away the sleepy fug. Taid, I remembered, was in Nantwich on a liberation site reconnaissance mission for the Association; my mother had not yet surfaced. This was odd. Her bedroom door was still shut and the bathroom free. I slipped in, locked the door and turned on the radio. I was under the shower, honing my argument for skipping the end of term and going straight to London, when I thought I heard the sound of Maldwyn's enhanced exhaust filtering through Edith Bowman's voice and the steaming hot water. I couldn't be sure but, by the time I was dressed and making my way downstairs, Mam was on the front porch picking up the post.

'Morning!' she said sifting through 'dull' and 'interesting' as she made her way into the kitchen, throwing 'dull' straight into recycling and reaching for the letter knife. She sounded cheery.

'Rather a late lie in, Mam?' I chanced without thinking. Not a good move, considering we'd had words the previous evening. I helped myself to orange juice from the fridge.

'And what makes you so early for a change?' she quipped, ripping open an envelope like she was clipping me around the ear.

'Well, I was hoping we could set off for London,' I replied quite innocently.

She looked up from the letter. 'Today? Are you mad?'

This was a bit harsh, I thought, but I let it go. 'Why not?'

Mam shook her head and went back to the letter. 'And what would Joy have to say if I told her "*quick! Get packing! You're evicted!*" How much organising do you think it—' Her voice trailed off.

I threw some bread in the toaster and tried another tactic. 'Well, how about tomorr—'

Mam's hand went up, cutting me off. She slowly folded the letter and raised her head. 'I can think of a better reason why we can't go today or tomorrow for that matter, sunshine.'

The toaster slots were glowing brightly. She held out the letter.

My eyes went to the amateurish Deiniol High logo, the result of an all-school competition. The letter was addressed to Mrs Price and signed by Mr Griffiths MA. I scanned the contents, browsing over 'altercation', 'dim view' and 'if our thoughts, opinions, emotions or feelings cannot be expressed in words, then it must be considered a weakness in us'. It went on: 'punishment', 'battle of words', 'last day of term'. Then I reached the final paragraph: 'Failure to take part in this school debate will result in both parties being expelled for the new term.'

The toast jumped out. Somehow I wasn't hungry.

'Over my dead body will we go to London this weekend,' said Mam, snatching the letter off me and making her way past. 'Now shift. I'm making coffee.'

Another knock. Another setback.

'So, this is the price you pay for helping a mate, is it?' she said, reaching for the cafetière. 'Come to mention it, Gareth's not taking part, I see. Only Lynton Chivers?'

She was right. I'd missed that bit. 'Yeah, he scarpered.'

'Some mate, letting you take the patsy,' she tut-tutted. 'You wait till I see him.'

'I wouldn't bother,' I shrugged. 'Anyway, don't you mean pasty?'

Now it was Mam glowing brightly. 'I'm the linguist around here. Look it up!'

'Yes,' I ventured sheepishly. 'Best get cracking. Got a debate to prepare.' I tried to sound jolly and made for the door. 'Oh, and when you see Maldwyn next, tell him I want a word.'

'What do you want to tell him, exactly?' I heard her ask, following me to the door as I dashed out of the house and up the steps. It wasn't a matter of me telling *him* anything. I wanted him to tell *me* how his pigeon came back but hearing her fearful tone, it felt right to leave her hanging. It sounds mean, I know, and I really did want her to be happy but her second chance, as Taid had called it, had come too soon, or at least too early for me to give it the consideration it deserved. Maldwyn's candidacy as a suitable recipient for my mother's affections would have to wait.

From the gangway the perfectly still strait glistened in the morning sun. I stepped inside the loft, hoping to see Mister Lloyd back from his escape, happily treading his perch, no questions asked. But no; it irked me to see his nest so clean and now, worst of all, *occupied*! Reluctant to accept these new young lovebirds, I made my way to Darwin HQ, carefully side-stepping the red plastic bath, filled at the ready. Just in case.

Still there. It faced me. A happy moment, captured. There we were, close up, laughing outside Taid's shipping container with Mister Lloyd perched on my head. I could still remember the tickling sensation I'd felt on my scalp as Mister Lloyd's feet shuffled around on top of me. I moved the framed photograph aside, to switch on the computer's hard drive. I slouched back on the chair, listening to the computer's burps and rumblings, waiting for it to boot up. I straightened my back and stepped over to the shelves, running my finger along the book spines: *From Hero to Zero*; *The Pigeon's Life Explained*; *Catch the Pigeon and Other Useful Tips*; *The Pop Up Book of Pigeons*; *Pigeons in the Great War*; *How Not to Lose Pigeons and Influence Them*; *The Gilded Gutter Life of the Street Pigeon*; *Good Dovecote Keeping*; *Rich Pigeon, Poor Pigeon – How to Make Money from YOUR Racing Pigeon*; *The Million Dollar Pigeon*; *The Good Pigeon Guide*.

The shelves went on and on, book upon book. My eyes glazed over. The computer mooed electronically, waiting for further instructions.

I logged on to Report Strays Online. Elvis was not online. It being early, no one was on MSN either. With the selected books in a pile on Taid's desk, I had no choice but to make a start. I opened a new document and stared at the blank screen. I typed:

Dear Simon Blake,

Thank you so much for news of your sighting of Mister Lloyd and for taking the trouble to let us know. It was good news and bad news. When you said 'The Greater London Vicinity', where did you mean specifically? My racing pigeon's disappearance is a mystery but, with your note, I am sure he is out there somewhere. Your email proves it!

We will be visiting London in a week. My Mam won't let me come any sooner as I have to finish term – got a school debate to win – so I wanted to ask you whether you could keep your eyes peeled, hold the fort until I arrive. Check any ledges; look for any green-ringed birds mixing with the feral. Wheelie bins, etc. I have seen on Google that Tower 42 is on Broadmarket.

Do let me know if this is convenient for you.

Yours sincerely and thanks again,
Mostyn Price.

I copied and pasted the letter into a new e-mail in Outlook and pressed send, cheered, even when I got an instant reply. Then I scanned the subject line.

> **From:** Simon Blake [simon@systems-fidelity.com]
> **Sent:** 09 July 2005 08.23
> **To:** info@reportstraysonline/mostynprice
> Subect: Out of Office Autoreply: Mister Lloyd Sighting!
>
> Good day!
>
> On annual leave – HOORAY! – and I won't be back in the office until Mon the 11th of July! I'm sorry about this! I need my holidays! But don't be shy, don't be nervous, my colleague Charlene Eccleston's at your service! If urgent, contact the IT Helpdesk
>
> Best!
> Simon Blake
> **IT Systems Analyst**

Collapsing on the keyboard seemed to help. After a while the computer whooped, jerking me back upright.

> **Lowri:** STIL WID SEGALS? LOL
> [Laugh Out Loud. I certainly hadn't for a while. Lowri was shouting at me from her corner of the chat room; I was glad

of the distraction.]
Me: LOL Pijins!!! U not down town? ☺

Another window bounced open.

Misterlloydfanclub invites you to Chat.

Lowri: WOT DUZ LOOK LIKE? ☹
CAN I CUM ROUND? BORD ERE

TheWingedAthlete: U got your caps
locked. Soz. U cant cum round. I'm workin.
[But when I hit return I saw I had sent it to
Elvis.]
Misterlloydfanclub: ??
TheWingedAthlete: Soz wrong window.
BRB
Misterlloydfanclub: U in chat with s'one
else?
TheWingedAthlete: Ys. BRB

Lowri: U STILL THEIR?
Me: Soz working. *THERE Lows.
Lowri: OOPS (*Blushing emo-
ERROR!*) NE WAY. YOU NEED
HELP.

Misterlloydfanclub: U talking 2 UR
girlfriend? U R aren't U?
[I was taken aback by this new direction.]

Me: NO I AM NOT TALKING TO MY GIRLFRIEND
[I was definitely shouting but the cursor was still in Lowri's window. ERROR!]
Lowri: Beg Pa'rdon? Was that 4 me? U not talking to me? ROFL! DUDE I'm OFFRIN TO HLP!!!! WHERE U GONE?'

Misterlloydfanclub: ooooooooooooooeeeeeeeeeee. sum1's rattled.
TheWingedAthlete: Can't tlk now. Another time.

Lowri: Hello?
Me: PLZ, cum round HLP me wid debate. BTW, what's ROFL again?

[The pencil began to shake furiously]
Misterlloydfanclub: Boyfriend then?
[I froze, but had to answer.]
TheWingedAthlete: No!
[Did it matter? My mistake was to continue the dialogue.]
Misterlloydfanclub: So u have girlfriend?
TheWingedAthlete: Yes!
[I lied, just to shut him up.]
Misterlloydfanclub: Name?
TheWingedAthlete: Lowri
[This was getting worse.]

Misterlloydfanclub: How long u 'n' Lowri bin 2gether?

[What a mess.]

TheWingedAthlete: LOL ERROR! We're not.

Misterlloydfanclub: 1st u say you have. Now u say u don't.

TheWingedAthlete: Nooooooo!

Misterlloydfanclub: LOL. Keep ur hair on. U not fallen in <3 b4 Mostyn?

TheWingedAthlete: What? NO.

[I suppose I had, but I didn't want to get into this line of conversation. This was cyber-stalking, bordering on grooming. It had gone too far. I hurriedly copied in a link to chat room etiquette and typed]

TheWingedAthlete: I know the rules. U R harassing me. Won't B meetin up or NEthing.

[I dropped in an angry emoticon and went Code 9, letting Elvis know I was about to leave.]

Misterlloydfanclub: LOL. Wot makes u think... I'm root—

I didn't even bother finishing his message. I signed out of Report Strays Online and resolved to send Elvis a note later. In it I would thank him for his support but go on to explain that he had crossed a line and, reluctantly, I would have to block him as a user.

Then Lowri piped up:

ROLL ON FLOOR LAFFIN!! B THER
IN 10! TURRAH

XV

Wheelie bin, London

It takes a while to calm the nerves but, when he
accepts his sorry fate, stuck in that stinking bin,
replete with food, the exhaustion takes over and Mr
Lloyd falls into a deep sleep. Let's hope he is dreaming
of Graceland. I have lost count how many hours he
sleeps. Remiss of me, I know, but it is enough to recharge
his worn-out body. It's an engine roar that we hear now.
It's loud enough to wake him from his slumber. In fact
it's getting louder. The sound is strange but it is not
unlike – yes, he remembers the sound of The Beast. There
is a screech and the roar softens to a low grumble, not
moving now, but pulled up beside the wheelie bin.
Against a background of hissing and banging the
occasional human voice can be heard. Was it that
Maldwyn Jones from The Beast? Taid? Or better still
Mostyn, having ridden all the way in the cabin to rescue
him? But alas, through the cushioned interior Mister
Lloyd does not recognise the accents of home.

With a jerk the unwieldy bin is pulled, gyrated and
pushed, *vibrating!* Mister Lloyd looks terrified. It is like
an earthquake; his surroundings shake him to the bone.
All around him bags dislodge and fall, debris thrown all

111

about him while voices boom, penetrating the interior, deafening Mister Lloyd.

'Blimey, this one ain't budging easily,' says one of them. 'Bloody awful castors!'

The noise has a doomed resonance. The men seem to be lining up the wheelie bin with another metallic structure, which can be heard screeching and clanking ominously beneath. They groan and push with a final heave. Mister Lloyd is about to go on the kind of ride people actually pay to experience: the eerie silence, the slow ascent, the mid-air suspension, the flip and release! Gravity gives way and he watches the bin bags that have given him air to breathe, food to eat and a cushion on which to rest his weary head fall away from him, farther and farther. *Hold on!* There we see it: an enormous front-loading dustbin lorry. And now Mister Lloyd is sliding towards it, into daylight.

'Hey did you see that?' asks the voice.

'What?'

'That pigeon flying off. Look!'

Mister Lloyd's liberators watch him go.

Oh, how we love London!

CHAPTER SIXTEEN

Darwin HQ, Bangor

S he knew the way, lived close by and had said ten minutes, but after some time I worried where Lowri had got to. Every so often I would receive a progress report via text. I was still rattled by Elvis and was trying to get back into work but her missives were becoming more and more disruptive. I'd write a couple of sentences, print a page of research here and there, and sure enough she'd touch base again, disturbing my train of thought with the digital sound of galloping horses racing towards me through the computer's loudspeakers, alerting me to yet another helpful, urgent message.

Soz. On root, lol!

Finally she arrived, with a flurry of chaos not seen at Graceland since Taid hosted the One Loft Race when all three hundred of its young participants clapped their way into the sky. Almost to the same sound, Lowri pulled both doors open, like a diva making her stage entrance, and walked into Darwin HQ with a loud sigh, throwing her bag down on the sofa.

'Sorry, sorry, sorry, Mostyn bach! Took me forever to get out of—'

My stare said it all.

'What's the matter?'

113

Something about the way she looked was so at odds with her stagy manner: the brushed hair and the simple wrap-round dress. Whether it was that season's must-have, I had no idea, but she looked pretty. I worried that if I told her the truth she'd snap my head off. 'Um. You look different.'

'Talk about statin' the bleeedin' obvious!' she shouted. 'Course I do. I got no make-up on and I'm wearing this really prim, niminypiminy, prissy nambypamby excuse for a dress.' She stood upright and pirouetted.

We both laughed. 'No, that's not what I meant!' I was about to tell her that I liked it, but Lowri held up her hand.

'Enough already. You don't think I'd normally go out looking like this, do you?'

I tried to get the words out in time. Words that would tell her she looked beautiful, that if it wasn't for me being so het up with Mister Lloyd, I'd probably fall in love with her right now, maybe already had. But I was tongue-tied and she wasn't.

'Ohmygodwhatdoyoutakemefor? Only my mother would make me wear this dress. Insisted I wore it when I said I was coming to your house. Respect for Taid or something. Hence late. Bit of a row. All that jazz. Still, I'm here now.'

'Taid's not here,' I said, wondering if she felt the same as me and just couldn't say it. I hoped she was using him as an excuse.

Lowri looked to her bag. 'You what? She'd slung it on the sofa and brought out a pair of jeans. 'Why didn't you bleedin' well say?'

'How was—' I glanced over my shoulder. The clock ticked. Louder, it seemed. 'Never mind.'

'Don't you worry. I smuggled a change of clothes out of the house. Anyway what was that silly message you sent me about not talking to your girlfriend? Have we had a virtual row or something? LOL. More importantly, how come you got a girlfriend and I don't know about it?'

'No, somebody on another chat room asked if you were my girlfriend and I said you weren't.' Lowri was staring at me at this point. I carried on. 'It was Report Strays Online and I mixed up my windows. Hilarious, that. Always doing it.'

Eventually, her eyes slipped past me, wandering round Darwin HQ. 'They got a chat room on there now, have they? How you've got the time to be on Facebook, MySpace, MSN and conduct this search, I will never know.'

'Lows, cariad, I *don't* have the time. Let's get on with it.'

She smiled and held out her trousers. 'Moment I put these and some eyeliner on, Mostyn bach, it'll be all hands on deck, you'll see.' She began to pull them on under her dress. 'That's better. Oh! Almost forgot. Guess who I rescued on my way here, which, I hasten to add, is another reason why I was late?'

'Mister Lloyd, by any chance?'

Lowri stopped, her jeans halfway up. 'No. As if! A straggler checking one of your posters up the road and Looking. A. Bit. Bored.'

'Who are you talking about?'

'Gar, you nitwit. Pop your head round the door while I finish getting changed. He's taking a gander at your feathered friends.'

'Gar?' The one friend who I didn't want to see, or rather

115

I didn't want my mother to see. If I kept those two apart, my story might just hold water: that it was Gar who was being bullied at school and not me. To this day I don't know why I even said it. Tired of being the victim, I suppose. Shame, most probably. I ran outside.

He was on the gangway, in full view of the kitchen, his hands blocking out the glare of the afternoon sun as he peered through the loft's window. He must have seen me reflected in the glass.

'Hey, dude. Whassup?'

'Get down from there!' I shouted as loudly as I could.

'Charmin',' he replied, clearing the web that clung to his face. 'Great to see you too!'

My welcome, I admit, was hostile. 'Keep your voice down or you'll frighten the pigeons!'

Gar kicked the red plastic bath as he sauntered along the gangway, causing it to splash everywhere. Not intentionally, granted, but I was agitated.

'Hey, don't worry. We're here now,' he announced with a swagger as he took the last few steps. 'Chill-ax, Stressed Eric, and let your amigos kindly unburden you of this punishment the headteacher impolitely hath bestowed on thee.'

'Cooee!' shouted Mam from the blind spot in the backyard.

Quick. Think. 'You were right about patsy, Mam,' I called back, shoving my unsuspecting friend into Darwin HQ.

'Oi! What you doin'?' protested Gar, put out by Darwin HQ as much as my manners.

'Zip it!' I said with some urgency.

'Told you,' I heard Mam reply. 'Just off del supermercado, carĩno!'

'Champion!' I shouted, pulling the Darwin doors. 'Laters!'

'Sorry. On edge a little,' I said as I pressed them shut. 'It's just Taid's away and I'm in charge.'

'Are we not supposed to be here or something?'

'Something like that, yeah. It's *top* secret, don't you know?'

'Cool. Nice one. Loves a drama, me,' piped up Lowri, newly eye-lined and checking her tousled hair in Taid's shaving mirror, which also revealed a stupefied Gar. Darwin HQ was familiar to me but I forgot what it must look like to the outsider. Each tread-worn rug guiding you to a library, a bedroom, sitting room or kitchenette and all filled with Taid's books, trinkets, 'useful' aides and, of course, his medicine.

'Jeez. Are all these pills and tinctures for your Taid?' asked Gar.

'Some are, but most are for his birds,' I explained. 'He stores most of it in the hospital.'

'Ysbyty Gwynedd or Bangor General?' enquired Gar innocently.

Picking up one of Taid's books, Lowri gave out a laugh. 'No, dumbo! Gramp's got a small pigeon hospital next door.' For someone who claimed little interest in my hobby she was remarkably well informed.

'Might've known,' said Gar flatly

'*Rich Pigeon, Poor Pigeon*?' exclaimed Lowri. 'It says here that a racing pigeon was sold last year for one hundred thousand pounds. Politely, I will ask if this is the truth I am seeing before my very own eyes?'

'Now you understand why this place is top secret.'

'Top secret and messy, if you ask me,' said Gar.

Lowri slotted the book back into its place. 'You didn't tell me you could make money from pigeons!' She cricked her fingers. 'I'm ready. Come on,' she ushered us to the computer. 'Let's get cracking!'

For the rest of the afternoon we settled down to a routine. I selected all relevant information, references and interesting facts, be they historical, biological, anthropological, topical, physical, zoological, in fact any 'ical' I could think of, while Gar dictated them to Lowri, who, being the deft typist she was, churned out an impressive amount of words per minute. Together we managed to compile a document I could see would be powerful ammunition against Lynton Chivers. It was turning out to be a good afternoon, until I heard a knock on the door.

It echoed round the container. The three of us looked to each other. Frozen.

Knock. Knock. Knock.

'Mam's back,' I whispered. 'Quick! Hide!'

'But where?' they both cried. It was a reasonable question. Stuff being everywhere, it was not going to be an easy undertaking without an almighty kerfuffle.

Error Carried Forward. 'I dunno!' Fretful and feeling ridiculous I looked all around me and settled on the small space nearest to us. Under Taid's desk.

'You are joking me,' Lowri protested, though I'm sure she was quietly enjoying the hoo-ha. 'There's no room there!'

The rusty door handle began to squeak.

'Loves a drama, you said. Down you go!' and, with both hands, I pushed Lowri and Gar under.

'Animals get treated better than this,' muttered Gar.

I parked myself on the old wheely chair and pulled myself towards the desk. I must have knocked Gareth at this point, because I heard him groan. I began to type. Gibberish pressings of the keyboard: 'sqojlaczvkgksn,xbvola;kvaKnak'

Mam stepped in and stood at the doorway.

'Oh, hi there.' I smiled and waved.

'You're not still working, surely? Aren't you overdoing it?'

''Fraid I am!' – I was – 'Still working, I mean.' When I turned my head back to the screen I felt my knees being knocked against the filing drawers. I yelped.

'I was actually trying not to frighten you. You OK?'

'Fine thanks,' I enthused. 'Just a knee-jerk response to a really exciting project. You know how cheek-by-jowl it is in here.'

'Rargol, I've given up on this place, Mostyn bach. Anyway, listen now. How about some din-dins? I mean, you need a break.'

'Tis true, Mam. Tis true,' I agreed, my eyes glued to the screen. 'Half an hour?'

It wasn't enough. She was walking towards me, clearly wanting to know what was taking up all my concentration. A hop and a skip around a pile or two was enough for her to realise she was dragging something along with her heels. She picked up Lowri's dress and held it up with both hands. 'What's this?'

My stomach clicked into auto-spin. *Quick! Act dumb.*

'Urm, I don't know.' I began to rub my chin – I'd seen people do that on a game show but Mam was still looming – *'I'm afraid I'll have to hurry you!'* – and having no one to confer with I offered, 'A dress?'

'I know perfectly well what it is, Mostyn,' she said, folding it carefully and placing it on the arm of Taid's wing chair. 'But you see I was wondering more on the lines of what it's doing here and, more importantly, whose dress it is? I mean, is there something you want to tell me?'

'What do you? Me? No!'

I spun back round. 'It's not that uncommon, you know. Cross-dressing. Experimenting at your age.'

'No, no, no!' But before I had a chance to explain a blast of raucous laughter blew me out of my seat. Mam recoiled, shocked to see Lowri and Gar spill onto the floor, rolling about in hysterics.

'Good God, Lowri. What were you doing there?'

'Oh, I'm so sorry, Mrs Price,' said Lowri, wiping the tears of laughter streaming down her cheeks. 'Hands up, it's mine. I brought it here, you see. My mother made me wear it, but I'm more me in jeans.'

Gareth struggled to his feet.

'And you here too, Gareth?' said Mam, walking over to help him up. 'What brought you here? Guilt?'

I cringed.

'We're ever so sorry, Mrs Price. We know we're not supposed to be in here. And we won't ever say to anyone we've been, will we, Lows?'

Lowri winked. 'Our little secret, Mrs Price.'

Mam raised her eyebrow at me. 'Whatever gave you that idea?' Gar and Lowri looked at each other. 'You're most welcome, I assure you, but I have to say I was surprised by what I heard this morning. Disappointed in you, Gar, letting my son take the flak for your misdemeanour. Is that why you're here: come to help with the debate because he' – pointing at me – 'had to stand up for you?'

'I don't understand, Mrs Price,' said Gareth before it dawned on him. 'Whoa, excuse me.' There was a distinct tremor in his voice and his eyes were wide when he turned to me. 'What have you been saying? You've been on edge with us all afternoon. Lows and I, we've come here to help you get out of this mess you've got yourself into and now your mum's telling me I'm here cause I didn't stand up for you. And,' he continued, not even pausing for breath, '*and* I haven't had as much as a biscuit all afternoon because we've had to hide here.' He turned to Mam, visibly shaken. 'You know what, Mrs Price, I wasn't even there. He's brought it all on himself, picking a fight with—'

Mam caught my eye. 'Lynton Chivers?' she said, her expression one of triumph.

'And I'm bloody well glad he did. Lynton C deserved all he got,' said Lowri with her elbow resting on Gar's shoulder. 'He's been giving Mostyn a hard time for ages and ages.'

'I knew it all along,' said Mam and kissing Gar on the head. 'I just wanted him' – pointing, again – 'to tell me the truth.'

I nodded.

'Such a shame,' added Mam. 'That Lynton used to be a sweetie.'

'That's what we thought, Mrs Price, but he's not the boy

he used to be.'

'Neither is this one by the looks of it,' piped Gar.

'Look, I'm sorry,' I said, going on to explain The Quiet Life, The Not Wanting a Fuss, The Shame, The Wanting to Protect Mam from the Truth, and The How One Thing Led to Another.

'Well, one thing's confirmed, Mostyn,' proffered Lowri, still leaning on her friend. 'You're a bleedin' cretin.'

I grinned sheepishly, but knew there and then I'd blown it with Lowri.

'Right,' said Mam, rubbing a corner of her eye. 'You've all been cooped up in here too long – and on a lovely sunny Saturday, an' all. Come along. Pizzas. My Kitchen. Half an hour.' She turned and held the door open. 'You two, help me bring in the shopping from the car so we can get started. Mostyn's cooking.'

'Right you are, Mrs P.' Lowri stuffed her dress into the bag and hop-scotched her way to the desk, grabbing *Rich Pigeon, Poor Pigeon* and narrowly missing a half-empty can. 'Don't worry, I'll bring it back,' she whispered in passing, grabbing Gareth on her way out. 'Would that be the yellow car, Mrs Price?'

I envied her cheek.

'Here's the key,' Mam called after her and throwing Gar the set.

'The stuff's in the boot, and Lowri—'

'Yes Mrs P?'

'It'll be the only car on the drive, whatever its colour.'

I let out a small laugh and set about replacing Taid's books. Running my fingers across the shelves, I deliberated, trying to remember the proper order – author or subject? –

when Mam landed at my shoulder. *Elvis, help me!*

'*Used to be a sweet boy...*' she sang, ending with a nervous laugh. 'Morrissey. My teen idol and still one of my favourites.'

I smiled blankly. Did she mean Lynton or me? Did she mean Dad? I picked up a few more books and stared at the shelves in defeat.

She pulled me in tight. 'Just tidy as much as you can, for now. Taid should be back soon. And on your way out remember to close the doors. Don't, *whatever you do*, let in the draughts!'

'I've made a right mess of things all round, haven't I?'

Mam caught my tremulous smile.

'About time you stood up for yourself.' She put her hand on my shoulder. 'You can tell me all about it. When you're ready.'

I thought of acts of kindness. Kind people helping and how, sometimes, we reject them. I hoped kind people were helping Mister Lloyd. I turned to Mam and nodded. 'I won't be long.'

'Just get through this week, cariad, because after that London's calling.'

123

XVII

Liverpool Street Station, London

Oh, look how he speeds through the air, making his onward journey, we hope. Fly away home, Mister Lloyd; that gash in your abdomen is healing nicely. If only he could hear us. He recognises the grey light of dawn but nothing, he soon realises, seems familiar. London is waking up to a new day but it greets Mister Lloyd with contempt. True, he has begun to feel steadier in his flight but he is growing befuddled by his rusty orienteering skills. He zigzags from one building to another. What could be the matter? Closer. Yes, come closer. Ah there, you see? Look at those ledges; they are no better than a bed of spikes! The welcome here is decidedly hostile to the pigeon world, and Mister Lloyd takes it personally. One would hope this would spur him on to find his way home, and at the double, but it's looking like the usual routine. The Sun – check, coming from the east, need to go northwest – is a distant memory. Even his arithmetic is in doubt. On top of this, grease from the bin bags has rubbed off on his lovely plumage and – oh what a shame – it has given him a scruffier appearance. Lady Grey would be cross, telling him he was definitely 'not at all right for London' and, normally, he'd agree. Mister Lloyd was not born to this. A look to the road shows him a red, high-sided box. It must be a painful, if fleeting, reminder of Darwin HQ but when he sees it move he's reminded of the shipping vessel that had served them so well. Wanting to recapture the magic, Mister Lloyd hitches a lift to Liverpool Street Station.

Here, there are signs of life. Mister Lloyd, glad to see a few of his own kind loitering, decides it's a good place to ask around. He wants to know about pit stops, the way home – general stuff. He hops from the double-decker's roof onto an adjacent bus stop where several crouch.

'Good Morning,' braves Mister Lloyd, squatting at a suitably distant length. Aware of other pigeon's spaces since his Graceland days, no doubt, he hopes this tentative approach will work. It doesn't. Two or three briefly glance over but their look suggests they think him mad – stark raving bonkers, in fact. 'Something I said?' No one turns. 'I was only trying to be friendly. Where I come from, you talk to each other.'

No one replies.

He looks around for interesting things to see, although we could argue he is mostly looking for his dignity. He is aware of their whispers. They are a shifty-looking lot, he decides, and is about to go when the dandier-looking one approaches.

'Forgive me, but there doesn't seem to be any other way of saying this—'

'Do carry on, by all means,' replies Mister Lloyd. Is

he hoping this polite approach will shame them into a more courteous exchange? That would be a good move, Mister Lloyd.

'You're—' continues the smart one. His coat is purple and beaten-pewter.

'Go on,' nudges Mister Lloyd.

'Well, you're stinky. Sorry, fella, but you are.'

Ah. Maybe this wasn't such a good move, Mister Lloyd.

'I see,' is all he can muster. He begins to nod uncontrollably, a rare twitch in pigeondom but one that is usually a sign of suppressed anxiety. His inability to think of a witty riposte seems to make matters worse. 'Thank you for your concern,' he manages, ashamed by his dull plumage. 'I'm perfectly aware I need a good wash. I was about to ask you for some directions to the nearest bathing station but, as you can appreciate, it's a bit difficult when no one replies,' he coos to that effect.

The dandy looks behind him. He confers with the others and then turns to Mister Lloyd. 'Follow me.'

Mister Lloyd does as he's told and we see, despite earlier unwelcoming sights, he manages to clock some fabulous perching opportunities along the way. The dandy leads him through London, passing St Paul's Cathedral, then west, down a narrow street until it comes into a huge open space ahead. Oh, this is a spectacular sight and Mister Lloyd finds himself enchanted by its baths, statues, paving steps, walls and the number of his feathered fellows flying around. We are at Trafalgar Square. This must be the liberation site, thinks Mister Lloyd, the terminal to home. He turns to show his gratitude but finds his guide gone.

'Oi! Up here!'

He looks up and sees the lone bird perched on the shoulder of a tall statue stood on a column. The site dominates the square and Mister Lloyd flies up to join him and Admiral Nelson.

'Take special care,' warns the dandy. 'Mind you don't slip on the epaulette. That's it: Descend. Slow. Stand by to grip. Grip! Atta boy! They're trying to wean us off this geezer with some slippery gel. It's one of the reasons why you won't find many of us up here.'

Of course, they do not know what gel is, but they know this substance is making life difficult for them so we may as well call it slippery gel for now.

Mister Lloyd manages to get a grip on the stone shoulder. 'Wow, what a view!' he says.

'Well, it's a bit different to how it used to be. Many of us have had to move on. Since The Incident...'

'Come again?'

'I'm struggling to keep it together,' says the dandy, 'but my nerves ain't what they used to be. Never mind, where was I? Oh yes. Despite it being a bit chilly up here, it's a handy little spot to show the newcomers. Down below you'll see there are two baths to choose from, but I reckon – top tip and strictly NFT – the one facing west is best. More tropical, see.'

'NFT?' asks Mister Lloyd.

'Not For Tourists.' This is a rough translation but he means it is classified information that he is imparting.

Very kind of him, seeing as we're hoping our friend is only that: a tourist, passing through.

'Right, well, the name's Dorian.' (It's a good name, isn't it?)

'Mister Lloyd.'

'It is an honour,' says Dorian. 'Welcome to London.'

'Thank you,' replies Mister Lloyd.

He must be so glad to have found a friend and the prospect of a bath! He slips off the epaulette into mid-air.

'We need to improve that take-off of yours,' coos Dorian as they land on the fountain. 'It's a bit provincial.'

CHAPTER EIGHTEEN

Kitchen, Bangor

Traditionally it would have been a dove, but the symbol of peace that evening came in the shape of a twelve-inch margarita pizza. It had such a great success in improving diplomatic relations that Mam was of the opinion that her decision to go to the supermarket was bordering on the sixth sense. In the car, driving home, we laughed as we had done over supper. There'd been some ducking and diving, of course, a few digs thrown over the kitchen table but I knew it wiser to suck it up, which I did until Taid walked in through the door, his arrival prompting a change of subject.

With Lowri and Gar dropped off, I felt lighter in spirit than I had done for a while. Turning on the radio, I stumbled across a familiar voice coming through the loudspeakers. Elvis Presley singing *Always on My Mind*. We both fell silent, gripped by a glimpse of what was, what is and what could be. Then we turned into our lane and saw the mustard-yellow Mid-Life Crisis had made itself quite at home on the flat of the drive. Ousted from our usual perch, we lost reception, Elvis dissolving into static.

Mam didn't say anything, but looked around her for a better purchase on the sloping tarmac. I tried to be Taid, happy for her, but had to make do with the 'fake it 'till you make it' approach. Maldwyn was easier as a concept than parked on our drive. His tale of success meant there was a chance Mister Lloyd too might come back. But his presence meant Dad would not. Staring at his car through the windscreen, I saw Maldwyn as both an angel and a demon, his presence offering a glimmer of hope and a looming threat. Mam agreed. She didn't say so, but I saw her head turn at that very moment.

You were always on my mind... (white noise)... your sweet love hasn't died.

It could have been Elvis. It could have been Mam. It could have been the radio. The reception was always sporadic whenever we turned this corner.

If I made you feel second best... (white noise).

I switched it off. Mam's foot slipped off the brake and the car rolled down. 'Well, I'm glad he's here,' I said cheerily.

Mam pulled the handbrake and slotted the gear stick into reverse, neutral, eventually settling on first. 'Are you?'

'I wanted a word with him, remember?'

Mam seemed lost, staring at the windscreen ahead and all its wedding ring scratches, evidence of many a rainy day and desperate attempts to demist the windscreen with the back of her hand. For years we couldn't work out how they got there, till the wedding ring was off and the scratches stopped getting worse.

'Come on,' I said, and dashed out of the car, running past The Mid-Life Crisis. I did it for me. I did it for her. 'Snap out of it', our family motto. But when I turned around, urging her to follow, I saw her head had slumped back on the headrest. I lip-read 'give me strength', followed by some other Mam-ism, switching herself on, maybe off.

Sure of my lines, I turned into the backyard and flung open the door to find Maldwyn and Taid sitting at the kitchen table in a blaze of low sunshine, enjoying a beer. 'Maldwyn!' I called out. 'I wanted to ask you something.'

He was spruced. Oyster pink shirt, open neck, even a whiff of eau de something.

'Howaya, lad?'

'Dear boy!' said Taid, decidedly unimpressed by my manners and shooing me away. 'I think you'll find we were in the middle of a conversation before you interrupted. Wait your turn.'

I had forgotten old house rules. Taid may have given us free rein of his house but only, it seemed, when he was up in Darwin HQ. 'Don't go far,' he warned, 'because I too want to ask you something.'

I made my way into the pantry.

'Deeply sorry, Maldwyn,' he continued. 'Now where was I? Oh yes. No, no, no!' His fist came down on the table with a bang. 'I'm not sure you're right, after all. What you have to offer doesn't satisfy here. Past mistakes aside, we still don't have a clue, do we?'

No we don't. What had I interrupted? The pantry had only so many walls for me to look at. With my back to the feuding adults I opened the upright fridge. I saw goose fat, bacon, cerveza, vine-ripened baby plums. Not enough; I scoured the shelves some more: tonic water, Ami du Chambertin, Tropicana, rhubarb crumble, butter – unsalted, salted – Crunchie bars and film-wrapped lemon wedges.

'No, we certainly don't, Professor,' agreed Maldwyn with what sounded like a smirk. 'But—'

Olives. Watercress. Two full-cream milk bottles, one semi-skimmed. Cava. Laughing Cow and last night's dressing.

'—I reckon – and I stand by this – the two of us are a perfect match and, quite frankly, you should marry us together.'

Tomato puree. Capers. Bitter, bitter capers. The tumult inside me spread to the fridge. Is there a doctor in the house? I could feel my heartbeat surge to a record speed. Doctor Pepper. I need Doctor PEPPER! I reached for the fizzy drink bottle but it dislodged from its compartment and fell on top of me. I caught it. Just.

'Butter fingers!' shouted Maldwyn from his chair, sounding remarkably jovial. I bet he was.

Taid looked over his shoulder with a menacing grimace I swear could have stopped a London bus. They couldn't possibly be talking about wedding plans already? I began to rearrange the mess I'd caused.

'I do apologise, Maldwyn,' said Taid. 'I can't hear too well with these trifling activities going on behind me. Now, do you mean *marry* the two theories?' he asked, bending his ear pointedly.

'"Theory", that's the word I was looking for, ay,' said Maldwyn. 'On the tip of my tongue,' he continued. 'If you combined Matthews "Arc of the Sun" theory with Keeton's Magnetic Cue one, yeah, I reckon you could just about nail this homing mystery.'

If there were a paper bag to hand, I would be trying to breathe through it now. I knew exactly what theory lay behind Maldwyn's fantastic homing instinct. It began with Paloma and ended in Price but it didn't seem appropriate to suggest it. I quietly shut the fridge door, plastic bottle in hand and tiptoed past the debating table in search of a clean glass. In the distance an immobiliser bleeped, Maldwyn's Magnetic Cue Theory locking the car and walking up the driveway.

'Throw a bit of Morphic Resonance in there,' said Taid, his voice sounding more and more clipped, 'and you wouldn't be far off, I'm sure, but if it's baffled scientists since the days of Socrates, I hardly think we're likely to solve it over a beer on a Saturday night in Bangor. Another?'

'You're right, Professor,' said Maldwyn holding out his empty bottle, his pigeon tattoos just showing under the cuff of his shirt and the Swiss watch telling us it was half-past eight. 'But I like to picture myself in The School of Athens, if only now and again. That would be a laugh, ay! Have you been to Athens, Professor?'

I could just about see in the blinding sun we were not far off high tide, two worlds about to collide.

'Not yet. It's on the list,' said Taid reflectively.

'Sheer chaos, but mind-blowing,' offered Maldwyn. 'Not into Ouzo, mind.'

Taid smiled and handed him a fresh bottle.

'Thanks, Professor.' He took a sip and motioned me over. 'Anyway, what did you want to ask me, Mostyn?'

If I made you feel second best...

Over my shoulder Mam was ambling past the orange begonias. Quickly I grabbed my drink and walked over to the table. 'So Maldwyn—' It was already too late. The back door opened and Maldwyn rose to his feet.

I'm so happy that you're mine...

Always on his mind, the sight of her set Maldwyn's face

133

gleaming. 'Here she is!' he exclaimed, knocking his chair back against the stove and standing like one of Taid's Blue Pouters, puffing out his expandable chest and blowing his crop. 'My very own Miss Bangor 1987. Also Ran 1988.'

We looked on, open-mouthed.

He held up his beer bottle. 'Sorry, sorry. 'S gone all to my head, ay! Oh well, what the heck,' he sat down, deflated but looking delirious.

Taid burst into an uncharacteristic giggle. Mam's secret was out.

'Yes, well whatever, Maldwyn,' she said, her face taking on a crimson hue. 'Thanks for reminding me. This boy wants to ask you a question. So you carry on. I need to go and make a phone call. Lovely shirt, by the way.'

'Thanks, guappa—'

Mam rolled her eyes and left us in the kitchen.

Phone calls were always made in the dining room. We had plans for going cordless, underlined several times on the to-do list when we took over the house. Somehow we had never got round to it, possibly fearing it a slight on the previous regime. I pulled a stool from under the table and sat next to the blue pouter and his increasingly purple hackle. 'Listen now, Maldwyn. Tell me your good news.'

'Perpignan, it was, in the South of France,' he began, darting a poorly disguised and wide-eyed look through the hatch, where his girlfriend was untangling the cord of the telephone, the two of them knowing Taid was a cinch but me, not so.

The strong summer sun was flooding the kitchen. I pulled down the roller blind.

'Yes, back in, well, before you were born, Mostyn, and

certainly before I left for Dubai. Anyway, there'd been a solar eclipse only the day before.' Maldwyn turned to Taid. 'Do you remember reading about it, Professor?'

Taid nodded.

'It was meant to be a straightforward race – Perpignan to Penchwintan Road, you know – ought to have taken a couple of days at the most.'

Same with Mister Lloyd, I thought. 'How many made it back?'

Maldwyn stared at his bottle and took another sip. 'It was well over two thousand, five hundred birds flying that day, or thereabouts, ay. If you think, in your average race how many lose their way, what would you say, Professor?'

'I'd say five to ten per cent.'

'Really?' I felt strangely pleased.

'Yes, really,' agreed Maldwyn. 'You're not alone, ay. Anyway, of the thousands taking part only around three hundred or so found their way home. Can you Adam-and-Eve it? Birds were spotted all over the place. I mean, we're talking Barcelona, Madrid, Toulouse, even Venice.'

'Ah, *La Serenissima*,' said Taid. 'The Queen of the Adriatic.'

Another one to look up later.

'Mine was spotted on the French Riviera apparently,' Maldwyn continued, 'near whatjamacallit.'

'Monte Carlo?' I suggested, thinking of how much I wanted to take Lowri there.

'That's the one, ay; anyway, it took days for him to find his way back home again.'

'Yes, but he did come back within the three week period.'

'He did. Nearly broke him, mind. Had to be re-released. Funny, we were just talking about that now, weren't we, Professor?'

Taid choked on his beer. 'Narrow gullet,' he said, as he did every time. Then he mentioned something about crossing a bridge, but I couldn't quite make it out.

'So what was the reason, Mal?'

'Funnily enough, I was reading an article a mate of mine handed to me at the railway depot, only this last week gone. It was about a Belgian study which had found a link between these strange occurrences and some serious disturbance in the Earth's magnetic field caused, it said, by solar storms, sunspots and solar eclipses. Which incidentally is why, Professor, I tend to go with that Keeton's Magnetic Cue Theory.'

Taid, taking a sip from his bottle, was wagging his thumb like a Roman spectator.

'No disrespect here, Maldwyn,' I cut in, seeing my grandfather's doubtful response and reading it as permission to speak. 'I'm sure you're not talking some baloney here, but Mister Lloyd got himself lost without the inconvenience of a solar eclipse. Then just to rub salt in the wound, he was spotted only to disappear again later. So my bird must fall into the boring five-to-ten per cent category.'

Maldwyn glugged. 'Listen,' he said, pulling the bottle from his mouth, 'there might be a lot of theories being bandied around as to why pigeons find their way home or not, but there are a thousand more reasons why yours could have got lost. Your belief that he's out there is as magnetic as a pigeon's homing compass. You can but try, Mostyn, you can but try.'

Damn him. It would be him that said the right thing. He was Elvis, I was convinced. I never wanted to feel this hope. I mean, I wanted to feel hopeful, but not thanks to him. It felt wrong, somehow. I poured some Dr Pepper into a glass, knowing this feeling was all I had. Taid got up from his chair and passed behind me, where he rested both hands on my shoulder.

'You're looking perilously low there, Maldwyn. Have another.'

'Don't mind if I do, Professor.'

'Oh, and by the way,' said Taid on his way to the fridge. 'I passed on a few posters to the Nantwich club. Said they'd make their own enquiries. Now what did I want to ask you?' He pulled a couple of bottles from inside the door and as it shut he clicked his fingers. '*Rich Pigeon, Poor Pigeon*. Any idea where it is?'

How on earth?

'Lowri borrowed it,' I confessed, watching him amble from pantry to kitchen. 'Said it was her new money spinner. I'll get it back, don't worry.'

'I'm not worried. It's just that I like to know these things,' he informed me, scrambling about the kitchen table. 'Now where did I leave the bottle opener? Maldwyn? Any idea?'

A loud bell resonated through the house, signalling the end of the phone call. The sun still shone brightly and, casting a shadow onto the roller blind, Mam's silhouette could be seen preening.

'If it ain't broke, don't fix it.' This was Taid, struggling with a drawer and muttering. 'Where does she keep the blessed thing now?'

Seeing my chance, I turned to Maldwyn and whispered. 'Are you Elvis?'

'You what, mate?' he asked rather too loudly.

'Keep your voice down,' I urged him. 'Come on, Maldwyn. You know. User name Misterlloydfanclub. Report Strays Online chat room?'

Maldwyn looked mystified. 'Rargol, never knew they had a chat room, ay.' He held up the bottle opener. 'You left it by the fruit bowl, Professor. Here.'

Taid took it and walked to the sink.

I tried again. 'Look, someone's been contacting me on that website. They won't reveal who they are and they're sending me weird messages of hope. I don't think it's you, but thought I'd just check.'

Maldwyn drew a blank. 'Not guilty, m'lud.' He leaned in, looking serious. 'Is someone cyber-stalking you?'

'Don't be daft.' I heard two bottles fizz open. 'Zip it.'

'Breaking News,' Mam announced as she entered, her face beaming. 'London. You. Me. Next Saturday. Best I can offer.'

Life's moments didn't come much better. 'For real?'

She nodded.

'Yes!' I shouted, feeling a step nearer. Carried away by the moment, I high-fived Maldwyn. He answered my call with a winking eye and a quick glance thrown over to Miss Bangor.

I know why I did it: I wanted his good fortune but, to this day, I don't know how I blurted out: 'You are coming with us, aren't you, Maldwyn?'

It was Maldwyn's turn to choke. I saw him dart a panic-stricken look at his girlfriend who seemed unable to throw him as much as a rubber ring. 'I...I ...I don't know,' he ventured. 'I mean, what would I do with my pigeons? Who'd look after them?'

'All taken care of,' said Taid, handing Maldwyn another beer.

I was about to compose my 'thanks but no thanks' note to Elvis when I found this message waiting for me. Mam and Maldwyn were in the sitting room watching *The X Factor*; I had said I was looking over my notes.

> **From:** Simon Blake[simon@systems-fidelity.com]
> **Sent:** 12 July 2005 18.36
> **To:** info@reportstraysonline/mostynprice
> Subect: Re: Mister Lloyd Sighting!
>
> Mostyn!
>
> So sorry I missed you! Was on hols, as you know. We had a blast! Anyway, cut to the chase, I know. I've been having my fags on the roof and walking the streets around the building these past couple of days, looking for Mister Lloyd, checking the pavements and the wheelies but, alas! I have no news. I even timed it with the refuse collection outside our building this evening, but I didn't see anything. I know it's no consolation really, but when you come to London, consider this area covered. You'll have enough groundwork of

your own!

I WILL GIVE UP SMOKING! LOL

Best!
Simon Blake
IT Systems Analyst

XIX

Trafalgar Square, London.

'**M**y advice to you,' offers Dorian, new best friend and London guide, 'would be to find your perch ASAP and stick to it. That's the secret. They get snapped up quickly round here since them spikes started to appear. Is the water all right for you?'

Mister Lloyd is splashing in the western fountain of Trafalgar Square with Dorian bobbing up and down the ledge, talking nineteen to the dozen, and noise coming from all around: water, footsteps, sirens, screeching, laughter. Mister Lloyd drifts back to bath time at Graceland with Mostyn. That lovely warm water, just the way he liked it. Dip in, splash about, make room for the next, out you go. Afterwards more fun: standing in front of the bracing hairdryer, feeling his feathers turn fluffy in the hot air and Mostyn laughing loudly.

'Did you hear what I was saying?'

'What?' replies Mister Lloyd, flinging himself out of the cold water, his plumage this time his own to dry. Still, he feels better – and looks it too. 'It's a bit noisy round here, isn't it?'

'I was just saying, Taffy boy, you should try South Africa House. My mate Parker had a place there. He's

141

just vacated so his perch is unexpectedly back on the market. Very quiet, apparently.'

'Sounds great, but not sure how long I plan on staying around,' replies Mister Lloyd.

(Well, that's a relief to us but back to their conversation we must go.)

'I see,' says Dorian, taking himself off the ledge. 'Makes no difference to me. Anyway, if you're not interested, I'll be off. Loads to do.'

'No! Yes,' he protests. 'I am interested.' (We must remember Mister Lloyd is alone and in an alien place. He panics.) 'Would you mind showing me?'

Dorian begins to flap his wings up and down and bids him follow.

Mister Lloyd is looking around the colossal square and we hope he is scanning it for a clue, a pointer for home. None is forthcoming, it seems, for he takes off with Dorian. We must go with him and keep an eye.

'This friend of yours Parker,' coos Mister Lloyd once he has caught up with the dandy flyer. 'Where did he go?'

'Rumour has it,' replies Dorian, 'he's in *La Serenissima*.'

Mister Lloyd looks at him blankly.

'Venice,' explains Dorian helpfully. (In the feral pigeon world, Venice is paradise, friendlier too.)

'Was that after The Incident?' We hear an innocent timbre in Mister Lloyd's coo. Dorian shoots up, leaving him flying aimlessly through the square, nearly into the path of a red London bus, every passenger sitting on its

142

top deck looking just as startled. Mister Lloyd swerves at a right angle.

'Watch the traffic!' It is Dorian from above. 'Up here!'

'My, my, I've got a lot to learn,' coos Mister Lloyd lightly. But Dorian doesn't respond. They both land on a piece of cornicing that surrounds South Africa House, our friend out of breath.

'Got a death wish or sumfin'? (Thought I'd give him a cockney accent.) If you're not careful, you're not going to be around here much longer anyway. I was trying to spare you the harsh realities but I can see you need it spelt out. Look. Where. You. Are. Going!'

Mister Lloyd must wonder when life is going to get nice again.

Not for a while, sadly, for Dorian's words of fury still flow freely. 'There's no way I'm going to let a bumpkin like you drag me down and put me in danger. It's tough enough round here as it is.' Dorian stops. Perhaps he knows he has said enough. 'Right, let's find Parker's perch and I'll give you the lowdown.'

They circle the yellow Portland stone building. With its balconies, balustrades and parapets, it is another fine building but, alas, it is no match for Graceland. That's what Mr Lloyd is thinking as he finds himself heading towards a mesh banner tied to the side of the building. Although he swoops himself out of danger, it is another clumsy blow for our friend, the bumpkin, as Dorian indelicately put it.

'You're a bleedin' liability.' This is a chuckling coo,

143

just to be clear. 'In a nutshell, that net's more obstacles for us. Same with them spikes, but I'm happy to report we've made good progress there. Some even build their nests on 'em. I wouldn't recommend it though. Air conditioning units are the new up-to-the-minute trend.'

'So, where is Parker's place?'

'I'm having trouble remembering,' mutters Dorian, a touch embarrassed. 'I only visited it in the dark, see. He used to have some wild parties, old Parker.'

Mister Lloyd is nonplussed. It has taken them three goes and they're none the wiser.

'Parky always had this idea that the best perches were to be found between the second and fifth floor of any building. Them were the desirables: elevated enough to protect you from people but not so high as to make you miss out on what's happening down there,' he coos in the direction of the pavement below. 'Got to keep your eyes peeled on the food front, see.'

'So why are we circling the roof, looking for this blessed perch then?' It is a fair question, I think we would agree.

Dorian looks at him. 'Alrigh', alrigh', Taffy.' (Dorian doesn't really know he is Welsh, but he can hear Mr Lloyd's coo is different and I am taking artistic licence here.)

Saying nothing Mister Lloyd does a back-flip roll and nose-dives to what he presumes was Parker's fifth floor. If only Anne of Grey Gables could see him now. Dorian follows suit and in passing suggests he cover the lower rung of the building while Mister Lloyd scours the

144

higher. Their starting point we observe as the corner of The Strand and St Martin's Place, and the two follow the façade round in an anti-clockwise direction.

'Found it,' shouts Dorian from beneath. 'It's all coming back to me now.'

'You don't say,' we can just about hear Mister Lloyd coo to himself as he swoops down to join his guide.

'See that gap in the wire? Parky picked at it. There, see?'

Mister Lloyd hovers by to check it out. It is a perfect spot for him to rest and the views are magnificent. 'I'll take it,' he announces, and sets about rearranging some of Parker's old things more to his liking and adding his unique scent.

'No squatter'll come near it now, Lloydy. It is well and truly yours,' exclaims Dorian, hovering around the ledge. There is not much room for both of them so he keeps himself airborne. 'Happy now?'

'Most definitely. I only hope Venice is as nice as they say it is. I'd hate to think of him missing home.' Mister Lloyd takes time to think about what he has said. Still, he has made a friend in Dorian and with that things seem somehow easier, more bearable. 'So, when does the roof get put on?'

'Roof? What you see is what you get, mate. Who the bleeding hell do you think you are? Perches don't get much better than this.'

'Oh,' coos Mister Lloyd. It is all he can say, for if he protests some more, another telling off might bring about another panic attack. He tries to reassure himself

145

it is all **OK**. It is all right, Mister Lloyd. Get a rest and set off home. He looks down on the view and tries to rustle up a brighter outlook. 'I can see what Parker meant,' he coos, thinking sometimes we have to fake it till we make it. 'Far enough from danger, near enough for bounty.'

'Precisely! And what's more, my friend, look what you got down there.'

'What?'

Is that a sigh, Dorian? He goes on. 'Only one of the finest eateries in London.'

Mister Lloyd takes another look but sees only humans beneath a shelter, waiting.

'The Bus Stop!' exclaims Dorian with a dramatic sweep of his wing. 'Them over there, see, they eat as they wait for the bus. Some eat while running for the bus. Bus arrives. No food allowed on board. Hey presto, fast food at your disposal. On most days we can offer you half-eaten burgers, fries and bagels. Do look out for daily specials, samosas being one of my favourites. But keep your eyes peeled. They get snapped up quick, so you've got to be *quicker.*'

Now Mister Lloyd looks genuinely pleased. 'Show me the other hot spots – that is, if you've got time. Do you say that here in London? Hot spots?'

CHAPTER TWENTY

Deiniol High, Bangor

'And now the moment you've all been waiting for,' announced Mr Griffiths. If Elvis were here, there'd be searchlights, a drum roll and a fanfare. 'An additional treat for us at the end of what, I can categorically tell you, has been a very successful year at our beloved Deiniol High.' The headteacher paused dramatically, his head bobbing gently as he scanned the hall. 'You're going to love this, kids. Oh yes.'

The whole room tittered knowingly. The debate had not been advertised but news of it had spread round the school like the plague.

'Last week I was set an extraordinary challenge when two lads from year seven were caught fighting over the plight of a pigeon, would you believe?'

Wearing a gown he stood in the middle at his lectern, Self-Help Ms Hughes seated at a table beside him. Behind, on rows of chairs, were teachers and prefects, and in front me and Lynton at a lectern on either side of the stage. Mister Lloyd had been missing nearly two weeks now and time was running out, but here I was about to be punished. I'd once seen someone looking like I felt right now; it was an illustration in a history book, crosshatched ink of a face scrunched and broken, caked with rotting food, crowds shouting and jeering at it. Mine was tomato-crimson, said Lowri later, even from where she sat.

She still laughs about it now but, to be fair, when we were called to the stage, she tugged at my sweater with a rooting smile. 'That day,' Mr Griffiths resumed, 'the two were clearly lost for words and so, in order to help them clarify their thoughts, I suggested a battle of words, right here in front of you as a lesson to them. And, I hasten to add, a lesson to any of you out there who may harbour any similar ideas. This stage is the only place I shall allow such battles in my school,' he banged on his lectern. 'The rest of you Goody Two Shoes can sit back and enjoy the entertainment. So, without further ado, Lynton Chivers and Mostyn Price have five minutes each to discuss the motion: Pigeons: Friend or Foe? Ms Hughes, stopwatch at the ready, if you please.'

Lynton was invited to begin the debate. I looked in his direction, casually leaning on his lectern as he was. No notes. *He had no notes.* I glanced down at mine. Twenty-three ruffled sides. I went over Taid's main points: be passionate, believe in your cause, convince them you're right, en-*un*-ciate – and for God's sake be brief.

'Pigeons: Friend or Foe? Discuss,' Lynton exclaimed. He paused. Then like a human cannonball he launched himself from the lectern and landed at the front of the stage, throwing his green sweater to the audience like an aging rock star. From where I stood he had on what looked like a plain white T-shirt but the school fell about laughing. It wasn't until he swaggered back to his lectern that I saw the 'I HATE PIGEONS' logo emblazoned on his front. It was a cheap trick and a lousy argument but Lynton had to wait for the adulation to die down. 'What, I ask you, is there to discuss, yeah? Pigeons are *discuss-ting.*'

Silence.

Was that it? Was it over to me that soon? Restless stirrings now came from the gormless crowd. I wanted them fickle, but their dispirited murmurs spurred Lynton on and his ensuing speech became a tirade.

'I mean, I ask ya, they're disgusting!' he shouted. 'When you're roamin' the streets of Bangor, yeah, on a Saturday with your mates, cos that's what we usually do, or it could be anywhere else for that matter, yeah – doesn't have to be Bangor – it could be New York or Llandudno – there's nothin' worse than when a pigeon flies right in front of your face when you're quietly mindin' your own business. My nana is truly frightened of 'em, right? She's getting on a bit these days. Fifty-one come the March, yeah, and she done nuffing to aggravate them, you know. She said it caused her accident when she fell and cracked her knee on the High Street. It was when a pigeon flew straight at her head, missing it by millimetres. Anyway she tried to get compensation, yeah, for all the hurtin' and trauma, and not even Cash Injury Direct could help with her claim – 'No Win No Fee' they say but in the end, yeah, she owed them money cos you can't sue a pigeon, no?'

The audience giggled.

'First time in the history of Cash Injury Direct apparently. Me? Well they put you off your chips, yeah, because they're full of germs – more germs than Brommers!'

More titters.

'You're so going to regret that, Chivers!' protested a muffled voice from Lynton's posse.

'Where are ya, lad?' shouted Lynton, by now quite at home behind the lectern.

Bromley shot up and bowed to the cheers.

The whole school laughed; even Mr Griffiths and Ms Hughes found it hard not to. Bromley, he of the spotty face and curly peroxide hair, had become Specimen Number One and it was a right crowd pleaser. I looked down at my notes. It read worthy, page after page of it. But it was all too late, I couldn't change it now. I was stuck with Plan A: A Speech Called Worthy. I looked over to Lowri, Gar and Tim. They had been gesturing wildly, trying to flag my attention. They made a slitting throat gesture. Hardly a time for charades, I thought.

'Get on with it, Chivers!' shouted Mr Griffiths. 'You have three and a half minutes.'

'Right, where was I? Yeah, to me, pigeons are like rats and we all know how much germs they carry and the only difference is these got wings, yeah. Rats with Wings. Suppose that's a good way to describe 'em, ay.'

'Oh, that old chestnut,' I wailed, slumping my head down on the lectern.

'My dad works in the bank by the big clock in the High Street,' he continued, now on a roll. 'He says their dung is full of germs and diseases – and acid as well. It eats into the buildings and before they got the nettin' on the front of the bank it was covered in dung. He told me if they'd done nothin' abou' it, it would have disintegrated, yeah. I tell ya, it's a disgrace, ruinin' buildings like that. That's why Conwy Castle looks like it does, apparently. Ruined.'

'Rubbish,' heckled a voice in the audience. It sounded like Taid's. I looked over the enchanted crowd towards the backbenches, reserved for visitors who cared to drop in on such days. It was him.

'It's what I heard,' retorted Lynton to my side. 'Anyway now they've got the nettin' on the building my dad says he can stand outside the front door and have a quiet fag now without fear of bird-shit dropping on his bald head.'

Great. The bird-shit trump card. As predicted, the school fell about once more. I began rifling through my notes again, looking for tricks that might capture this audience. Be inspired by your opponent, I could hear Taid say, *not* defeated. All very well, but how? I looked to Lowri, Gar and Tim for help. Their arms still gesturing wildly, for a second I thought they'd switched allegiance. But a pattern and a rhythm emerged and I realised they were trying to tell me something. The audience cheered.

'No, hey, stop laughin' now, this minute, yeah,' Lynton was saying. 'My dad could have died a horrible death from touching that poo. Cos that's what happens. And you lot are laughing. He could've got pneumonia—'

'Eew,' cried the audience. Among them three fingers pointed at me.

'Yes, vomiting,' shouted Lynton.

I mouthed back to the three in the back. '*Me?*'

'Eew!' cried the audience again. Among them three heads nodded, followed by three hands coiling like the action of a writing hand.

'Ay, diarrhoea even,' continued Lynton.

I held up my notes with a questioning look.

The audience was squirming but I kept my eyes on the three heads nodding urgently, followed by the three hands lifted to respective open mouths, tapping their top lips. It was, no mistake, a yawn. My notes were boring.

'Thirty seconds, Lynton,' shouted Mr Griffiths.

'Listen now, yeah. There are millions of pages on t'interweb which say the same thing as me, with names of diseases I'd never even heard of. Don't worry, everybody, my dad didn't have any of those diseases – which, is a shame really, because I could have rested my case there. But that's not the point. He *could* have had any of those. The honest to God truth is pigeons are a bloody nuisance and they're bloody everywhere. They poo on your head, in their own nest, they smell, they're dunces. Basically, right, they are the most hated critters not just in Bangor, not just in north Wales, but in the World and its surrounding area. I rest my case.'

The audience clapped loudly but all I could see were three fingers slashing three throats, followed by three pairs of pinching fingers working back and forth. The message could not have been clearer: tear up the notes or die. *But I had worked so hard!*

Lynton walked to the edge of the stage and took a bow, his T-shirt glowing in the bright morning sun as if he had walked into his own spotlight. The audience clapped and cheered, giving the clown the benefit of the doubt.

'Well, thank you, Lynton,' said Mr Griffiths, 'on behalf of everyone in the hall, for that enlightening insight. And now I call upon Mostyn Price to defend the pigeon.'

Three thumbs raised high took my eye to the rear of the hall, where Taid too was miming the tearing of pages and pointing to his heart.

I heard a small cough and felt a tap on my shoulder. It made me jump.

'Mostyn Price, did you not hear me?'

My mouth was too dry to answer; all I could manage was a nod.

'Right, well, without further ado, please give Mostyn every fair play as he presents us with his own views on the subject, Pigeon: Friend or Foe.'

I'd not noticed the ticking clock above the proscenium arch before. Friend or foe, I thought. It was getting louder. There was a clap, two claps, more claps. My name. I heard my name. *I'm thinking.* Where to begin, don't panic. *Think.* I looked behind. Ms Hughes was urging me on. *I'm thinking!* To my side Lynton was leading the commotion. If I close my eyes, it might go away. *I'm thinking!* I'll close my eyes anyway. Rotten food. I could smell rotten food from the kitchen wheelie bins. Cabbage hurtling towards me. I lifted my hand high above the lectern to catch something putrid. Caught. I heard cries of hush darting round the room. Slowly I opened my eyes. My hand was raised, fist closed. There was no cabbage. In fact, the place was falling silent. I had commanded their attention and they had obeyed. I looked behind again. Ms Hughes in the lotus position, meditating. I brought my hand down to rest on my notes and looked hard at the entire school. *I was thinking!*

The silent room.

'Friend or Foe?' I began. *Sound challenging. Doesn't matter if you don't mean it, just sound it.* 'You know—' I paused. *Buy some time.* 'You know, as different as we may look, I believe there are more similarities than you think between Pigeon and Man.'

The audience burst out laughing. I had wanted laughter, but I didn't think it was that funny till I saw Mr Griffiths perched behind me in his black gown, head bobbing.

'Well, some of us more than others, right?' I said with a knowing smile. The shaft of sunlight that had basked Lynton in glory was now dappled the shadow of a flock of pigeons, feral, flying above and giving me the focus I needed. 'Seriously, however, this debate tests our attitude to all animals, even to our own friends and foes, wouldn't you say, Bromley?' I picked up my notes. Mister Lloyd pattered about happily on my head. *Come on, Mister Lloyd! Let's fly!* 'See these?' I said, showing them to hundreds of eyes. 'Thanks to Lynton, these notes don't matter anymore.' I began tearing up each sheet, one by one, tossing them onto the stage to the sound of gasps and flutters. Seconds ago this would have been torture, sacrilegious even, but this moment of theatre kept my audience spellbound. It was all in me and had been all along. 'I don't have to remind you that the gentle dove is a kind of pigeon. In Welsh we use the same word for both: "Colomen". The pigeon and the dove are both descendants of the original Blue Rock Pigeon and have lived on this earth far longer than we have, but while one became a symbol of peace, the other, and Lynton isn't far wrong here, has became a symbol of *shit*.'

The very word was an attention-grabber. Some guffawed, others smirked with embarrassment. If it had worked for Lynton, it would work for me. I carried on tearing, my eyes firmly fixed on the audience. 'I was going to try and explain how pigeons were respected before they flew into this public relations disaster, how with their extraordinary homing ability they became messengers, bringing urgent news and saving thousands of lives, but,' I paused, thinking I'd give it a try for dramatic effect, 'Lynton knows best. I was going to try and explain,' – this was good – 'how in the Bible the pigeon, and I shall call it a pigeon, brought news to Noah and his ark of animals that the floods were waning, how it became a symbol of the Holy Spirit in the New Testament, how it helped Charles Darwin come up with his theory of evolution. But no, there's no point because,' I repeated, liking the rhythm, 'Lynton knows best.'

(The previous night at Darwin HQ, Taid had told me about repetition. Useful, he said, before telling me about this character called Mark Antony in some Shakespeare play, who liked to repeat things to get his point across. Anyway, it seemed an interesting tactic and worth a go.)

'I was going to tell you how the world's largest news agency, Reuters, began life using the pigeon as messengers, as did one of the world's largest private banks, and how even today pigeons are big business, changing hands for thousands of pounds, top racers earning their owners up to a million dollars in some cases. But there's not much point telling you that, as—' I put a finger to my ear this time and bent it towards the crowd. Right on cue, the whole school joined in.

'Lynton knows best!'

The last of the sheets flew into the air. 'So how come we're in this mess in the first place? Well I'll tell you why. I own a pigeon, my Taid owns several and it is my interest in these creatures that has ruffled our friend over here,' I pointed at Lynton but held my gaze on the audience. 'It's this problem that we have between us, this difference of opinion that got us into trouble and which is why I am standing here before you today.'

Lowri, Gar and Tim were sat upright but I felt shy of

looking at Taid just yet.

'You know, there's a word for people like Lynton. He is what they would call a Peristerphobe – someone who fears pigeons. And I would argue it is an irrational fear. Look, I'll be honest with you. Those pigeons, the ones you see on Bangor High Street who allegedly shit on balding heads, although it's physically impossible for them to do so when they're on the move, the ones who traumatise Nanas and bring medieval castles tumbling down, according to Lynton. They've more than likely escaped from coops, dovecotes, or lofts like my Taid's. At one time the country was riddled with them, dovecotes everywhere, but over hundreds of years, just like man, they escaped to the city. And why? Quite simply, we made it lovely for them. We provided buildings which are just like the rocks they dwelt on for thousands of years. We provided food, lots of lovely food, thanks to people like Lynton, so generous with his chips on a Saturday afternoon. Incidentally, yes, pigeons carry diseases, up to twenty-six in fact, but there is no evidence that they can be passed on to us humans. None!'

Silence. I banged my fist on the lectern. Accidentally. It hurt but I tried not to let it show.

'If people didn't make it such a wonderful experience for them to roam our streets, then it would mean fewer pigeons, the stronger ones would outlive the disease-ridden ones and, hey bingo, bob's your uncle, the problem is indeed solvèd. It's up to us, not them.'

I turned to my opponent and noticed Mr Griffiths pointing to his watch. I didn't care. I was having too much fun. 'Lynton, pigeons have a nasty image because of people like you who continually encourage their behaviour;

overfeeding means overbreeding, yet I'm the one who gets it in the neck just for keeping one as a pet.'

Lynton shrugged his shoulders and looked flushed.

'Now a couple of weeks ago, my racing pigeon went missing. It was flying back from a race in Belgium. I'd trained it for years. I'd looked forward to this moment and when he was released, he never came home. Missing. Lost. Disappeared.'

'So much for its homing ability then!' shouted a jeerer in the audience.

'You wait till your dad's Sat Nav breaks down,' I snapped at whoever. 'Look, try to imagine a pound of flesh flying through the sky and finding its way home from a distance of five hundred miles at a speed of fifty-miles-an-hour from a place it's never been before. Hey, so I was unlucky—' I found that bit difficult to say. I cleared my throat. 'But it hasn't lessened my wonder, which is why standing here before you makes me more determined than ever to find him. So in a way,' I added, pointing my thumb in Lynton's direction, 'I ought to be grateful to this geezer. So thanks, Lynton! Your work is done. And so is mine, Mr Griffiths.'

The headteacher looked at his watch. 'You have one more minute.'

'No thanks, sir.' It was enough.

The headteacher was already on his feet. 'Well, I think that dispenses with any need for a casting vote. Now shake hands.' He started a solitary clap. Under duress or not, Lynton and I met halfway and duly obliged. I turned to Lowri, who stood up and burst into applause, her rapture prompting the whole school to follow. I closed my eyes and pictured a thousand pigeons released into the sky. I wished them all a safe journey before Ms Hughes woke me with a gentle prod and my torn pieces of paper.

'They might come in handy,' she whispered in my ear. 'You never know.'

I looked back to Taid. He'd gone.

'Did you really have to announce the sweepstake to the whole school?' I asked Lowri. We'd stopped off by the poster, on our way home, the whole of the summer holidays ahead of us. 'Now everyone's got money on whether or not Mister Lloyd comes home.'

'Oh, do shut up,' said Lowri from her position behind the camera. 'Now move in a bit closer, Mostyn. Tim, you're out of shot.'

'Look on the bright side, now we're all on the lookout,' proffered Tim as he entered the frame.

'Well, you lot can keep it casual,' I admitted through a pained grin and feeling like a ventriloquist. 'A quick-glance-under-the-table-while-sipping-a-Cappuccino-on-the-terrazzo type thing. Just check their feet – green ring, always a sign of a quitter.' I made it sound so simple.

'OK. Say cheese!'

Click. Lowri took the photo and handed me back my phone.

'Right, send us it now,' demanded Tim. 'I'll post it on my site so we can all do our bit, including you, Gar.'

'I've done my fair bit. LOL,' said Gar.

He could see I looked worried.

'Fret ye not, lad. I'll send you pics of any sightings from The Algarve. You never know, your Mister Lloyd might be sunning himself by the pool, on an all inclusive, no doubt having a right ole laugh.'

'Same here from the Eisteddfod field,' added Lowri. She and her parents were off to the cultural festival, staying in the caravan, as they did every year. 'He'll be hobnobbing with the druids, you'll see! So, babycakes,' she shouted, poking me gently in the ribs, 'when you off to Londinium?'

'In the morning.'

'Right, well I want you back with your pigeon and not them airs and graces,' said Tim.

'I'll remember that, thanks. Taid's over the moon, of course, with a house full of people landing on him. Still, he won't venture out much beyond Darwin HQ, I'll bet you, with his stove and his birds. Which reminds me, Lowri: *Rich Pigeon, Poor Pigeon.*'

'Chill-ax, Mostyn!' she protested. 'He'll get it back when I've finished my notes. Me and the Professor had a friendly chat about it earlier in assembly.' She tapped her nose. 'We have an understanding.'

'Well, understand this. Whatever you do, don't spill anything on it,' I said portentously.

'Hark at you,' smirked Lowri, pointing at the stains forever imprinted on the posters. 'You've got an awful lot of pinning to do, by the way. London's a big place, you know.'

I rolled my eyes.

'Anyway,' she continued, 'my mother, the vulnerable—'

'Venerable!' we all shouted.

'That too. The venerable Mrs Levald of Britannia Close, told me to tell you, yeah, that if you're ever lonely in London, go stand on Piccadilly Circus for long enough and you're bound to see someone from Bangor. Remember that, yeah?'

'How could I forget?' I said, before we all burst into hysterics.

'Well, take care then,' said Gar, offering a group hug when the laughter had died down.

We all threw ourselves in.

'Send us a postcard!' said Lowri, pulling away. 'Prince William on a London Bus, please.' She sounded suddenly sniffly. Lifting a sleeve to dry her eye, she walked away, turning at a safe distance to yell 'TTFN!'

With a final 'Hwyl fawr!' we watched her tidying her hair for home until she disappeared from view. Tim, Gar and I shook hands and went our separate ways.

School was out. Tomorrow, London.

XXI

Trafalgar Square, London

'**B**y the way,' says Dorian as they fly over the café housed beneath the North Terrace, 'If you're going to do your business, try not to do it on any of them awnings. It gives us lot a bad name and we've got enough public relations problems without our very own species making it worse for ourselves.'

Mister Lloyd is very obliging. He bears it in mind but this is one of many things he has had to take on board. 'What's over there?'

From his new home on South Africa House, they had flown around the Royal Parish, also known as St Martin in the Fields. Taking in a quick view of The National Gallery – more of that building later, Mister Lloyd is assured – they fly over towards Whitehall. Admiralty Arch looks a fun place, he muses, before being ushered past Canada House and warned to make preparations for landing.

'I'm afraid it's the Gel Crash Landing method for this one too,' says Dorian, getting his feet into position.

Quite a number of fellow flyers have gathered on The Fourth Plinth, Mister Lloyd observes, as he prepares to go through the drill. Slow. Standby to Grip. Feet out.

Land. And not a bad attempt, Mister Lloyd.

'Come and plonk yourself down here, mate,' says Dorian rather loudly. 'Up on that epaulette you can get a sense of scale but down here's better for atmosphere,' he explains as he wades through his fellow citizens, shuffling along the edge of the plinth rather brusquely, many jostling in retaliation. 'Sorry, an' all that. New kid on the block, so to speak,' he shouts, although the joke falls flat.

Mister Lloyd bobs his head politely and joins Dorian on the edge. Robust, confident Dorian, who speaks nineteen to the dozen, who was always dishing out good advice, is all quiet for a change. Mister Lloyd waits for some worldly-wise words but Dorian just stares at the view of Trafalgar Square, its visitors, fountains, traffic and noise all a blur. Eventually he turns.

'It's like *The Day of the Triffids* round here compared to what it used to be.'

Mister Lloyd hesitates. 'Are you going to tell me what happened?' He has been here long enough – too long! – to know it was a sensitive subject.

'When I was a young squab there were literally thousands of us here. Plenty of food to go round, an' all – you couldn't move for people throwing food at you. They wanted their photograph taken with us and we'd oblige in return for a few grains – you know, the old party trick of flying on to their heads, arms, what have you, and they'd love it. And *we* loved it,' he adds, turning back to the square. 'Then one day it stopped. Woke up one morning and everything had cleared. The crowds still came but, as far as we were concerned, they were empty-handed. Puzzled, we were. Stumped.'

'What did you do?'

'My old Pij used to tell me, "stand not on sufferance, my squab, but fly at once from those who bring nothing to the table." So we stopped. We stopped posing for their photographs. I mean, nobody wins at the end of the day. Our numbers began to dwindle. Then *he* arrived,' points Dorian with his fan tail.

Mister Lloyd looks over but his view – and ours – is blocked by the milling human gatherers. Move out of the way, you lot, we want to shout, but no one can hear us. Finally one male eating an ice cream and reading his guidebook is called over by another nearby. He gathers his things – gosh, he is slow – and eventually clears the view for us and Mister Lloyd. Oh dear. Maybe we were too quick in wanting the male gone. He should have stayed there eating his ice cream, because Mister Lloyd is, quite understandably, looking more petrified than the stone plinth he's standing on.

'That loud-mouthed geezer, The Falcon—' Dorian stops. He has spotted Mister Lloyd's pearlescent hackle changing colour. 'Upsetting, isn't it? Right, well, keep your eye out for him. It ain't pretty what happens. His owner apparently doesn't feed him so he gets all funny and hungry by the time he starts his shift here. It's bad enough when we lose one but then you have to deal with all the screaming humans around you. It's distressing.'

'Spare me the detail,' interrupts Mister Lloyd. He lifts his wings and flies off the ledge, hovering in front of Dorian and showing him his healing wound below the rear of his keel.

Dorian winces at the sight. 'You've been through the mill, my friend.'

'It's how I ended up here,' explains Mister Lloyd, coming back in to land. He decides against telling Dorian his old mate Parker is unlikely to have got as far as their paradise, Venice. Possibly not even as far as the end of the square itself.

Deep down, maybe Dorian knows it too. 'Tis the land of milk and honey for The Falcon,' he coos, reflecting on the view. 'Funny that,' he adds. 'It used to be ours. Right, let me show you what to do in an emergency.'

Oh, the harsh realities of the city, the country, of life!

CHAPTER TWENTY-TWO

Sitting Room, Bangor

'Is it flipping well worth it?' she shouted, to herself most probably, as she cleaned out the bath. A change is as good as a rest, they say, and boy, did Paloma Price need one. She had been tidying, polishing, wiping and cleaning until the early hours. This morning – two weeks since I last saw Mister Lloyd – it was the bathroom's turn. 'I mean, it's not as if I'm going to benefit from all this work! It'd better be as good as this when we come home.'

Lord knows who she was talking to up there but the Rathbones and their four children certainly couldn't hear her. I was downstairs, busily writing the *Welcome!* note in the sitting room. My handwriting is haphazard at the best of times; that day it was all scribbles as I set down beach and castle recommendations, pto's, asterisks and its conclusion, *'Have Fun!'* halfway up the margin. Joy, most likely, was delivering much the same address their end as the Londoners got ready for their holiday between the sea and the mountains of north Wales while we, the Prices were making the same last minute preparations for our trip to the metropolis. Very last minute.

'Will you, for God's sake – how many times do I have to ask you? – remove your duvet cover and finish your packing?' she shouted from the top of the stairs. 'Do I have to do everything myself?'

I was over the moon at the prospect of swapping houses for a fortnight, but sprinting from sitting room to hall, making my way up the stairs, I passed Mam halfway and it dawned on me the task of getting everything organised on time had fallen almost entirely on her shoulders. Half-hidden as she was behind a large holdall, towels and a couple of down pillows, we could barely exchange a glance. I squeezed my way past and did as I was told.

Last in: the posters, packed with the same care as pilfered Egyptian treasures, except these were recycled multiuse photocopying paper sheets. To me they were The Rosetta Stone; drawing pins boxed jewels, and let us not forget the dazzling brilliance of ring-binder sheet protectors, all neatly cushioned on a suitcase full of clothes, books and all my printed correspondence. On top I placed a freshly laundered and perfectly folded duvet cover. And a sticker marked 'Fragile' slapped on. Destination London, and only six days left to find him.

Taid was to stay at Darwin HQ, while Maldwyn was to join us in a few days. Catching up with some outstanding paperwork was what he said. That morning, however, both had been enlisted and by the time I appeared on the driveway, Maldwyn's head was burrowed under the bonnet, Taid's half hidden under the tailgate.

'This one on its side, please, Taid,' I said, placing the suitcase down on the concrete level. 'I don't want my posters squashed.'

'I'm already trying not to squash your Mister Lloyd's basket.' He sounded tetchy. 'Where am I going to fit all this?'

'I don't know why you're looking at me like that, Taid. There's more stuff in the hall. I've passed two suitcases, a picnic basket, vanity case, hair rollers, toiletries, four kimonos, a bag of groceries, a newly laundered dress and a pair of shoes for every conceivable occasion!'

The bonnet slammed shut. Maldwyn walked towards the back of the car, wiping his oily hands. 'Hope you don't mind, Professor, but why don't you fill the empty basket with some of the odds and ends Mostyn mentioned? That way the basket won't cave in and you won't lose out on any space.'

'Genius, Maldwyn,' Mam called out, carrying a tray of tea and offering mugs all round.

Maldwyn looked suitably abashed but took the mug into the driver's seat for the next job in hand.

'Why couldn't you come up with that?' said Taid under his breath, glaring at me from the corner of his eye. With a heavy sigh he began to rearrange the contents of the boot.

I sipped quietly at my tea until I was upstaged by a loud shriek.

'No, Maldwyn, No! What do you think you're doing?'

Here we go, I thought, and peered through the gap between the headrests, the cry of protest coming from the driver's side. Mam was leaning over the open door, an elbow on the window, the other on the roof.

'I told you. I know the way!'

'You say that now ay, Paloma,' Maldwyn said, fiddling around on the dashboard. 'You never know, it might come in handy.' He was wiping a small patch of the windscreen to secure better suction for the Sat Nav Maldwyn and I had agreed to transfer from The Mid-Life Crisis. 'Traffic systems change all the time down there in the big smoke. I'd much rather you had this than me.'

Maldwyn, poor unsuspecting Maldwyn was taking the flak for what was my idea. Living in my homing pigeon world, I was curious to see how this at-the-time recently invented contraption worked. Named Bonnie, it had up till now been Maldwyn's only companion. He merely thought he was being kind.

'Don't be so bloody sexist! How many times do I have to tell you, Maldwyn? I've been there loads of times – practically lived half my professional life there!' She slammed the door with a growl, catching sight of me in the gust of her swing. 'And what are you squinting at?'

'Maldwyn says she's pretty spot on,' I muttered.

Mam glowered at me, snatched the empty tray off the roof of the car and marched back into the house. 'There are bags waiting in the hall!'

'First tiff,' I suggested to Taid quietly.

He sniggered and went back to his rearranging.

'Yeah well, you've got to take the rough with the smooth,' said Maldwyn, seeing me in the wing mirror. He sounded surprisingly unperturbed but I began to think he wouldn't last the course. That suited me, of course: Maldwyn in my head, safe in a box labelled 'Comedy Action Hero Who Got His Pigeon Back'. I caught his eye in the mirror once again and worried he had read my mind. He winked. 'What's the postcode, lad?'

I quoted it off pat and leant on the window.

Bonnie La Brea, or Bonnie for short, was an American. Maldwyn had bought her in a shop on La Brea Avenue. He had attended The International Los Angeles Liberation and

Racing Pigeon Conference that had been organised by the Culver City Racing Pigeon Club a couple of years back. His American hosts took a shine to his 'quaint' Welsh accent – *'what's this "ay" business?'* They adopted him as Maldwyn 'The Liberator' Jones. He liked it and it stuck.

'That's it,' he announced, pressing Done. 'The dock's a bit dodgy, mind, so careful she doesn't fall out. Now, let's see if I can get back into the other girlfriend's good books again.'

Oil-scuffed and carrying her vanity case and rollers unembarrassed, Maldwyn was indeed soon back in favour. To and fro, back and forth, he filled the car to bursting point, leaving just enough room for Mam to see through the rear view mirror. Tailgate shut, he pulled out a piece of chamois leather tucked under his belt and began to wipe the glass.

'Right,' said Mam. 'Before we go, Taid, quick recap.' She was looking at her watch and marching him to the garage. 'I just want to go through with you what meals I've prepared. I don't want you calling us in London, asking where's this, where's that, where I keep things, complaining that I haven't explained things properly or, heaven forfend, clearly!' She yanked open the chest freezer.

With Maldwyn cleaning the car windows and Mam and Taid discussing lobscouse, it seemed a good time to sneak off for a quiet moment. 'I'm just popping up to Graceland, Taid. Won't be long.'

'That's right, my boy,' said Taid waving from deep inside the freezer. 'Better check that Mister Lloyd hasn't come home before you go.'

I could see how that joke could work but I sloped off without a retort. I wanted to take one last look at the place before we set off. I needed a word. With myself. I followed the crazy steps up to Graceland, imagining Mister Lloyd flying towards me. There'd be a no-questions-asked welcome as we made our way along the gangway, him flying to his loft as if he had never been away, parading the compartment to the cheery fluttering of friends and family. Then, landing on my head, his feet tickling my scalp, he'd find his balance. Once steady he'd survey his surroundings, no longer lost.

No such happy ending greeted me as I turned the knob of the door. I stepped inside to the sound of murmuring pigeons. 'Only me,' I whispered as their alarm faded. All quiet. I'd come to tell myself that if by any chance I didn't find Mister Lloyd, if by any chance he didn't return, that if I had to go back to school without news of his homecoming, I would still hold my head up high. I would have done my best.

I edged towards Mister Lloyd's compartment – it would always be his – and saw Anne of Grey Gables and Grey's Anatomy sitting there contentedly in their brand new nest bowl. They knew it was me, recognised me straight away. I peered inside. They didn't flinch; I could see how well they had settled in their new home, the one I'd scrubbed clean. It had irked me then and it still did now, for they were squatting as if they had lived there all their lives.

I don't know if it was to show me or if she was simply on the turn of duty, but Anne of Grey Gables got to her feet, revealing two eggs she had been incubating overnight. My heart skipped a beat. I looked over to the spider-webbed windowsill where Taid kept a box of matches and a candle, useful, he had shown me once, when he wanted to do a quick check on the development of an embryo. Slowly and carefully I walked over to the window, struck a match and lit the candle. I was keen not to alarm the two, and so began talking to them in a low voice – silly things, nice things – as I tiptoed back to the compartment. I was right. The young couple were on the turn of duty, swapping places, Grey's Anatomy about to start the incubating shift. I liked it that they both took turns. Still talking I put my hand inside the compartment and began stroking Grey's feathers; he buffeted me gently with his wings, even pecked a little at my hand, but despite being territorial he wasn't alarmed. With one hand I began lifting him gingerly out of his perch and with the other I took hold of an egg from his nest bowl and carried it over to the candle. It was cruel, I know, but between finger and thumb, I wanted to examine the speckled shell against the flame. It was there. Through the delicate, now translucent shell, I saw the dark shadow of an embryo.

–*The wonder of you*, said Elvis in the candle-lit reflection.

I nodded. There was no mistaking. There'd be two young squeakers waiting for me when I came back.

'Beep! Beep! Beeep!'

'Iesu Grist!' Mam was tooting the car horn. I nearly dropped the egg on the floor, only managing to save it in the palm of my hand. The kerfuffle brought about tremulous, alarmed stirrings and anxious fluttering in the normally calm, Zen-like atmosphere of Graceland.

'Beep! Beep! Beeeep!'

'All right! All right!' I said, whispering loudly, the delicate egg rolling about in my shaking hand.

–*Return to sender!*

The loft cooed in outrage and I hurriedly placed it back

with its rightful owner. 'It's unharmed, look!' I protested but Grey's Anatomy began pecking heavily at my hand. 'Sorry, sorry, sorry,' I uttered, unable to make amends. It would have to wait till I got back from London.

I stepped out, shutting the door behind me with a dull thud and caught sight of the candle in the window – *Blow it out, you fool!* – I rushed back into the still indignant tittle-tattle. Another Graceland disaster averted.

'Oh and by the way,' Mam shouted, reversing recklessly, issuing her last note through the open window as Taid and Maldwyn walked us down the drive. 'The microwave is actually kept in the utility room these days. Instructions on top. See you, Mal!'

'Prepare to turn left in Five. Hundred. Yards,' Bonnie announced innocently, her electronic Californian voice very supportive. Each. Word. Sounding. Like. The. Beginning. Of. A. New. Sentence.

'What's she doing here?' shrieked Mam, slamming on the brake. Bonnie slid off her dock and fell into the foot well.

'She's trying to tell me now how to get out of Bangor, is she?' I reached down for the discarded contraption. 'I've only been living here all me bleedin' life. I've told you, Mal, I don't want her! I've half a mind to throw it back at you,' she fumed, her neck stretched out the window.

Maldwyn leaned in and kissed her on the lips.

'Oh, give me strength!' she sighed and put the car in gear.

'It's my fault,' I confessed, slotting the American back into the dock. 'I thought it would help me understand how pigeons find their way home.'

To which she had no answer.

I grimaced and fastened my seat belt. 'Come on, Mam!
'We need to get going!'

'Ring when you get there,' Taid called out.

'So long,' added Mal with a final, foreboding wave.
'And good luck.'

We were on our way.

XXIII

Trafalgar Square, London

Duck your heads! It is Dorian flying low, above and through the pedestrians of the North Terrace. And here is Mister Lloyd following! See how he is getting the hang of it; Dorian's advice has come in handy: *'Look. Where. You. Are. Going!'* These city ways! Mister Lloyd could fly in this fashion all day but we don't want him to enjoy himself too much. This could be dangerous. Dorian lands on the stone ledge in front of the National Gallery, where dozens of humans are milling around.

'Thought we'd do the rest on foot,' suggests Dorian, sounding perkier for their distance from the Fourth Plinth. He begins bobbing along the stone ledge, never in a straight line, mind, forced into small detours here and there, jumping onto the grass verge as and when humans block their path. 'See what's beneath you now?' he asks, checking his friend is following.

Mister Lloyd looks down. They are treading on grass. It was everywhere at Graceland. 'Yes, and?'

'Good for minerals,' coos Dorian. 'Grown nowhere else on the square, so it's in your interest to know about this place. Up above you'll see this building. Unremarkable apart from a few prize meeting places.'

He is pointing at The National Gallery, would you believe. 'Handy for Accidents and Emergency. See her over there?' he asks, twitching in the direction of a female human who is making her way towards a mixed gang of her own species sat on the grass.

Mister Lloyd nods. The woman's name is Mrs Wanda Petrovsky – you'll meet her soon. They don't know this name, of course, but they will refer to her as Kind Lady.

'Checks up on us, she does,' explains Dorian as he continues along the human queue gathering outside the gallery. 'And if you ever get into trouble, have an injury or feel poorly, bob up and down this grass verge – if you can, like – and, don't ask me how, she'll find you. Proper kind lady,' he hovers close to Mister Lloyd and indicates to his left. 'Rumour has it these people here, them we're walking past now—'

Mister Lloyd sees the mixed gang the Kind Lady was talking to. They seem to be scruffier in appearance than most of the other humans around.

'It's said they pass on the message,' continues Dorian. 'Birds then disappear. Come back fully recovered. Marvellous, when you think about it.'

Mister Lloyd clearly thinks this is more than marvellous. He pats about on the grass, most probably contemplating a whole new world full of possibilities. Truth be told, we don't want this, we don't want him to settle down. We want him to fly home. Back to Mostyn.

Up the steps to the main portico entrance of the gallery, they fly to a quiet spot. From here, they can see beyond Nelson's Column down towards Whitehall,

Downing Street and, in the distance, the Houses of Parliament and Big Ben. Dorian turns to Mister Lloyd. 'You know, I think the world hates us right now.'

Mister Lloyd shrugs his wings. Let's hope he's thinking of Mostyn. 'Really? I thought we're supposed to be a gregarious lot. Love socializing and all that.'

'We do! But here we're quite the unloved. Such a shame, that,' says Dorian quietly. He turns to Mister Lloyd and eyes him up and down. 'So, are you a quitter then?'

'I'm sorry?' coos Mister Lloyd in reply.

'I see you got a ring. Tells me you were brought up posh. Left home, did ya, or was you pushed?'

Mister Lloyd coddles and preens his waxy plumage. He must be recalling the elsewhere, home and Mostyn, because he seems suddenly lost in melancholia. He isn't *un*loved!

'Don't get upset,' coos Dorian, 'there's a good chap. We're survivors. My gramps was also a quitter.'

Mister Lloyd looks up.

''Cept he called it something else,' adds Dorian. 'What did he call it? That's right, an escapee. A survivor!' Dorian nudges Mister Lloyd's wing. 'Hey, I wouldn't be perched here talking to you now if he hadn't! We're just like them humans, he said to me, flocking to the cities. And where they go, we follow. He hit the big time, you know, took to it like when you see ducks in the water in St James's park. You adapt, and I'm sure you will, so bill up, ole bird.'

Mister Lloyd's iridescent hackle changes colours.

Yes, he thinks it's nice here but what if he's lost forever?

'Tell you what, Taffy,' says Dorian. 'Would you like some chips? I know a good place.'

And so this is where we first met Mister Lloyd. Remember? After chips, with Dorian gone. Here is The Accidental Quitter, all alone, perched as he was on the cornice that surrounds South Africa House.

Oh Mostyn, where art thou?

CHAPTER TWENTY-FOUR

The car, Oxfordshire

'You have reached your final destination,' Bonnie announced, as fresh as when we set off, happy to have delivered such wonderful news.

Speechless, we stared through the windscreen at the vast concrete expanse of a disused airfield. An air of idiocy surrounded the two of us as we sat peering through the windscreen, stony faced and rocking with the rush of the wind buffeting the car. It was a barren landscape, save for a lonely cabin standing like an ancient monolith at the end of the runway.

'GPS signal lost,' Bonnie confirmed before vanishing.

'This isn't bleeding London,' said Mam, defeated.

'Well if it is, it's gone awful quiet,' I quipped.

I tried to remember how it had come about, us two here. The journey from our town to the metropolis should have taken about five hours. Mam had opted for the 'scenic route'; Joy was taking that one and there was talk of a chance meeting. I favoured Bonnie's choice – the speedier option – the free-flowing dual carriageway. Seeing the slow progress we were making, Mam was soon swayed, and before long we were joining the M6 at Junction 16 and the heavy midlands traffic. Slowly Stafford came and went, as did Cannock, Wolverhampton, Walsall and West

Bromwich; at Birmingham we ground to a halt and Bonnie fell out of the dock.

'Prepare to leave the freeway in. Two. Hundred. Yards,' Bonnie had said with a hint of surprise when I had fixed her back to the windscreen. She sounded persuasive and, longing for London, we had put our faith in her short-cut, which had led us away from the urban sprawl of the Midlands, through the pleasant views of the Black Country, in totally the wrong direction. Our suspicions were first aroused when we began to see signs for Stratford and Warwick. An hour later the problem klaxon really went off when Bonnie confidently ushered us down a series of rutted tracks and grassy lanes brushing the underside of the car.

'Where's the map?' Mam asked, holding out her hand to receive it.

I closed my eyes. 'I left it at home.'

'What?'

'Well, you said you knew the way!'

'I do,' she snapped, 'but not from a rutted track in the middle of God knows where!'

'GPS Signal Lost,' blurted Bonnie as if she had been woken from a deep sleep. Gingerly, with my index finger, I waded through the options – Destination, History, Avoiding Hot Spots, Alternative Route – and with each mode I was given the same negative sting. I looked at the screen. It had frozen at Windrush.

Even up to a minute ago, it would have been over her dead body, no, never in Europe; but now Mam knew she had no choice. It had to be done.

'Call Maldwyn,' she demanded. 'I'm too cross to speak to him.'

I rummaged through the cubbyhole behind the gearstick. It was where my mobile phone was kept. I went straight to Contacts and selected Maldwyn only to realise, when I put the speaker to my ear, that I too had lost signal. Mam's sigh was enough to take on the whistling wind. She rummaged around in her handbag.

'Might be worth a try,' she said thumbing the keypad of her own phone and handing it to me. 'I have a different network provider.'

I put it to my ear and waited for a ringtone. Success.

'Hey, what's up, sexy? Missing you like crazy here,' said the voice at the other end.

'It's Mostyn,' I cut across.

Maldwyn cleared his throat. 'Oh sorry, mate. It's just that your mother's name flashed up.'

'I gathered.'

'So, did you reach your *Final Destination*?' he asked, mimicking Bonnie's enthusiasm.

'Urm, sort of.'

Maldwyn was silent.

Mam took the phone. 'No, we have not arrived, Maldwyn! We are lost. Courtesy of Bonnie Bee or whatever she's called. Thanks to that rubbish *thing* you attached to my car, without my permission I hasten to add, we are now sat in this disguised runway in the middle of nowhere. Have we arrived? No!'

'Disguised runway?' asked Maldwyn, confused.

'I mean disused!' My normally articulate mother was in a fluster. 'Doesn't matter what it is. Thanks to your cruddy machine, we are lost!'

Back in Bangor a deep breath was being taken. 'Paloma,

darling, there is nothing wrong with my machine, ay. Have you been messing about with it, dare I ask? Pressed the wrong button or somethin'?'

'We have not pressed the wrong button,' shouted Mam.

She may not have, but I had, I now realised. When Bonnie fell into the foot well at Birmingham. I tugged at Mam's sleeve and held up my hand. She turned and gave me a quizzical look.

'Well, we may have,' said Mam with a sigh. 'But that's not the point! How are you going to get us out of this?'

'Me? Don't you mean, how is *Bonnie* going to get you out of there?'

'Oh, spare me,' wailed Mam.

'So, a disused airfield, you said. What's it near?'

I grabbed the phone and turned on the loudspeaker. 'We just passed a tiny place called Windrush,' I shouted.

'Oh, I *see*. Now I know what you did, ay,' said Maldwyn. 'You must have pressed the History button. By accident, mind, of course,' he added hastily.

'Right,' said Mam, clearly not following.

'It's a racing pigeon liberation site. Been there loads of times, ay. It's on Bonnie's history list. We released Mister Lloyd from there a few weeks back, Mostyn, do you remember, ay? You were in school at the time.'

'Of course! So we're in Oxfordshire,' I said, thinking of the happy memory of Mister Lloyd completing that long distance race, the qualifier for the ill fated—

'Correct,' said Maldwyn. 'Right, you got no signal there, have you?'

'No.'

'Do you see a freestanding toilet at the end of the

181

runway?' he asked.

'What on earth—?' shouted Mam, peering passively into the distance, 'Oh, is that what it is?'

'Yes, we do,' I said into the phone.

'Right, you've got a signal there, and it's near the old main entrance. Mind, before you go, select your destination.'

I passed the phone to Mam and took hold of touch-screen Bonnie.

'On the left hand navigator you'll see three options: Destination, History and, I can't remember the other one,' Maldwyn called out.

'Hot Spots?' I suggested.

'Ay! Hot Spots. Now press History. Do you see it?'

'Yes,' I said. 'Nothing's happening.'

Maldwyn suggested I rub my fingers in my jeans to warm them up, maybe wet them with a bit of spit. It worked: a history of all Maldwyn's destinations came up as he said it would. 'Scroll down to NW3 thingummy and enter.'

An affirmative chime for all three of us to hear.

'Now, skip to the loo my darling,' announced Maldwyn, 'and see how you get on from there.'

'Ay, well just remember how the rest of the nursery rhyme goes,' warned Mam as she passed the handset back to me. 'You nearly lost your partner, then what would you do?' She turned on the ignition.

I looked at her blankly and then at the handset. Maldwyn was laughing in the palm of my hand. 'Bye sugar lumps!' I heard him shout.

Mam drove in the direction of the Port-a-loo and, right on cue, Bonnie La Brea woke up, chest out, and took us to the capital.

XXV

Trafalgar Square, London

Looking back maybe he shouldn't have followed Dorian down the back alleys of Leicester Square, and yet his guide had been so cagey about where he went of an evening that it had just aroused Mister Lloyd's curiosity. Oh, how we'd all like the benefit of hindsight before we embark on these adventures! If it was just the once, he'd think nothing of it but Dorian kept disappearing every night, refusing to tell him his whereabouts and then showing up at breakfast the following day looking the worse for wear. No wonder Mister Lloyd is concerned. 'My nerves ain't what they used to be,' he remembers Dorian saying, 'but I'm keeping it together.' What did he mean by that?

Breakfast at Kind Lady's is part of their routine, and for Mister Lloyd it is a reason to start the day. He has become increasingly depressed, not only by the physical decline in his sole friend, but because his old life is slipping further away. Mostyn and Graceland are a hazy memory and day in, day out, as the sun rises, Mister Lloyd opens his eyes onto the same nightmare.

Breakfast affords a diversion. It is served outside the Getty Entrance to the National Gallery. Quite a flock waits each morning for the arrival of Kind Lady and her plastic bags of delicacies. Mister Lloyd exchanges daily niceties with the rest of the diners as he gads about in line, gorging the scraps and saving a pecking place for his mate Dorian. But today, as the first sitting comes to an end and his fellow diners realise Dorian is a no-show, the niceties are dispensed with.

''Ere, who you 'ogging that food for?' asks one disgruntled regular.

'Urm. My friend Dorian, actually.' Bless Mister Lloyd, so thoughtful in trying to safeguard his friend's share of the food. It shows good breeding.

'Course you are. Well, whaddyaknow?' says the regular, looking over Mister Lloyd's shoulder. 'Here he comes! Phantom Dorian.'

Mister Lloyd falls for it. Of course Dorian isn't there but by the time he realises it, Dorian's food has disappeared down one disgruntled gullet.

'Do us a favour,' he says, walking away. 'Tell your mate he needs to confirm his booking in future.'

'Excuse me, did I hear you say you're a friend of Dorian's?' says a wizened old hen who has been watching Mister Lloyd with her gimlet gaze from behind one of the Corinthian columns. Her figure is gaunt and her coat lacklustre, matted like a derelict slate roof, and Mister Lloyd is struck by her crazed look, which becomes scarier as she approaches. 'Stay away from him!' she coos, her breath smelling as if she has been pecking at cigarette stubs all night. Mister Lloyd recoils slightly and, as he does so, she bobs her head further forward. 'Stay away from him, do you hear me? I'm ruined 'cause of him.'

The wizened hen vanishes as fast as she appeared, leaving Mister Lloyd visibly shaken. '*He ruined me*,' her words echo. Look how his hackles change colour uncontrollably! Is there no one to come to his rescue? Dazed and confused he hobbles away from the hostile scramble that has become Kind Lady's breakfast (she's long gone, have you noticed?) and opts for the grass verge, feeling on edge. He hops into the air. No, Mister Lloyd, that is only *your* shadow! Although what is this larger one towering over him? He turns around and sees an object hurtling towards him as if thrown from the sky. It is one of the mixed gang's rucksacks.

'Why me?' he coos to himself and, fleeing for his life, Mister Lloyd shoots out of danger and onto the stone ledge. He needs to move further away! 'I mean, thanks for the food and all that, humans, but no thanks!' Not knowing what he could have done wrong to warrant this persecution, he gains speed, part walking, part taking off, until his tail fans out and he flies off to the Fourth Plinth, where he can be safe and alone. Slow. Standby to grip. Feet out. He lands.

Here he can calm himself down, gather his thoughts and tidy himself up a bit. The Kind Lady reappears on the square. He watches her chat away with the gang. Then when the sun is high in the sky, Dorian breezes in on the square. From his vantage point Mister Lloyd spots him immediately. It does not go unnoticed that he is flying past South Africa House, without as much as a glance at Mister Lloyd's perch. When Dorian lands on the steps that lead from the North Terrace to the fountains, Mister Lloyd decides to stay close and spy on his friend in the hope of solving the mystery of his long absences. Discreetly he flies down, walks around a bit, looking for a strategic hiding spot behind one of the stone balustrades. From here he can see Dorian has lost his looks and has grown fatter. The waxy shine of the feather coat he wore on their first acquaintance has gone, replaced by an overall browny-yellow tinge, which gives him a scuzzy appearance. Yet he seems in good spirits as he coos around the café area, chatting to some fellow birds. But wait, how has he developed that limp? Absorbed and anxious Mister Lloyd fails to notice the approaching danger. It is too late. He senses a kick from a small human narrowly missing his wound and it sends him shooting off like a bullet through a gap in the balustrade. He lands in the middle of Dorian's circle.

'Mister Lloyd!' coos Dorian with a surprisingly pleasant tone. 'How good of you to drop by! Everything alright?'

'Yes, I think so,' says Mister Lloyd, trying to regain his balance and dusting himself off, all the while keeping his eye out for danger. 'Just been chased by a small human. It's not been a good morning.'

Dorian looks in the same direction, his blotchy eyes opening wide as he spots Kind Lady approaching. 'Yikes! Quick, come with me,' he blurts. Oh, how this is a mistake, Dorian! 'We must get lost in the crowd,' he insists, leading the way speedily despite his limp. Mister Lloyd follows nervously, as must we.

'She's seen your ring, that's what it is.'

'Kind Lady? But why? What could she want with my ring?'

'Search me! All I know is you ringed ones, Quitters, so-called, never come back from her clutches to tell the tale. So march on!'

'Whoa, whoa, whoa, wait a minute!' Mister Lloyd is confused but picks up speed anyway. 'You told me she helped our guys out when they're in trouble.'

'The Quitters never come back. Forgot to tell you that. Come on, I'll explain later!'

'But Dorian,' coos Mister Lloyd. He is struggling to keep up. 'Correct me if I'm wrong, but you look like you're in a bit of pain. You're injured. I mean, don't you think she could help you, then?'

'Shut up!' he shouts, turning without stopping, and seeing that Kind Lady, unfortunately for us, has given up.

'Dorian, won't you listen to me? I'm worried about you. Are you OK?'

Dorian stops, turns and limps towards Mister Lloyd, whose gullet is tightening as sharp pain shoots down his crop.

''Course I am,' he says in a softened tone. 'Now, I've told you it's no concern of yours. I've saved you from Kind Lady. That's what matters to me.'

We cannot be sure if saving Mister Lloyd was his main concern or if he simply does not want to be saved himself; truth is, Dorian is at a stage when he doesn't want to be helped, and the sight of Mrs Petrovsky is a signal of the end of the road for the good-time pigeon – possibly now for Mister Lloyd as well.

His tail fans out in preparation to take off. 'Got to go!'

'Dorian!' coos Mister Lloyd. 'What's so good about where you're going all the time?'

Dorian, circling up above, does not answer.

'And what will we do about breakfast? We can't show up at the diner again. Well you can, but I can't.'

'Samosas, at the bus stop,' is the heedless reply as Dorian speeds off into the sky.

Right, thinks Mister Lloyd, and follows.

CHAPTER TWENTY-SIX

Hampstead, London!

Even from the North Circular, I loved London. Taid had once said to me, quoting someone famous whom I have since found out was Samuel Johnson, 'When one is tired of London, one is tired of life'. I thought of Mister Lloyd.

Merging with the flow of the ring road through the drab outskirts had the same thrill as landing in another country. I wound down the window and felt the heat and smell of elsewhere. Bonnie and I were hushed as Mam psyched herself up for the slip road to Hendon Way and its humdrum ribbon housing: red bricks, clay roof tiles, extended semis, even billboards lining suburbia. We left the garden suburbs and turned onto the mansion blocks of Finchley Road. A few landmarks poked their way through gaps in the distance, teasing me with the enormity of the place. It made me feel uneasy. You see, I didn't actually know where to begin. London was fast approaching and I had no game plan, as such. What if I never found him, dead or alive?

'Blind spot.'

'What?'

'Can you check my blind spot?' Mam asked, sensing my faltering. I supposed she had not been led all this way for me to crumble now. 'I'm indicating, aren't I?'

'OK, left,' I declared. She switched lanes and we climbed

Frognal Lane into Hampstead village, still bustling in the warm evening sun.

'In. Two. Hundred. Yards. You will have reached your destination,' blurted Bonnie, ever hopeful but not quite forgiven. According to History this was her first visit to Hampstead and I felt sure that, had she sight or imagination, she would fall for its charm like so many of her fellow Americans.

Oh my, I almost heard her say. *Don't change a thing!*

Here she was – *Adooorable!* – driving onto a film set: the Georgian terraced houses of Church Row– *so* Anglais – past Louis – *A must, no you MUST* – and round to the High Street – *The Coffee Cup is a DARLING* – the shutters, the narrow cobbled lanes leading off – *say, can I get to meet Keats? Brunch maybe? Or even Ian Fleming, if he's available? It'd be so enchanting. And what about a martini with Dame Judi?* – I digress. We pass the pastel painted bricks and the sympathetically disguised McDonald's.

'Alfie's still at the flower corner, I see,' noted Mam, cruising the street like a native. Their friendship last year had stretched to a few extra stems and a couple of pounds off but we knew, even then, he wasn't the marrying kind. Still, there had been changes. Mam's favourite greengrocer was now a sushi bar, the ironmongers' a shoe shop, but, in what I took to be a good sign, The Three Pigeons Tavern remained, albeit in gastro-refurb glory. I continued to clock our way down the High Street, all the while my eyes flickering up to the sky, across buildings, down to the pavements, just in case I saw Mister Lloyd. Barking mad, I know. It gets worse.

Bonnie announced our arrival at Pilgrims Way.

'Hooray,' I cheered as we reversed into a slot between a Porsche and a Citroën DS. Suddenly, not knowing exactly how to begin, I decided to go back to my first instinct. 'Mam, I want to get some posters out straight away.'

'Not before unloading the car you won't.'

I frowned the kind of frown I was told I'd regret one day but Mam was too busy monitoring her manoeuvring through the rear view mirror to notice. She pulled the handbrake and turned off the ignition.

'You know what the traffic wardens are like round here, Mostyn bach. If you help me unload now, I can take the car round the back and lock it in the garage. Come on, it won't take us long. Then we can both go! I'm not having you walking the streets of London on your own just yet.'

I went to open the boot.

The house on Pilgrims Way was a three-storey terrace, evidently built on the foundations of a much older house, since it was more modern than those that surrounded it. What was so modern about The Fifties, I wasn't quite so sure. Also from north Wales, Mam's friend Joy Rathbone had married an Englishman called Clement and had settled in London after university – but the distance that separated them had affected their friendship very little.

Mam fumbled for the house key in the agreed hiding place. I singled out my suitcase and lugged it down the few steps to the front door.

'Oiga, don't forget to come back for more, guapo,' she shouted, holding the mobile to her ear. 'Dad, we've landed.'

I tackled the stairs to the first landing; new wallpaper, I saw, but its quirky, painted doors, the handiwork of the teenagers, were still preserved. One was a harbour scene, another a collection of road signs, and the penultimate a red and blue vortex pattern. The last one, entitled The Throne Room, was the bathroom door and had always been my favourite, with its surreal depiction of an outside lavatory in a Magritte-like perfect blue sky, and an oversized sponge and toothbrush. 'Yes, don't change a thing,' I said with a grin and continued up to the attic bedroom. I had assigned it to myself without as much as discussing it with Mam. I laid the case on the divan bed and walked over to the picture window that spanned the width of the room. There it was: central London, waiting for me in the distance. Ahead of me the BT Tower, The London Eye, which I had glimpsed earlier, and St Paul's Cathedral, all clear to the naked eye. Others, such as Nelson's Column, would need the assistance of binoculars, a pair of which I could see on the bookish windowsill.

Where have you been? they asked when I took hold.

Like a mariner at sea I scanned the horizon. Left a bit, towards the City of London, and – land ahoy! – there was Tower 42. I opened the suitcase and re-read Simon Blake's last email. I agreed my short time in London was best spent covering other areas. I looked around the room and saw the computer at Clement's desk. The thought of Elvis was spooking me. Strange I wanted to share all of this with him.

The bell at the top of the stairs rang loudly. It was Mam, pulling on the rope of the makeshift intercom that linked the attic to the ground floor.

'Excuse me, Mostyn Price, I thought we had a deal!' she shouted. 'Sooner we finish the unpacking the sooner we can go.'

We abandoned the odds and ends, including Mister

Lloyd's basket, in the hallway and set off at the golden hour, both of us donned in shades like natives. We were on the prowl for suitable trees, community boards and the likes on which to pin Mister Lloyd's poster. There must be a decent success rate to this method, I tried to convince myself, from the number of Have-You-Seen-This-Cat posts around the place. But how much of that same success could be applied to a poster alerting the world to my lost racing pigeon, I wasn't sure. That evening, as we walked past the yellow-scorched Heath, I knew it was worth a go. There must always be hope. We could but try, I heard Maldwyn say. We could but try.

We settled on a well-positioned tree at the bottom of Willow Road, its location ideal for several reasons: the Heath's popularity at weekends, plus the impending fair, a shoo-in; its proximity to the popular beer garden on the corner and the seemingly permanent ice cream van at the bottom of Downshire Hill, an added extra. Dozens of rusting staples and drawing pins agreed it was a perfect choice.

'Stranger things have happened, Mostyn,' said Mam, handing me a set of pins. 'Locals and visitors alike work all over London, you know. It'll give them something to look out for as they shuffle to their offices every morning. Might get some of them through the day; Lord knows, some of them are bored with their routines. They could be playing Spot the Quitter! Anonymous eyes working on your behalf, see?'

I pressed in the last pin and turned to look at my mother in the dappled evening sun. I could see what Maldwyn had meant by her beauty: her face was radiant, still untouched by years or trauma. She beamed as she assessed my work, her eyes acting as my spirit level; never, I realised was she off-duty.

'Mam, I thought you were trying to prepare me for the worst.'

'Well,' she said, a little taken aback by her own transparency, 'whatever's round the corner isn't always bad.'

'Meaning?'

'Let's just say things are looking a bit brighter.'

'Didn't sound like that to me from where Taid and I were standing this morning,' I said, recalling the spectacle with the Sat Nav. 'It was just as dark at Windrush,' I added. 'Well, dark and funny.'

She laughed it off. 'Oh that was something about nothing! I was only playing! In fact, it was this morning I knew I'd turned that corner.'

I frowned again. 'How come?'

'Because,' she began hesitantly. 'I was never comfortable enough to be that truthful with your dad.'

I managed a brief smile and swallowed hard.

'Maldwyn texted, by the way. Got ahead of himself with the paperwork. So he's coming tomorrow.'

First I had wanted him with us; now I didn't, especially when playing happy families was also just around the corner. 'We're not hanging around waiting for him to arrive. I want to start searching.'

'Oh, don't you worry. It'll take him all day in that jalopy!'

We both laughed but I felt I had to give in. It was the deal we'd struck on the drive down, between Newport Pagnell and Watford Gap to be precise. Scouring every street for Mister Lloyd was futile, we'd agreed, so we came up with a compromise: visiting attractions as normal but looking out for Mister Lloyd along the way.

'Anyway, you've got Simon whatshisname checking out the City, so you and I can make a start on Trafalgar Square and the National Gallery in the morning. We'll have plenty of time before Mal—'

I cleared my throat. 'Right, well, how do you fancy turning another corner?'

'What do you mean?'

'This one over here onto Downshire Hill,' I explained with an arch smile and pointing at the crossroads. 'Can we go and try some Sushi? I'm starving!'

TheWingedAthlete: Well we're here!
[Clement Rathbone's computer wasn't much faster than Taid's.]
Misterlloydfanclub: Hey. Gd 2 hear frm u. Soz about last time.
TheWingedAthlete: It's ok. Bit freaked. I still don't know who u r.
Misterlloydfanclub: Wuu2? [What are you up to? ('Never apologise, never explain' goes the saying. With that in mind I kept it all to a minimum. Elvis wanted news; I wanted support.)]
TheWingedAthlete: We put posters up. Mal's coming tomoz
Misterlloydfanclub: The birdman liberator? Gr8. Been doin sum research 4 U.
TheWingedAthlete: LOL. So have I. Will keep u posted. Wot u know?

> **Misterlloydfanclub:** Check out Wanda
> Petrovsky ;-) She might know. Night.

I could hear Mam walking up the stairs. Night, I typed hurriedly, then quit chat, forgetting to copy and paste. What had Elvis said? I'd missed his last note, the name. It was too late. In the rush I had closed down the window. What had it been? Wanda something? I got up from the chair. Mam knocked then popped her head around the door.

'Nos da, cariad.'

'Nos da, Mam!' Good night.

XXVII

Various streets, London

Up here! Mister Lloyd has switched to spying on his friend from the air, at once confident Kind Lady won't follow but also still aghast at Dorian's words: 'you ringed ones never come back from her clutches!' This is true, but it is not the whole truth. We know why! But we cannot interfere and there is nothing we can do except observe. How cruel it is to know this as we watch Mister Lloyd rise high above the crowds that have gathered, in hard pursuit of Dorian. And yet watch we must. He skims the roof of The National Gallery. Not since the Falcon chase has he been so determined, only this time he is not the prey. His tactic, we must presume, is to stop off at various posts and rooftops to keep a regular check on Dorian's direction. He begins with the cupola above the gallery. And if he worries about being rumbled, he soon sees there is no cause for alarm, for his quarry doesn't even look back.

Behind The National Gallery, the streets narrow, grow darker and grubbier. These are the back alleys of Leicester Square, the ones we don't always like to tread, on the borders of Soho. Dorian is speeding through one of these streets when Mister Lloyd is hit by the

197

overpowering odour of food coming from the inverted honey-comb ground. His hackles change colour mid-air, can you see? It's as if he's retching. What we smell up here is fatty grime. Hold your noses! Could it be this that is so appealing to Dorian, who we can see is now preparing to land? Mister Lloyd watches from this position above a red brick building overlooking a busy crossroad. Dorian narrowly misses one of the many passing vehicles as he descends. The unremitting Mister Lloyd follows suit. Oh, do be careful, please!

Down on pavement level he hides behind walking feet, using every possible gap to spy on his mysterious friend. Dorian is a fast hobbler, despite his limp. Mister Lloyd, seeing him disappear down the side of a building, gasps in panic and sprints after him, landing at the corner of the very same building. Mindful not to be noticed, he peers around, quite unprepared for what he sees.

Ever since he landed in this strange city, Mister Lloyd has been hoping he would turn some corner, any corner, and stumble upon Graceland. Instead what he now beholds is a hostile street where the highs and lows of the pigeon soul are to be observed. Hundreds of his fellows flock up and down, pleasure seekers drawn to the grime and grease that covers the cobbled surface, pecking at food and each other. From where he stands Mister Lloyd watches Dorian limping pitifully into this other world, dodging a barrel of fat which is being poured into a drain. Worn-looking pigeons are scrambling for scraps thrown from the back kitchens that line the street on either side, kitchens that serve restaurants and cafes on the other, more pleasant side of life in London. Some lap in the atmosphere, having the time of their lives, while others fight and bicker. In a bid for survival, wings have been clipped, limbs lost; the solemn and the comical walk side by side and Dorian seems drunk with the excitement of it all, strolling around his very own temple of pleasure, before he disappears behind a white delivery van parked clumsily on the pavement. So this is his paradise, thinks Mister Lloyd. Not Venice, certainly, and it is a far cry from Graceland. Mr Lloyd has seen enough.

He turns back and walks straight into Dorian's path. He must have fluttered back over Mister Lloyd and has been standing behind him, waiting.

'Did you follow me?' There is an aggressive tone to him that Mister Lloyd has not recognised before, not even during their first encounter at Liverpool Street Station. Dorian steps forward and corners Mister Lloyd in between two wheelie bins. He begins to nudge at him with his beak, all around his once-fine coat, gentle yet intimidating at first, till the nudges turn to pecking. Pecking feathers, pecking his healing gash. The last one thrusts Mr Lloyd against the wall. 'Do me a favour, Taffy. Stay away from me and this crowd. This ain't for you.' Dorian leans in ever closer and stares at him with his bloodshot eyes. 'Do you hear me?'

Mister Lloyd nods timidly, his heart beating faster and louder than the engine roar of the white van that is coming this way. Fly out, Mister Lloyd, we want to shout, but he is too shaken, broken in spirit and strength.

'You have made me very angry,' says Dorian, sounding as crazed as the wizened hen. 'I'm not a nice pigeon. Understand?'

Dorian steps back but holds his raging gaze on Mister Lloyd, unaware of the roar getting ever louder as the van careers nearer. He takes flight back towards the alley. Mister Lloyd sees the van accelerating towards Dorian, tries to shout – *Look Out!* – but it is too late. Smack into its windscreen. The van bears Dorian's inert body clean away onto the bonnet of a passing London cab and from Mister Lloyd's sight forever in a puff of feathers.

CHAPTER TWENTY-EIGHT

Hampstead, London

'Thanks for ringing, Dad,' Mam said. 'Must dash. It's pigeons and Picasso for us today. We're off to Trafalgar Square and this boy's tugging at my arm.'

It was a Sunday and our first full day in the capital. From my bedroom a beautiful summer's sun shone over London. It augured well for my Big Campaign, I thought, as I packed my bag for the day. Taid had rung to say that he had enjoyed the lobscouse from the freezer, The Rathbones had arrived safely – but late – and today were spending the day on Llanddwyn beach, while he was about to set off to Maldwyn's coop for a briefing.

'Well, whatever you do,' said Taid, 'he's only got six days left to find him. And he's not got much to go on—'

'Thanks,' I cut across. 'You're on speaker phone. Now, can you wrap it up, please? We're wasting valuable search time!' I took the handset off Mam. 'Bye.'

When I would write the book on How to Find a Lost Pigeon – an inspired idea, I thought, looking to the future as we set off down Pilgrims Way – one of the many pieces of advice I'd pass on would be to avoid The London Underground. True, one or two were carried through its tunnels but, generally, it was a no-no. We were to take the number 24 bus, destination Pimlico, from South End Green, a little further down and at the end of Willow Road. As well as being able to travel over ground, the walk down to the bus stop also gave us the chance to see how well the posters had fared overnight: updates, interest or lack thereof, copies in need of replacing.

As we strolled through the sunshine towards our favourite spot, I was quietly optimistic, particularly when I saw my poster was already attracting attention. A father and daughter, I presumed; she sat on his shoulders, pointing and – *surely not* – laughing. I turned to Mam.

'What are they laughing at?'

I began to sprint towards my ridiculed masterpiece, just as the father and child, still chuckling, stole away towards the ice cream van. Their laughter rang in my ears. I got to the tree, out of breath, and scanned the sheet. There, defaced. A prankster, no doubt overnight, had drawn three-pronged pigeon footprints all over it and written a short postcard-style greeting:

A blow. I swung my bag round to my front and began to unfasten the buckles.

'Oh, come on, see the funny side,' said Mam.

'Ha. Very witty, I'm sure.' I could sense she was trying to smother a laugh.

'At least they put it back in its plastic sheeting.'

Open-side up, we were later told, not that either of us noticed then, me too incensed, Mam too amused.

'Nobody understands how I feel!' I grunted, rummaging inside my bag, funnelling aside the flat-pack cardboard box and the binoculars, reaching for another sheet. 'That's a waste of a poster now.'

'Wait a minute! Where did you get those binoculars, may I ask?'

'What binoculars?' I said, trying to stuff the precariously jutting pair back into the fisherman style bag.

'Are they Clement's?'

I thought a reassuring smile was required here. 'I was just borrowing them. I thought they'd help me spot Mister Lloyd's ring quicker, know what I mean?'

'*Oiga*! *Por favor*,' exclaimed Mam, her arms folded tight. 'What is it with you? They're not yours to borrow. Lose them, you replace them, understood?'

I looked to the ice cream van and nodded.

'And what's the flat-pack cardboard in aid of?'

'That's in case we find him.'

'Oh Lord-y lord,' said Mam tut-tutting loud tut-tuts. 'I suppose I should be glad I have a son who is willing to fight his own battles.' She paused. 'Look, there's no point swapping it for another. The message is still clear and, see, already it's made people stop and take notice. Come on, let's go.'

I stuffed the clean sheet back in to the bag and, tussling with its bulky contents, I almost let drop the binoculars. I grabbed the strap and cast a last steely gaze in the direction of the ice cream van. The father and daughter had gone. I hurried after Mam to the bus.

We made for the best seat. Top deck, at the front. At once I began digging out the binoculars and pointedly hung them round my neck. All lost on my mother, of course; she having settled down to texting Bangor's answer to Antonio Banderas.

The idea was to clock as many pigeons as I could, focus on the feet of those close enough and, hopefully, spot a distinctive green ring, in the event of which, I would shout 'Stop! We have a quitter, everyone!' and we'd be off to the rescue. Zoomed in on, however, the world seemed especially speedy, and I wanted to shake my fist at the CCTV camera in the corner ceiling and tell the driver to slow down. After Fleet Road and the junction of Mansfield, I rested my elbows on the bars in front and soon got the hang of it. Behind me loud girls sang '*Go baby, go baby go.*' Ahead, north London's feral pigeons fanned out as the bus sliced through the Prince of Wales Road and the Fiddler's Elbow, Mam with her grip on the yellow bar and still texting, as I saw when taking one eye off the action.

'Just what are you texting, apart from The Rosetta Stone in emoticons?'

'Directions for Maldwyn,' answered Mam matter-of-factly, also affording just the one eye. 'Let's just say revenge is sweet.' She pressed Send. 'Gosh, it's hot.'

I laughed and went back to my magnified London. We

continued onwards through Mornington Crescent, down Gower Street and Bedford Square, cooling air blowing in through the open window as the bus sped along.

'Taid would hate this,' said Mam, shutting her eyes and taking in the welcome breeze, freckles beginning to sprout under the sheen of her face.

The pigeons of High Holborn came into my radar now. After that, Denmark Street, then a left turn introduced me to the inhabitants of Charing Cross Road. When the bus came to the corner of Cambridge Circus I saw it. Not him, I knew straight away, but still I recoiled at the sight: a dead pigeon lying on the bonnet of a London cab idling at the junction. A red light turned green and we watched the poor critter slide off, limply landing on the road to an even more undignified ending. Mam's arm settled over my shoulder when her phone rang.

'So you're setting off now? Marvellous, darling,' she said, sounding all London.

Triumph, Splendid, even Brilliant. Five Stars greeted us everywhere as we rode down the rest of Charing Cross Road, the billboards of Theatreland cheering us one by one. I didn't feel any of the above, yet their support was nice, uplifting, as if telling me to keep going. Then we came round onto a view of the church of Saint Martin in the Fields, marking the opening onto Trafalgar Square. The two of us wowed together as the bus pulled to a stop outside South Africa House and we hopped off into the heat.

'Look! Look!' Mam gasped, pulling and nudging me as we joined the queue for the exhibition. 'Have you noticed the banner?'

I turned in her direction and lifted the binoculars.

Hanging in the portico of the National Gallery was a huge blown-up image of a painting.

'It's Picasso's *Child with a Dove*,' she explained, 'a red haired boy too! I think it's a sign!'

With my hand as a visor I gazed at it dreamily, a single portrait of a child standing all alone and holding out a dove. It was what I wanted most of all: to be back there in Graceland, holding Mister Lloyd in the cup of my hands. 'I do hope so.'

I couldn't put my life on it but I could almost smell his scent.

XXIX

South Africa House, London

We must be thankful that he too did not fly away in the same direction as Dorian, otherwise Mister Lloyd's fate might have been the same. The pecking, although cruel and painful, has not defeated our hero. He is still hovering over the streets of Soho, in shock at what has happened. Nowhere seems safe. He skims the thoroughfares up and down, flying mid-air, checking any human head in case he comes across Mostyn's strawberry-blond hair. Maybe if he turns this corner he will find him; maybe the corner after that he will be back home.

'Have you seen Mostyn Price?' he coos at a pigeon that crosses his path. 'You know, short guy, blue eyes, freckles, funny cow's lick? No? Excuse me,' he coos at another, 'do you know how I can get to Graceland from here. No? Graceland, anyone?' Oh what is the use? And if only he knew that Mostyn Price had landed, here, in the capital!

Worn out and dispirited, Mister Lloyd at last returns to his perch on South Africa House. Until he finds his way home – *home* home – this is his only refuge, yet there is little comfort to be found in such surroundings. He wants to forget what has happened, to rest, to close his eyes, but all around and below him there is the increasing buzz of the square. And when he tries to distract himself from the noise, everywhere he looks brings back painful memories of his lost companion, the brilliant yet brutal Dorian: the high column; the fountains; the café; the steps; the gallery where all those people are crowding in and out; and the cupola, that good viewing point on its roof, where his ill-fated stalking had begun. 'Samosas at the bus-stop': the last pleasant words Dorian had said to him. Or at least the last words of the Dorian he thought he knew. He gazes down at the waiting bus below. Strange how the block of red always reminds him of Graceland. Ah! He must get away from this hostile place, the excited squeals and kicks of the young humans, all the fun everyone else seems to be having, away from all these memories. And away from that Kind Lady too, before the next morning. To somewhere shady and peaceful, wherever it was. Mister Lloyd looks up to the blue sky and tries to work out the moon's position in relation to the sun – come on, Mister Lloyd! – but his attempt to free himself of his hell is thwarted by the distractions of the square. Dithering and in a quandary, he watches the bus move off. Wouldn't his weary wings just love a ride on the roof? They move so slowly between stops and they haven't started smearing that gel on them yet. He could easily hang on; he has done it before. Anywhere except here, he thinks.

CHAPTER THIRTY

Trafalgar Square, London.

Thunderous clouds were forming a backdrop to my view down to Whitehall and Big Ben. Beset by the close atmosphere of a hot summer's day, I settled on the steps of the North Terrace, peering around the close-up square, following the pigeons wherever they went and hoping that, if I sat there long enough, Mister Lloyd might come by.

Overhead a helicopter flew past, bringing home the Prime Minister, so I imagined, while further over towards the new wing of the gallery, pigeons danced to the rhythm of a busking band. Loftier ones gathered at the foot of the columns outside the Getty Entrance. Two hours had passed since we emerged from the air-conditioned rooms, during which time Mam had sportingly accompanied me to attach one of my posters to the railings by St Martin's before leaving me free to roam the Square, scrutinising random groups of pigeons through Clement Rathbone's binoculars.

I trained them on as many as I could, clocking the defiant as they hobbled and glided among the reposing tourists. One took me up to a ledge on South Africa House, showing me the snapped wire in the building's pigeon-proof system, a sign of rebellion. It seemed the square had always been a place of protest. Mam had told me of the time when she and Joy popped down to join the gathering crowd who were voicing their anger over Margaret Thatcher's Poll Tax. They had ended up sharing a pot of Earl Grey at Maison Bertaux when it turned ugly and only realised it had become a full-on riot when they got back to their digs and turned on the telly.

I darted around the fountains, hopes raised, then dashed, raised, only to be dashed again. One feral flew across the square, drawn by blue flashing lights and bringing my attention to a middle-aged woman in a purple scarf. She was blatantly breaking all the rules: by her feet dozens of pigeons gathered; she was dispensing food all around her.

I turned to Mam, who was sat in full view at the café where we'd lunched earlier, ostensibly reading a book. 'Have you seen this? Someone's actually feeding the pigeons. It's not allowed.'

Mam looked up. 'Blimey, some people.' She looked at her watch and tapped its face. 'Don't you think it's time to go?'

It was hot and I was tired but I was reluctant to abandon the search for that day. I took to the binoculars once more. This time the very same woman was being marched to a waiting police car and taken away.

'Serves her right,' said Mam. 'Now please can we go?'

By this point I was doubling up on my sightings. Loath as I was to admit it, all had been feral, and some in a very parlous state: one stood on a Portland stone wall, balancing quite brilliantly on one leg, his other a stump. Another, club-footed, poked wildly at matted, greasy feathers, such a contrast to the waxy sheen of Graceland coats. Theirs was a tough life and I worried that the same fate had befallen Mister Lloyd.

To my left I heard a sigh: Mam squatting next to me. 'Can we *please* go back now?'

'I said not yet. You've had your time at the exhibition. This is my time.'

'So it's payback now, is it? I thought you liked it.'

'I did!' This was true; while I was there I had quite enjoyed the exhibition and I was particularly pleased with the poster my mother had bought me, as well as the Pigeons of Trafalgar Square T-shirt I'd got with my own pocket money. I lowered my binoculars. 'What if we're too late? You know, those fountains are just the kind of thing Mister Lloyd would love. What if we've missed him?'

We felt the rain. Mam marked her page and closed the book, large spots already begining to fall and swell the print.

XXXI

Pimlico, London

'**A**ll change!' shouts the driver and immediately the red roof stops trembling. Looking about him Mister Lloyd seems to like what he sees, wouldn't you say? Yes, we're still in central London but the bus has brought us to this fine area called Pimlico. It is behind Victoria station – don't let that put you off! It's really rather swish, although not as smart as its neighbouring Belgravia, of course. Still, there are some fine houses that line its streets and, by Jove, their prices would make your eyes water! Mister Lloyd flies down to street level to make a further assessment. It is busy here too but there is certainly a less stressful atmosphere for his poor, frayed nerves. He begins hobbling along its pavements, bobbing his head back and forth to get a better, three-sixty overview. Zigzagging from railing to post, he gently dances around walkers, delivery trolleys and traffic, passing cafés, dry cleaning shops and estate agents – didn't I warn you about the prices? Never mind. Mister Lloyd pecks at some food when he can, even though what he wants, what he needs even, is a good long drink.

Blindly he turns into the quiet curve of West

213

Warwick Place. Let us not ask why; this is fate, you understand. Here he sees parked cars all along the road – smart ones too – and he hopes to find puddles of water somewhere under their fine cool mechanical bellies. But the summer heat has created desert-like conditions. Having exhausted one side, he hopes for better luck across the road. He takes off from under a wheel arch but – *look out, Mister Lloyd!* – an oncoming car is careering round the bend from Clarendon Street and towards him. One of the residents coming home, no doubt, familiar with the delta but a foolish driver nonetheless. Quickly Mister Lloyd fans his tail – *oh, what adventures!* – and springs into the air, feet clawed. Miraculously unhurt he lands, by a kindly chance, in the basement yard of one of the terraced town houses that have an entire set of rooms below pavement level. Oh, London, what an endless source of fascination for us curious passers-by! For dehydrated Mister Lloyd it is salvation. Our friend has found himself in a yard whose centrepiece is a water feature, would you believe? Yes, yes, it is a smaller version of the fountains found on the Square, granted, but it is a blessed oasis for one weary traveller. Here in this yard, sandwiched between the house and its vaults, is as much water as he can suck into his beak and no one, yes, – he looks around – that's right, no one to disturb him. He dunks his beak straight in. This, you can tell by how he glugs the water, is as near to Graceland as he has ever found. He looks around. Surely Mostyn will appear any minute now with his red bath. Yes! Oh, shall we celebrate with him, dive in ourselves? That would be fun, wouldn't it? We've come this far! After three. One. Two. Thr— hang on, stop! Sorry, I got carried away and I must get this off the proverbial chest. Yes, sorry. Let's think for a second or two. Controversial, I know, but why does he expect Mostyn to come to him? Mister Lloyd is the one who's meant to have the homing instinct. For Mostyn to find him, we might be a long time. I hate to be the one breaking up the party. I know, I too got a little bit carried away, but we have to be realistic. Truth is, he might never find him. It is part of the game. Some get lost. That's life. Oh, I know, can we bear it? At best all we can hope is that a reminder of Graceland might spur him into action, kick-start his homing instinct once more and empower him to find his way back to where he *really* belongs. Sometimes I hate my job, disappointing you like this. Yes, yes, he is tired and, yes, he must rest. But I suppose we can hope that he and Mostyn will be reunited one way or another.

For now only the rain comes – and plenty of it. Mister Lloyd spies a window ledge tucked under the parapet of the street pavement, behind which lies the vault. There he falls into a deep, deep sleep. Oh, blessed relief! Now he shall rest, at least, he shall rest. He is OK. And breathe. Wait, did you see that? I thought we could see someone moving behind the voile curtain of this basement. Yes, there is definitely movement in the opposite window, the house side of the yard. Look! A face has appeared, yes, yes, obscured somewhat by the curtain but now that is being pulled! It is a young human making itself known to us. Is it him? I've never met him. All I know is Mister Lloyd's descriptions of him. So it is? Yes? No? Ah, fiddlesticks! I'm sorry, no it is not Mostyn, alas. No, this is a young female – a girl, you may say. She cannot see us, remember, but drawn by the rain she looks up and spots Mister Lloyd resting. Contact is made. I do not recognise this girl but I do know she is the type who will take care of our friend. No, she will, I promise. Mister Lloyd will be in good hands from now on, which sadly makes me slightly redundant. I did warn you, I did! I'm sorry, but we must leave him there, resting and safe. Let's hope one day he finds his way home. Let's hope that Mostyn finds him. And if it's not the outcome we want, we have to be grateful that he has found this shelter. It is his decision, remember. We cannot interfere and I certainly cannot be there if e'er the two shall meet. Come now, our job is done. Let's leave it to fate, and besides, I have another stray to find somewhere and make safe. I must dash. No, I'm afraid it wouldn't be right for you to come with me. You stay with Mostyn. Thank you so much for your visitation. I have so enjoyed meeting you. Hey, we didn't even do the introductions! Oh, how shoddy of me! Another time, eh? Now, goodbye Mister Lloyd. And to you too, goodbye.

CHAPTER THIRTY-TWO

Trafalgar Square, London

'Come on, Mostyn! I can't get my hair wet or it'll frizz.' To the get-set noise of thunder, people and pigeons began to disperse, fleeing the square. One of them being Paloma. 'I don't want Maldwyn to see me with frizzy hair, do you hear? Put those binoculars away. It's about *me* now.'

The sight of the emptying square prompted a truce. I packed my bag and followed my mother, who was running towards the bus stop with both her handbag and the plastic gift bag from the gallery over her head. I gave a final look to the sky, then huddled against the rain and watched the entire square reflected, scrambling for cover, in the high gloss of the wet pavement, like a watercolour I had seen in the gallery earlier. This canvas ran through with sprouting brollies and pop-out cagoules – organised trippers, unlike us. Mam squeezed her way into the bus shelter outside the gallery and pulled me in, having secured a tiny space in the reshuffle. I sorried my way under arms and over bags, landing squashed against the glass of the shelter. I tried to make myself more comfortable and turned my head towards the gallery, leaning against the clammy glass with the same reluctance as having to kiss goodbye to a prickly-chinned old aunt. Lightning lit up a huddle of pigeons at the foot of the Corinthian pillar. Alerted for one last fleeting look, I scrunched up my eyes. It was no use, even with my expertise. I could not pick out an identity ring through the runnels of rain.

I clambered to the muddy top deck, the rain pelting on the metal roof sounding like marbles dropping from the sky. Mam, having run on ahead, was stood hogging her own seat and pointing at mine a few rows down. Till Euston Road we sat apart, our view each way obscured by steamed-up windows.

'We'll have to walk through this at the other end!' I called out over my shoulder, my voice drowned by the struggling engine, the outrage of the rain and the tearing sloshes of wheels through water. 'It's like Noah's flood out there,' I shouted, trying to make light of my part in delaying our return.

'Shall we send out a dove?' teased Mam, holding out her hands as if to release an imagined bird.

'Mam, I'm sorry—' I began.

She shook her head. It was no use shouting so she searched her handbag and brought out her phone. I jumped when mine went off, alerting me to her reply. It read: 'I blame myself. Don't worry. I mean, flip-flops and no cagoules! What was I thinking?'

I was about to send one back when the gong of another message on Mam's phone beat me to it. Mam's sodden shoulders sagged and she forwarded it on to me.

'Lost, sugarlumps. Soz. Malx.'

The flood almost came up to my knees. Slowly we waded our way through the street to South End Green, guiding ourselves by memory alone. We judged where and when a kerb was due, latching onto a railing here, a litterbin there. Over the road frantic shop owners desperately tried to keep the damage at bay by sweeping the flood away. Walkers linked arms and shared brollies, some shrieked, others giggled but everyone agreed: it was unbelievable! We came to the pedestrian crossing, recognisable only by the beacon and its flashing yellow light, and tapped a few feeler taps with our feet. As we nervously crossed the road we saw it. Our very own beacon: the sight of the yellow Mid-Life Crisis, paddling its way through water and looking for Pilgrims' Way.

I got to the other side of the road, running as fast as I could barefoot, having lost my flip-flops in the water. I landed at the corner of Keats Grove, Mam in tow. We both waved frantically as Maldwyn desperately tried to work out his whereabouts, his large frame filling the windscreen, peering left, ahead, right, trying to read signs and squinting for any clues to the street name. I began to shout in the vain hope he could hear something through the rain-drenched soft top. In danger of driving past us, by some fluke he indicated right, turning into our line of sight. We jutted out onto the street and flagged him down. He, in turn, flashed his lights, both parties glad to have found each other.

'Iesu, Paloma, you look like a drowned rat, ay,' he said, leaning over the passenger seat to open the door. 'Get in at once!'

'I'm afraid for today, Maldwyn bach, what you see is what you get,' said Mam.

'A thing of beauty is a joy forever,' he replied. 'Now shut up and get in.'

'Yes, Mam! Hurry up!' I shouted.

'But it's a two-seater, Mal!' said Mam, battling it out with the noise of the rain as water poured down her face.

'Well, is it far?'

'No,' I said. 'Just up the road.'

'Well, hop in. You drive Paloma, and I'll follow on foot.'

'Are you sure?'

''Course I am. Iesu, what do you take me for? I've got a brolly, ay, now get in!' He swung open the driver's door and stepped out into the rain. 'You win, by the way,' he added as she climbed over the passenger side and slumped into the driver's seat.

'What do you mean?'

'I've only been going round the block for bleedin' hours. Should've taken Bonnie with me!'

He slammed the door shut and Paloma Price laughed through the jewel-like drops on the glass. She screeched the unfamiliar mustard-yellow Mid-Life Crisis into gear, out of the floodwater and up Keats Grove, Maldwyn alongside us, each guiding the other to safety. She knew the way, and he his car. My ears rang in the silence as I watched him signal instructions through the closed window, all the way to Pilgrims Way until we docked safely outside the house.

'Remind me to give you the resident's permit, Maldwyn cariño,' said Mam, unlocking the front door, clearly desperate to get in. 'No news from Taid?' she shouted before disappearing upstairs.

I went over to the answer machine in the sitting room, just in case.

'Flippin' heck,' said Maldwyn as he followed me into the room. 'It's like a stately home in here. You'd never think it, would you, from the outside, like. Are all these The

Rathbones?' He was pointing at the family portraits dotted round the place, ranging from eighteenth-century paintings to haphazardly strewn photographs on the mantelpiece.

'Apparently.' There was no flashing light.

'Just goes to show, ay? Never judge a book, an' all that—'

Suddenly two towels landed at the bottom of the stairs. 'Here, dry yourselves off with those before you catch your death,' Mam called out from above.

I grabbed one and ran upstairs.

From a distance London looked unaffected. Day one and my expectations of the metropolis crushed. I looked from the bedroom window to the bedside clock. Six twenty-six. Taid's news hour, I suddenly remembered. What we'd just seen might make the news. I hurried on a change of clothes and rushed back down to the sitting room, calling out and rattling doors and passing Maldwyn on the stairs with a bucket in his hand along the way. 'Mam! Maldwyn! We might be on the news!' I turned on the television and settled down to the local headlines: 'North London Lashed! Battered! Forty-Five Minute Deluge!'

'It's on!' I shouted, rushing over to the doorway to pull the bell-rope.

The headline sting continued throughout other top stories: teenage stabbings, post strike, jail for congestion charge dodger, hospital cuts – all of them dramatic.

'Maldwyn! Mam! Come *now*!' I called out again, the hum of the hairdryer a clear sign of the biggest drama of the day. Maldwyn was dotting containers all around the top floor, desperately trying to catch the water dripping from the leaking flat roof.

'Be down in a sec, ay,' he called.

I gave up and ran to the sofa to watch. Apparently London had never seen anything like it. They repeated that several times over. In a while I heard speedy trampling down two flights of stairs.

'You've only gone and missed it all,' I said irritably as Maldwyn entered, half-dressed and wrestling a jumper. 'They showed blocked drains, flooded tube stations, traffic jams galore.'

'So I may as well put the kettle on, ay?' said Maldwyn, or something like that. I was still waiting for the closing headlines.

'And finally,' piped up the news presenter, 'they are Trafalgar Square's most famous inhabitants.'

It could only be. I sat up.

'What do you say, Mostyn? Kitchen's through here, innit?'

'Stop mithering and sit down, Maldwyn,' I shouted. 'Can't you see this is important?'

Maldwyn turned to the television screen and saw a close-up shot of a pigeon and realised the magnitude of the unfolding story. 'Sorry. Sorry,' he said, throwing himself next to me and trying to settle. With some difficulty.

'Yet feeding them is now an illegal activity,' continued the news presenter, trying to remain professional despite Maldwyn, who was now rearranging cushions and moving the books and newspapers off the sofa and onto the coffee table, 'and a costly one at that…'

'Shh! Stop faffing!' I said, elbowing Maldwyn in his side. 'Some of us are trying to listen.'

'First time I've sat on books, ay,' he countered with a

222

grin, attempting to whisper – badly. 'And you've got to hand it to me, no messin', yeah, I'm not still drying my hair like someone I could mention.'

I flinched and looked back to the screen.

'...when a woman was arrested earlier today for trying to challenge the end of a legal loophole. For years Mrs Wanda Petrovsky fed pigeons from a spot that did not come under the ban. But a new by-law means those days are now over. She was later released on bail but could face a fine of up to five hundred pounds.' The news presenter sounded, oh, *so* concerned. 'Here's our correspondent, Celia Blythe.'

So this is she, the Wanda that Elvis mentioned.

'I saw her today! It was her, the one Elvis—' I blurted, stopping just in time. Luckily by now both of us were listening eagerly, me on the edge of my seat, as Celia told us how Mrs Petrovsky was one of the original Save the Square's Pigeons campaigners, who protested against The Mayor of London's recent ban on the feeding of pigeons in Trafalgar Square. Their argument with the Mayor's office was that, given the pigeon population was admittedly a problem, their number should be reduced gradually and in a way that would prevent starvation. Finding a loophole in the law, Mrs Petrovsky had found a spot on the North Terrace where it was possible for her to feed the starving pigeons without fear of being arrested. Despite her arrest that day, Mrs Petrovsky was adamant she would be back.

'Oh yeah, I'll be back tomorrow if I can,' came the Londoner's voice from the television set. 'I'm not backing down. Someone has to look after them and that's all I'm doing,' added Mrs Petrovsky, now standing in front of the bronze lions in a distinctive purple headscarf and brown-tinted glasses, her name subtitled at the bottom of the screen. Finally I had found a kind person who may just have come across Mister Lloyd.

'She doesn't sound foreign, does she?' proffered Maldwyn.

The picture cut to images of the square but the voice of Mrs Wanda Petrovsky continued. 'For years now I've visited them every week, you know, two or three times a week sometimes. Seven thirty in the morning, you know. I check for starving and injured birds, some of the rough sleepers help me out, you know, and between us we look out for them. I take the injured home with me. I can't let them suffer. Oh yes, I'll be back. I'll find another little spot if I have to. Let them try and stop me.'

They cut back to the news presenter in the studio.

'Mrs Wanda Petrovsky there, ending Celia Blythe's report,' he read with a wry smile that implied Mrs Petrovsky was just one of the many eccentrics that characterised London. 'Now, over to you, Derek. Is there an end to this rain? Come on, bring us some much needed good news.' The shot panned over to the weatherman standing by his chart in a tropical shirt. 'Good evening!'

I turned the volume down and looked at Maldwyn. 'Are you thinking what I'm thinking?'

He didn't move but his eyes slid in my direction, his sights, I now understand, on other things.

'You don't mean tomorrow morning? I've only just arrived, driven for hours, got lost, got soaked and now I just want to relax a bit—' He stopped, saw my frown, sighed, then rested his head in his hands. 'I'm thinking exactly what you're thinking. How about Tuesday?'

'I was thinking Monday.'

'Tomorrow?'

'Tomorrow morning?'

'Right.' He did say that. I remember it clearly. Yes, he looked ahead to Derek, who was coming to the end of his forecast and, unfortunately, bringing more bad weather news, but he *did* say it.

'You heard what the man said,' mumbled Maldwyn, showering poppadom crumbs all over the table. 'It's going to chuck it down again tomorrow.'

'So?' I fumed behind my menu.

'It's now or never,' the tune went, a Bhangra rendition of the Elvis song. I tried to shut Maldwyn out but he went on.

'And Mrs Wanda Petrovsky isn't guaranteed to make an appearance now that she's a celebrity pigeon catcher,' he added, casting about in vain for an approving nod. Paloma hurriedly scanned the menu. 'Two or three times was what she said on the news.'

'Yes,' I said curtly, menu lowered. 'Did you not hear? Of course I heard what she said. Your point being?'

'*Tomorrow will be too late,*' the music continued over the restaurant tannoy, and the small, hushed chatter of other diners filled the gap in the conversation. I knew Maldwyn was one of life's Mr Nice Guys but not even he could live up to the exacting standard I had set for him. Right was a *yes*, correct? This was, after all, the very reason I'd invited him. To help me in my search. And he had agreed to come with me to Trafalgar Square the very next morning to look for Mrs Petrovsky. His first mistake was to suggest Tuesday, yes, ok, but he'd soon seen the error of his ways. When he showed his hand as a turncoat that evening in the Star of India, however, I felt it a poor show of the would-be-superhero.

'Rogan Josh. King Prawn thali, please,' said Mam, handing the menu to the waiter and a wink in Maldwyn's direction.

'I'd spend a lifetime
Waiting for the right time.'

From where I sat, opposite the loved-up couple, all I could see was a conspiracy to destroy my plan. The two of them were accomplices in a plot to prevent me from finding Mister Lloyd. Laughing, winking, laughing, winking. Screeching trolley castors wheeled main course sundries over to our table, jostling my high-backed chair. A spoonful of lime pickle missed my mouth. They laughed and suddenly I lost any interest I'd had in telling Elvis the latest about the so-called Liberator birdman.

Later that night, high above in the attic, I was kept awake by their laughter wafting through the floorboards like a bad smell. Under the duvet I turned my attention to those coming in to land: aeroplanes up above from far-away places, and the murmuring clatter of the underground approaching Hampstead station. I thought of all those travellers reunited with long lost loved ones, thinking very little of the couple two floors below who had been looking for each other all their lives.

'Well, tough,' I muttered and set my alarm for six o'clock the following morning. I was coiling myself into the duvet when my mobile went. I turned my head towards the bedside table and watched it vibrate, its flashing light begging me to answer. I reached over and looked at the screen. It was she.

'What are you doing calling me at this time of night?' I whisper-snapped into the mouthpiece.

'What's this? No howaya? No how's it going? How lovely to hear from you?' The she was Lowri. 'And what do you mean "this time of night"? It's only ten. Were you fast asleep or something?'

'Almost. Look, sorry. Bad mood—'

'You silly moo. Haven't found Mister Lloyd, I presume? Is that it? Flipping heck, you can't expect to. Not straight away, anyroads. As Romulus, politely, said to Remus: this effing Rome of ours won't be built in a day, mark my words. So what's really up? Quick, now. It's me next.'

I sat up, glad of a sympathetic ear.

Cut to half an hour later.

'Oh, bloody well go on your own then, FFS! It'll be fine. And if you get lonely, remember what my mother said: stand on Piccadilly Circus long enough and you're bound to see someone from Bangor. Go for it, Mostyn! Anyway, please can we talk about me now?'

And so we went on. Truth was, we both had our agendas, but I rather think it was Lowri's characteristic rebelliousness that tipped the balance.

CHAPTER THIRTY-THREE

Trafalgar Square, London

The following is a version of what had been reported to me a few days after my moment of mental aberration. It is the result of a detailed transcription of interviews with both Mam and Maldwyn.

'Mal! Wake up!' cried Paloma, running up the stairs and barging into the bedroom. 'Wake up, Maldwyn! He's gone!'

'Wha'?' Maldwyn was lying spread-eagled under the duvet, his face squashed against the pillow.

'He's gone. Get up, Maldwyn!' She threw herself on the bed, kneading his drowsy, lame body into action. 'Please!'

Maldwyn opened his eyes and turned over. 'What do you mean "he's gone"? Are you sure?'

'He's not here, Maldwyn,' she said, her face, I picture, ashen with shock. 'I've checked everywhere.'

'Well, did he leave a note?'

Paloma shook her head. 'It's not like him. Oh God.'

'Hey, hey, hey, calm down. Everything's going to be fine,' he reassured, reaching over to hold her. 'The naughty boy's probably gone down to the square. Have you called him?'

Paloma pulled away. 'The Square? On his own? This is London, Mal, not the bloody Penchwintan Road. You see it on the news all the time. Teenage stabbings.

Disappearances. Oh God. I'll never forgive myself.'

'Hey, hey, stop it!' said Maldwyn as he grabbed both her shoulders. 'Now you're being silly. Have you *called* him?'

'No!'

'Well get dialling,' he urged, pointing at the phone on the side table. 'Iesu, I knew he was set on it. I never thought he'd be so bloody-minded.'

Paloma waited nervously for the rings but she was sent straight to the Voicemail of Mostyn Price telling her that I was unable to take the call. She sat on the side of the bed, distractedly rubbing her forehead and desperately trying to clear her throat when prompted to leave a message.

'Mostyn, it's Mam. Please phone me back as soon as you get this.' She hung up, dropping the phone onto the duvet, and began to sob uncontrollably.

Maldwyn shot out of bed and hurriedly threw on some trousers. 'I'm going after him.'

'You don't know the way!' she called out through the open door as he hopped his way downstairs. 'I'll come with you.'

'No! You need to stay here in case he comes back. I'll get a cab!'

I sat alone on the top deck with a small congregation of early-bird commuters. Almost all my posters had survived the storm's buffeting, thanks to their plastic protectors, but the most strategically positioned on the corner of Willow/Downshire had disappeared. I had allowed for some casualties and, although disappointed, I was nevertheless undaunted as I stepped onto the Number 24, even if my eagerness wasn't quite matched by any other passenger that Monday morning. The flood had subsided and Derek had found himself on that ever-expanding list of weather forecasting gaffes. From my perch on the front seat of this double-decker, I could see the glimmers of a bright day shining through the tall plane trees at the terminus, unaware that another storm was brewing, and this one of my own making. Gazing through the binoculars, I remained calmly in my own world.

Earlier that morning Mam and Maldwyn had been nowhere to be seen. I put my ear to the Vortex painted door. No sign, no stirrings. I even gave it a firm rap, in case they'd like to give it a second thought. No answer. I made my way to the Throne Room, brushed my teeth and corrected my slept-on hair to the murmuring duet of two snorers in the background. I spat out the foaming white toothpaste and rinsed my mouth, resolved to go it alone. I wouldn't have had to if Taid were here, I remember thinking. Right now he'd be preparing a flask downstairs and packing for an adventure.

Alone I gathered all my things. Binoculars, check; posters, check; watch, check; flat-folded cardboard box, check; banana, check; oyster card, check; mobile, *blast* – its whimpering low-battery signal reminded me I'd forgotten to charge it over night. Lowri had to go one better, as always, with her tales of woe. She'd prattled on for what must have been a good hour before I finally convinced her I really needed to get to sleep, had an early start, and that, by all means, we would meet up when I was back in Bangor. Bangor.

'*Don't look back in Bangor!* Go for it, Mostyn!'

Still Lowri's words rang in my ears. I paced between

kitchen and sitting room, cussing the snorers above for their self-absorbed behaviour.

'Don't look back in Bangor!'

I very nearly didn't leave a note, until the more charitable side of my character got the better of me. I scrambled around for a pen and paper and scribbled where I had gone, that they'd left me no choice and not to worry, the time I was aiming to be back by. Judging the mantelpiece as good a place as any, I propped the note upright, wedging it carefully behind the carriage clock. *There!* I picked up my bag – cagoule included – and made my way to the front door. Unable to resist a pointed slam, I pulled it shut with a bang, not knowing that all I had roused was my hand-written note, which swayed in the ensuing gust. We have since guessed that it slipped down the tiny gap between the mantelpiece and the wall behind, where we imagine it joined a small selection of family photographs and invitation cards, disappeared over time, lost, possibly never to be recovered.

I checked my watch: 06.54. Each stop was agonising and made worse by the wail of my phone reminding me of its low battery. *Please let her be there*. Simmering bile gurgled in my stomach. *Please let her be there*! Not hungry. *Eat something!* I went for my bag and pulled out the banana I had grabbed earlier. I took a bite but could barely swallow. I tried again, this time using my hand to squeeze my neck and force it down. This seemed to work, although the pressure made my eyes water. I rubbed them dry and wiped my nose, attracting the attention of the woman across the aisle as I did so. *Please don't ask me what I'm doing*. I stuffed the peel into a side pocket and then, looking down, I ran my finger along the seat's upholstery counting the pattern repeat. *Please let her be there!*

I must settle down, I thought. Not let my mind wander.

I had an inkling things had become muddled, even then. I thought of turning back but it was, by that time, too late. The bus was pulling into Trafalgar Square.

I stepped off to the half-past chime of the clock on St Martin in the Fields. Dead on time for Mrs Petrovsky. I looked out onto the pale-grey, empty square as it got itself ready for a new day. Pigeons on standby, it was almost quiet, save for the stammer of early morning traffic. Street cleaners swept up last night's debris while mopping machines glided like ice skaters. In and out they weaved through the fountains, past one another, leaving a snail-like trail as they washed the square clean for a new batch of visitors, now stirring in hotel rooms across the city, thinking of breakfasts and itineraries.

Back on the North Terrace, I was on the lookout for a lady in her late sixties, hopefully wearing a purple scarf and tinted glasses: an easy enough task in a quiet square waiting for life to begin. Taking in every worker, warden, commuter and laughing rough sleeper, I could tell, even without the aid of Clement's binoculars, she was nowhere to be seen.

What, *oh!* What had I done? Slumped down on the steps of Trafalgar Square, I drew in a large breath, hugged myself tightly before breathing it all out again. Loudly. Framed by the tall fountains, I must have cut quite a diminutive and lonely figure. Nelson stood with his back to me, his stony silence broken only by the laughing rough sleepers behind. The same ones as the day before, I saw: four or five gathered on the grass verge, dwelling under the gallery and huddled in a semi-circle, apart from one who lay supine on the wet grass.

To approach or not? Surely these were Mrs Petrovsky's helpers, the ones she'd spoken about on the news? I looked to Nelson, still sulking. I got to my feet.

'Harmless or not, I don't care,' I heard Mam roar, picturing her sat astride one of the bronze lions. 'You're not to do it!'

I turned to the Fourth Plinth. This time Mr Griffiths, addressing the whole square with a fact of life: We Were Not to Talk to Strangers. But, not that I was reckless, this was Mrs Petrovsky's patch and it was the belief that someone, *somewhere* might have seen Mister Lloyd that had brought me here in the first place. Dithering, I walked on, *no sit down*, got up, walked again in their direction. The lion roared. I stopped, started, traced the Corinthian columns of the Gallery as they faded into the new wing, now Big Ben, back and forth, somewhere called Apollo, another called Fancy That, back and forth until I saw one of the square's wardens begin his shift. This clinched it – I was safe! – and I approached the laughing rough sleepers.

I got to the stone ledge that separated the grass verge from the pedestrianised terrace and stood firmly on my side, wondering how best to intrude on their world.

'Oh, hi there,' I tried with forced enthusiasm, pulling one of the posters out of my bag. If in doubt, look busy, I had thought. Unfortunately the gang I faced had pretty much the same idea. Their cackling made me feel most unwelcome. I stood close to the ledge for a few seconds until they acknowledged my presence.

'Alright?' said one chap with a nod, nudging the others quiet.

233

I tried to remember all my manners. 'Excuse me, I'm sorry to disturb you.' I counted a beat. 'It's just that I'm looking for Mrs Petrovsky.'

'Who?' chimed one after the other with the same precision as the bell ringers of St Martin's. It ended with a resounding 'You what?' from an anonymous, reclining figure. 'What's this normy going on about, Bronco?'

Normy? Did he mean normal?

'Take no notice of him,' said Bronco, who looked to be in his fifties and seemed friendly enough. Getting to his feet, he added, 'Maxwell over here has issues,' with a tap to his nose, 'and we live with them every day, don't we, Max?'

Max remained hidden from view but let out a large grunt. The gang fell back laughing. 'Yeah,' came the reply. 'And rumour has it, Bronco my lad, you've got millions stashed away somewhere you're not telling us about.'

I made a mental scan of the rulebook and laughed politely, possibly feebly. Abashed, I looked down at the grass verge and saw Bronco's tremulous hand held out to greet mine. I hurriedly offered my own. 'Mostyn Price. Pleased to meet you.'

'How can we help?' he asked, the sound of his voice painting a much younger picture than what I could make out.

'Well.'

They stared at me expectantly. I struggled to find the next word. I made to swallow. Couldn't. Eventually brought my hand to my throat, squeezing it once more.

'You said you were looking for someone,' said Bronco, prompting me with his chequered smile, black holes where teeth once shone. I pictured that chequered flock coming

234

home.

'Yes,' I managed, beginning to recover. 'Mrs Petrovsky. I mean, the pigeon lady, you know – tall, scarf round her head—'

'Oh, that silly old bat.' It was Max. He shot up and began to sing the theme tune to a famous cartoon Mam had told me about. *'Catch the Pigeon!*. You mean, Wanda the Pigeon Catcher? *Catch the Pigeon!*' he sang again, encouraged by the raucous laughter. *'Catch the Pigeon!*'

'That's the one,' I blurted, thinking it wiser not to query the 'silly bat' comment.

'You'd never believe it,' said Bronco letting me in on another secret. 'but Max is a softy, really.'

His face wasn't. With his young-old complexion, Max had the corrugated skin of a middle-aged schoolboy. Appearing older than Maldwyn, his clothes shone with dirt, cloth buffed to leather-like patches. I was trying not to stare.

'Yes. Wanda, the pigeon catcher,' I stammered, hoping I sounded chummy. I had no idea. 'She was on the telly last night, said you helped her with finding injured pigeons. She was full of praise for you.'

Max thrust forward, shoving his disgruntled bell-ringing friends aside and landing like a falcon on the stone ledge. He faced me head on and spat as he spoke, eyes bloodshot and wide. 'You what? We were on the telly last night?'

'Yes!' I said quite bemused by the rush of excitement. Then I remembered I hadn't actually seen them on the telly the previous night, only heard them mentioned. I began to wonder how I would break this to him. Most people would be gutted. How was it that I, Mostyn Price, was now bringing bad news to the homeless? Half of school had put down Celebrity and Reality TV as career options. How was I going to explain to this poor man as I stood there in front of him, his forehead against mine, a whole laboratory of unidentified germs spraying in my direction, that this wasn't going to be his special moment after all?

'Tell me we *weren't* on telly last night!' he shouted, his breath smelling of pus and alcohol. 'Tell me!'

I didn't understand what he wanted and was too shocked to answer. With both his fists Max grabbed my shirt and lifted me over the ledge, throwing me onto the grass. I collapsed forward onto my knees, rolling over and landing on my back, and suddenly realised this was the very same verge I'd imagined Mister Lloyd had once pecked in search of his precious minerals. But I had no time to think about that now. It looked like Max was bringing out a weapon of some sort. I couldn't be sure. It happened so quickly. Something metallic, anyway. Gleaming in the morning sun as Max came after me, about to hurl his stinky body at me. I recoiled frantically. 'I mean, no. I'm sorry,' I shouted. 'Please don't!'

Bronco stepped in and pulled him away, shielding me and pushing him back amongst his fold. 'Don't, Max. Leave it – it's not worth it. The fella said no. He said we *weren't* on telly last night, you idiot!'

Nelson still had his back to me. I lay there motionless, yearning for the alarm clock, the banging of the stick, even a wet flannel: Mam telling me to get up and go down to Trafalgar Square and find Mrs Petrovsky! Maldwyn, having made a quick dash to the all-night deli, would be up waiting with a croissant and a coffee each, then off we'd saunter to the bus stop and hop on the 24.

Gar and Lowri always said when I laughed or got stressed they could see a vein strike through my forehead like a bolt of lightning. I could feel it throbbing now as Bronco helped me up. I thanked him, dusted myself off and noticed the green scuffmarks the fall had made on my jeans. Dash it all! How would I explain this mess and, oh no, shirt and all?

'Yeah well, you'd better be telling the truth,' Max bellowed over Bronco's shoulder before retreating to the grass. 'No one has the right to film me, do you hear?'

'No! I mean, yes, I hear you! It's just this Wanda Pigeon Catcher was on telly,' As I watched him retreat to his usual perch on the grass and rearrange his pockets, I quietly thanked God that Mam wasn't here. 'She – Wanda – mentioned some people, you lot for example, helped her find injured pigeons. Not by name, you understand, and we *never* saw your faces. That is the honest-to-God truth. You see, I've lost my pigeon and I thought I'd come and find you. In case. That's all. Honest.'

The child with a dove billowed pathetically in the breeze. Keeping my eye on the gang, I stealthily hobbled along the grass verge, gathering up the contents of my bag – binoculars, cardboard box – and saw I'd crossed the ledge onto their side. How narrow the divide between my life and theirs! Max can't have been much older than me, yet he had already lost his way. Lounging on a London lawn, the bedraggled group, drawn together by whatever life had thrown them, enjoyed one of the finest views of the capital. Their outlook on life, however, was bleak. My hands felt around the bag for a copy of the poster. I handed it to Bronco who passed it to Max.

'You Welsh?' he suddenly asked.

He must have deduced it from the poster. Whether it was the right answer or not, I could think of no other reply. 'Yes.'

'Snap!' he said brightly, advancing towards me. 'Whereabouts?'

I took a step back. 'Bangor?' I offered nervously, wondering if I should explain where it was. 'Can I ask why?'

''Cause I'm from Colwyn Bay, aren't I?'

I could see his eyes were beginning to glisten, as if it was the first time he had thought of the place in a while. He looked down to the poster once more, firming his grip on the wayward sheet as it flapped in the morning breeze. 'Me ol' man ran one of the large garages there, on the old road. Still there, d'ya'know?'

Max had softened. This must be the 'hiraeth' Mam told me 'us' Welsh feel when we long for home. I never imagined when I composed it that my poster would stir such emotion.

'I don't, sorry,' I replied wistfully. I was going to ask him which school he went to, because one from Colwyn Bay had thrashed us at basketball earlier that year. I had also liked the zoo there but maybe this was being too chatty. The Square fell silent.

'Hey up,' he chirped suddenly, pinching my cheek and pointing his finger towards the southern end of the Square. 'Pigeon Catcher's down Admiralty Arch. I sent her that-a-way.'

'So she is here?'

'Yes. I saw one with a broken wing earlier. She's gone to see if she can rescue it. Can I keep this?' he asked, holding up the poster with something approaching pleasure. 'I've not come across a bilingual pigeon before. We'll look out for him, won't we, Bronco?'

'And if you got any spare ones, remember to hand it to them wardens,' added Bronco in turn as a parting tip. 'They usually pins this kind of thing on the staffroom notice board. Bosses hate it, mind, but we all have feelings, don't we?'

I nodded, jumped over the stone ledge and began to run all the way down to Admiralty Arch, pausing only to give a grateful wave. Ignoring the forbidding lights I wove in and out, dodging the slow moving traffic, on the lookout for Mrs Petrovsky and keeping my hand on the binoculars. At the bottom of Canada House I almost ran into the path of a black cab as it pulled in by the kerb.

'Oi! Watch it!' shouted the driver, more concerned for his paintwork.

Out of breath, I managed a Sorry-Not-Looking-Where-I-was-Going type blurt and ran round the back of the cab and across the road onto the island in front of Admiralty Arch. *Please let her be there!* Was this it, I wondered, when I landed. Wanda Petrovsky was nowhere to be seen. I looked around. I checked. There was no other arch! If this was meant to be some kind of joke, my normally pretty good humour was failing me. Max had led me on a merry dance. All around me black cabs whizzed by, almost blocking my view. I turned to the grass verge to look for him, was just preparing a rousing rant to tell him he was a traitor to his own countryman, when I spotted a purple scarf through a gap in the passing traffic. There she was: Mrs Petrovsky, standing by the fountains.

Up till now I'd only seen her through a lens – my (*no, Clement's*) binoculars, when she was arrested – and, of course, last night's television, but even from where I stood it was definitely her and, sadly, definitely *not* Mister Lloyd cradled in her hands. The lucky bird was a feral and Mrs Petrovsky, now crouching by the lions, was placing it carefully in the basket by her foot. Without taking eyes off my quarry, I pressed the button for the pelican crossing. She picked up the basket and stood upright, appearing taller in real life. I crossed the road and quickened my pace, calling after her, my voice and the beat of my heart pounding around the buildings of the square. This was my moment.

'Mrs Petrovsky,' I croaked. To no avail. She was walking on ahead, waving to one of the wardens. I hurried after her, cleared my throat this time and tried again, much louder. 'Mrs Petrovsky!'

She turned and looked around. 'Yes?'

Her tone was kind yet apprehensive. I went on.

'Um, my name is Mostyn Price and I saw you on the telly last night. In fact, I saw you being arrested—'

'Oh I see,' she said, sounding a bit embarrassed. It dawned on me she might think I was one of her critics. 'Listen, pipsqueak' – I was right – 'you're not one of those peristerophobes, are you? Goodness knows I've had my fair share of those. So, if you've come to tell me off, you're wasting your time.' She turned on her heel towards the steps, basket in hand.

'No, no, no,' I said, horrified at such a comparison, and yet my protest wasn't enough to appease the rescuer. I ran after her. It was my one chance and I had to persist. 'The thing is, I'm *not* a peristerophobe. I have a racing pigeon called Mister Lloyd.' I had caught up and was trailing alongside her. 'You see, he got lost during a race and never came back and I think he is here in London somewhere and it sounds mad I know but I saw you on the telly last night and I thought I would come down on the off chance because you might come across these quitters from time to time bit random I know but I've had this dream he was here and then someone spotted him on Tower 42 then he disappeared again but I am convinced he is here.' Out of breath, I stopped, and saw Mrs Petrovsky had too. 'Somewhere.'

I managed a smile here, I think, and went to my bag, rummaged around and pulled out one of the posters. 'Here,' I said, holding it out. 'Have you seen him?'

Mrs Petrovsky put the basket down and began reading, lifting her glasses and mouthing the words as she scanned the page. Her eyes shot up in my direction. 'Green ring, you say. Not particularly unusual. 'Cept to you, of course.'

'Yes,' I said. My hands were shaking now. I clasped them together against my chin.

'You know, I think I have seen him.' She sounded very matter-of-fact.

Me, I pictured the *Dam Busters*, having watched it one wet Sunday afternoon with Taid. Unlike the Menai, adrenaline was bursting forth in my stomach like water gushing out of a collapsing reservoir. Not that Mrs Petrovsky could see this but it was sure to be seen in my eyes.

'Can't guarantee it, mind,' she added. 'Wouldn't want to get your hopes up. Seen it happen too many times. Though if he's the one I think I saw, then he was a stubborn little bugger.'

I could have gone home to Bangor happy at that point. 'That sounds like him, alright,' I said. 'Wary of strangers, you see. Only knows me, really.'

Mrs Petrovsky smiled.

'We do get quitters down here,' she continued.

'You call them quitters too?'

'Yes. Not often, mind, but some do lose their way and find themselves here, but your, what's-his-name,' she hesitated, lifting her glasses. 'Mister Lloyd, that's right. He kept running away from me. You know what they're like, taking off and landing, then, when you think you're getting close, *there*, gone again! No offence, mind, he was a proper bugger! Anyway, so I didn't get to read his identity ring, otherwise I'd've made a note of it, you know, got on that site you mention here,' she flicked the poster with her fingers. 'It was only a couple of days ago. Flying Tippler, wa'n he?'

I could have wept. All those times when I could have given up! I'd had people laugh in my face. How I'd struggled to hold on to my belief that Mister Lloyd was out there somewhere! The fact that Mrs Petrovsky could identify his breed without prompting. I looked down at the paving slabs, still wet from the mopping machines, and began to lose focus.

'Are you alright?' asked Mrs Petrovsky.

I nodded and gave her a smile. 'Did Mister Lloyd look OK to you?'

'Well, there was a slight gash to his abdomen, healing fine and nothing too untoward, shall we say. Judging by his reaction I'd say he was quite contented.' She stopped and shook her head. 'Sorry. Need to know basis. Listen, I'm sure he's missing his – what was your name again?'

'It's Mostyn.'

'OK, petal, I'm Wanda. Pleased to meet you.' She held out her hand to shake mine.

'Likewise,' I added.

'Mind if I hang on to this?' she asked, lifting up the poster.

'Not at all.' I looked at the lucky creature she had saved that morning. 'Will he be alright, do you think?'

'Broken wing; he'll be fine,' She picked up her basket. 'Few days at mine, right as rain! Listen, petal,' she added, steering my gaze to the North Terrace. 'Have you tried the rough sleepers over by the National, they're harmless enough and always on the look out.'

'I did, yes,' I replied, unable to meet her eye. 'They pointed you out.'

'Well, good luck,' she said and turned on her heel towards the steps. 'You obviously know where to find me.'

'Thanks!' I shouted, already wanting her friendship.

'I'll keep my eyes peeled, don't you worry,' she piped, her back to me and waving the poster in the air. She stopped and turned. 'Oh, and if you've got a spare copy of these, hand it to one of the wardens. They're always on the lookout for quitters, happens all the time. Usually pin this kind of thing on the staff room notice boards.'

'Don't tell me,' I said with a nervous laugh, amused as I was by this small act of rebellion, 'the bosses hate it?'

Mrs Petrovsky stopped. 'How did you know?'

'Oh, just one of the lads up there told me.'

'Did they also tell you to try Piccadilly Circus?'

My thoughts dashed to Lowri and her wild card theory. 'No, but d'you know what, Mrs Petrovsky? I might just do that.'

She winked at me. 'Fortune favours the brave.'

'Let's hope so,' I said, attempting a pathetic wink back. 'Let's hope so.'

'Right, young man, must dash. Turrah!' She took to the steps once more, anxious to rush the injured bird to her very own A&E.

The chimes of Big Ben and St Martin in The Fields told me it was a quarter past eight. I had a whole day ahead of me. I walked over to one of the famous fountains and sat on its ledge, listening to the sound of water as it cross-streamed through gushing copper fish mouths, the wind sending the occasional spray in my direction, washing me clean of Max. I shut my eyes and felt at peace, swaying and rocking to the patter of falling water. It almost sounded as if it was calling out my name. I pictured Mister Lloyd flying towards me. Mostyn! It became louder. I opened my eyes onto the brightening day and saw it wasn't Mister Lloyd. It wasn't my mind. It was a voice. Someone was calling out my name.

'Mostyn!' I heard it shout again. It seemed to be nearby but as for its exact whereabouts I was unsure. I scoured the square in search of my trailing name, straining against the noise of the traffic.

'Mostyn!'

I looked above the café. There. That's where it was coming from. I turned my body towards it and saw a man waving from the stone balustrade and sprinting along its entire length before landing at the top of the steps. Maldwyn. He ran down like the Blue Pouter he was, taking flight and skipping steps. A change of heart! I got to my feet to greet him as he advanced towards me. 'Maldwyn, what are you doing here? Changed your mind?'

'What am I doing here?' he asked, his broken veins crimson from running. 'I don't believe I'm hearing this. What the bleeding hell are *you* doing here?'

'Listen, Taid warned me the memory gets worse as you get older,' I said, throwing the strap of the bag over my head. 'Never mind. You're here now.'

'Nothing wrong with my memory. It's your head that needs examinin'.'

I bobbed my head back, just like Mister Lloyd would have done and stared at him. 'You know full well what I'm doing. I've come to see Mrs Petrovsky.'

'Not on your own you aren't! Jeez!'

At the time I didn't think it was right that he was shouting and I didn't think rubbing his forehead with the palm of his hands would benefit his wrinkles much either. He didn't seem to care. 'Who in their right mind? Do you really think your mother and I would let you go on your own in central London? If I'd've known you were so bloody-minded. Crikey, you're only eleven, Mostyn bach! Anything could have happened! Your mother is going spare. Are you OK?'

'Why wouldn't I be?' I asked and, thinking how quickly the paving had dried, I caught sight of the scuffmarks on my jeans. I must have been still in a muddle at this stage, because I couldn't think of anyone else except me. 'I gave you a chance, you didn't take it. Then I thought, well, I couldn't hang around waiting, so I went on my own. I left a note, didn't I?'

'What note?' he asked. 'We didn't see a note anywhere and, boy, did we look *everywhere*, your mother thinking you couldn't have lost your senses, completely.'

'The note I left on the—'

'Do you know what, Mostyn, spare me the details,' he cut in, patting around his jacket before delving into an inside pocket. 'I need to call your mother. She's going out of her mind.' He pressed the redial button and waited for the tone. 'Which reminds me, why didn't you answer your phone?'

The phone. I sat down, shut my eyes and took a deep breath. I went into my jeans pocket and pulled out my mobile. It was then I could see what a mess I'd created. The battery was dead.

'I've found him,' said Maldwyn into the phone, his hands shaking and trying to sound cheery. 'Everything's fine now. Exactly where I said.'

Thank God, thank God, thank God, I imagined Mam repeating via the satellite in space as I strained to listen; He, above, was sure to have heard.

'Do you want to speak to him?'

I was quite sure *I* didn't want to speak to her and signalled so with my hand. Mam must have said the same, because Maldwyn didn't insist.

'We're all pretty upset, Paloma bach, and I know he is. Why don't you just stick to your hair appointment idea, sweetheart. It'll do you good. I think we all need to calm down a bit, ay.'

I didn't quite hear what was said next but caught its end.

'Tell you what, I'll look after him for the day, ay. We'll go get some brekky and see you back at the house later, yeah? I will do, I promise. All's well, cariad. Yeah, me too,' He ended the call and sat down next to me. 'So, you're both too upset to speak to each other. What will we do with you, eh?'

I'm sure Maldwyn really didn't expect an answer. He was just an innocent Bangor lad caught in the middle of family peculiarities but, as he was about to put his arm around me, doing only what he was told and as he had promised Paloma, I shot to my feet.

'What will you do with me? I don't know, what *shall* we do with Mostyn Price, the problem child of your new girlfriend? You don't have to do anything. Mate. Butt out of it. You're not my—'

'Oh, that old chestnut!' he shouted, with a distinct tremor in his voice, as if for the whole square to hear. 'I was wondering when that was going to come out. Listen to me now, yeah, sunshine, I don't care who you are. I was the one who saw your mother's face this morning, white with fear, and I hope to God you never have to see that in your life. It was me who saw it, not your father, and I think that gives me some right to tick you off. Mate.'

'I have seen that face!' I yelled back, affronted but still more alarmed that I had not recalled that three-year memory when I should have done, earlier that morning.

'So why make your mother go through it again?'

I could only stare at him. We stared at each other, face-to-face, our silence drowned by the sound of falling water. I wanted to say something. Whether I was unable to find the right words or had changed my mind, I gave in and sat back down. Picking up the bag by my side, I tried untangling the binoculars from the strap, curious as to how it could have got itself into this knot.

'It's painful just watching you grapple with it,' said Maldwyn, his voice somewhat calmer. 'Here, let me help you with that.'

I didn't resist. He took hold of both binoculars and bag, tracing their straps to the knot. 'Where did you get this anyway?'

'It's Clement's,' I said, my eyes fixed on Maldwyn's hands as he unravelled the mess. 'This will come as a shock to you, of course,' – keep it light, I told myself – 'but Mam went mad with me for borrowing it. Thing is, I thought I could spot the rings better if I brought it with me.'

'I like your style,' said Maldwyn, untying the strap, separating bag from binoculars with a skill I'd not seen before. 'I might curse that hose on the back of The Beast but today it's served me well. Mind if I have a look?'

I smiled. 'Not at all. Just remember, "nice to look at, nice to hold…"'

'Let me guess, "if it's broken, consider it sold?"'

I wanted to dig him with my elbow but decided against it. 'How did you know that?'

'Mam – mine, that is – used to say that every time we got to the main entrance of Polikoff's, down town.'

'Sounds familiar.'

Maldwyn looked at me and gave out a laugh. With the binoculars in the grip of his hand he lifted them up to his corrugated face and panned the square. Left, right, he turned the lens clockwise, anti-clockwise, his lined face suddenly smooth.

'What's the matter?'

'Funny. I always thought I had twenty-twenty vision. Is there anything I'm doing wrong, Mostyn?'

'No. Why?'

'Well, I can't see anything.'

'Don't be soft.' I snatched the pair off him and looked through for myself, adjusting the lenses this way, that way, like he had done. Nothing.

Maldwyn steered the outer glass seemingly towards himself. I peered above the viewfinder and I saw his lip curl to one side. 'I think you'll find this is why,' he said, and flipped the pair round.

I was aghast. Both lenses had cracked. 'How can this be?' I protested and got to my feet. 'I was so careful! Mam's going to kill me.'

'Is she heck?' said Maldwyn, grabbing me by the arm. 'Look, let's get one thing straight. She's more concerned about you than a pair of binoculars. I mean, it'll be a pain in the proverbial to find a replacement, but we will, don't worry, and we could do it on the QT. She won't know. First, however,' he said, pulling me in, 'you need to tell me what happened.'

I looked to the North Terrace and the feral cluster on the grass verge. Picturing another altercation, I turned my timid gaze back to the Blue Pouter. 'Tell you what, I'll fess up over that breakfast.'

'Deal. Where would you like to go? My treat.'

'Well, Mrs Petrovsky said we should go up Piccadilly Circus way.'

Maldwyn squinted. 'That's a canny way of telling me you saw the legend that is Mrs Petrovsky, ay.'

I laughed. 'Bang on the money! And that's not all she told me. She saw Mister Lloyd and his green ring. She just couldn't catch him in time.'

'Do you mean to tell me that I have sat here for the last five minutes and you only mention it now?'

'I guess the mood wasn't right?'

'You bet your left one,' said Maldwyn. I didn't quite get what he meant. He shot up. 'Right, well, we'd better make our way to Piccadilly Circus.'

'OK.' I took a couple of sheets out of my bag. 'Just need to hand these to some of the wardens on the way.'

'Mostyn, what, now?'

'Well,' I said, sounding quite certain. 'You'll laugh when I tell you.'

CHAPTER THIRTY-FOUR

Piccadilly Circus, London

'You know, The Mid-Life Crisis was bought at that Colwyn Bay garage. Second hand. You can still see the sticker on the rear window. Bit brown and faded now, mind,' said Maldwyn as he handed the menu back to the tie-and-jacketed waiter with a foreboding look. 'That's sunny side up, yeah?'

Breakfast at the Criterion on Piccadilly Circus. I was stirring the tea.

'Listen,' he continued, 'some people just don't want to be found. And your Max is probably one of them. So when you mentioned telly, ay, he probably freaked because he was scared of being spotted. By his own family.'

'I'll say he did,' I muttered, not wanting to mention what I thought I'd seen Max produce from his pocket.

'Maybe he didn't want his mother finding out what became of him,' Maldwyn added. 'Too painful.'

I didn't say anything, my eyes now glazing over as I imagined the terror I had bestowed upon the house on Pilgrims Way earlier that morning: The Reaching of the Voicemail of Mostyn Price, my voice telling them I was unable to take their call. 'Um,' I said, clearing my throat and making for the teapot handle as our breakfast arrived. 'How do you take your tea?'

'Acid Gums.'

At least that's what I thought he said. I couldn't quite hear. I was making a mental note to delete all voicemail messages the second I'd get hold of the charger. I'd hate to hear my mother's voice sounding so distressed; it would haunt me for the rest of my life if I ever did. 'You've got acid gums?'

'What?' Maldwyn looked perplexed. 'No, I said "as it comes!" '

We both laughed and I poured the tea.

'Not quite the greasy spoon I had in mind, this place,' said Maldwyn, tucking into his fry-up as soon as it arrived. That A-frame sign outside had tempted us in with its two-for-one offer; what the heck, we had thought, we deserved a treat. 'It's like Dubai in here,' he remarked, craning back to take in the turquoise and gold ornamental tile work and gilded ceiling. The morning sun moved onto the tablecloth, blinding me momentarily, but when sight was restored, I saw Maldwyn was leaning to the side, his chin on the table, reaching towards the floor, fidgeting.

My eyes followed and caught him tucking his jim-jams back under the hem of his jeans.

'Fraid we're not exactly dressed right for the occasion,' he said, making light of his embarrassment and straightening in his seat.

I nodded, thinking I can't have looked much better with all that grass scuffing. I went back to forking my *oeufs brouilles et saumon fume*. When in Rome, I had thought when ordering.

There was an echoing buzz all throughout the turquoise and gold room, a chorus of yapping visitors, shoppers and business folk enjoying a 'working' breakfast. Yet the most important strategization meeting was about to begin right here, on table thirteen.

'So,' began Maldwyn, through with the chitchat. He put down his cutlery and leant back against the chair. 'Lowri's theory.'

Bingo. I had an ally.

'She says – have I got this right? – that if you're ever lonely in London, all you need to do is stand on Piccadilly Circus long enough and you're bound to see someone from Bangor?'

'Correct.' If my face ever reflected the colour of gold, it would be now, in this room. I took another mouthful of scrambled egg.

'Jeez. I've heard it all now,' said Maldwyn. He was pouring himself another cup. 'I don't mind telling you, that's ridiculous!'

'Oh, say it like it is, why don't you?' I retorted undeterred. 'Let me explain. It's not her theory as such. It's her mother's.'

'Mrs Levald?' shouted Maldwyn, causing a brief hush in the room. 'Of Britannia Close?'

'Correct again.'

'Blinking heck!' He looked around and leant in. 'Do you mean to tell me we're expected to stand out there all day just because of Mrs Levald and her crackpot theory?'

I nodded. Several times.

Maldwyn pulled the napkin down from under his collar. 'And this is good because... why?'

'Because,' I went on, my index finger brandished for the room's full attention, 'Mister Lloyd comes from Bangor, right?'

Maldwyn nodded.

'So if Mrs Petrovsky tells me she's seen Mister Lloyd on Trafalgar Square and suggested we should try here as well, *and* if Mrs Levald has this theory that if you stand out there long enough, you're bound to see someone from Bangor, then I reckon it is our duty to try it.'

'You are crazy, do you know that?'

I took a deep breath. 'It's called thinking outside the box, Maldwyn. The way I see it is this: I had a feeling Mister Lloyd had fallen out of the sky and landed somewhere in London. Someone contacts us to say they found him on Tower 42. Joy Rathbone then calls to offer a house swap and we are off to London for the Summer Holidays. Then,' I paused here and took a sip of tea, 'when we get to the capital, I see Mrs Petrovsky arrested, again later that evening on telly, and I get a feeling she has seen him, and oh, whadd'ya know, I'm right. She then tells me to try here and, because Lowri also mentioned it on the last day of term, I think, "do the maths". Don't you get it? It's fate, Maldwyn, and, OK, it's a little bit crazy but do you think I've come this far on sanity alone?

Maldwyn, I could see, was about to speak.

'And by the way, you don't need to answer that one,' I cut across.

'I'm flamin' well trying to finish me breakfast!'

When he did finish his egg he sat back in silence, his gaze fixed straight ahead, beyond my shoulders, at Piccadilly Circus. It could only be. I looked around and I too became blinded by the blazing light, the morning sun streaming through the revolving doors into the gold and turquoise grotto.

'Right,' he said, calling over to the waiter. 'What day are we?'

'Day sixteen.'

'Let's get the William, ay, and how about you tidying yourself up, otherwise your mam's going to do the maths an' all.'

Millions live in London; millions more pay it a visit, and so an unlikely pair such as Mostyn Price and Maldwyn Jones could stand looking for a lost pigeon in front of a famous landmark like Eros in Piccadilly Circus all day if we liked and no-one would bat an eyelid. Brought together by Mister Lloyd and Miss Bangor through a series of events and twists of fate, the two of us set about looking for Mister Lloyd, hanging around like a pair of train-spotters at the end of a railway platform. No-one could, or ever would, for that matter, count London's entire pigeon population, and yet Maldwyn claimed it was a tempting pastime as he contemplated the prospect of spending the whole day there, waiting for The Moment. Three times he had tried it, three times he had lost count and, as the hours passed away, the louder he questioned what he had done in a previous life to deserve being dealt a card such as this: Eros, him, me, looking for a lost pigeon on Piccadilly Circus.

I chose not to hear, of course, and instead sat on the edge of the aforementioned with an international delegation of other tourists, some of them sporting cagoules wrapped round their waists just like myself. *I had been so organised!* At the time I was unaware how ridiculous we must have looked, putting to the test a north Walian urban myth that most would take with a pinch of salt, but for me it was too important an experiment to cast aside. What if Mrs Levald was right? I scanned the Circus, clocking each pigeon as it flew or hobbled by. Ahead of us, advertising logos that made the place famous the world over – bright, even without their neon lights switched on – and around us, tributaries to elsewhere.

One pigeon guided my eye-line right, beyond the Trocadero, before it disappeared down Coventry Street and Leicester Square. I turned to my left and followed another, weaving its way through the heavy traffic that was coming up Lower Regent Street, up past Piccadilly and disappearing down the curve of Regent Street itself. Then I felt a tap on my shoulder.

'Are we just supposed to stand here?' It was Maldwyn, trying to catch my eye.

'Yes,' I said, darting mine everywhere and stepping off from the edge of Eros to lean on the railings nearby. 'And whatever you do, for heaven's sake, don't look at me while you're talking to me. You might miss him.'

'So,' I heard Maldwyn say, 'not only are we standing in central London in the same spot on one of the world's busiest junctions – *for a whole day* – and, as far as I'm concerned, looking highly suspect – I don't care how anonymous you say we are – but we aren't even supposed to *look* at each other now?'

With my attention drawn to the Trocadero vicinity, I didn't respond but I did feel him sidle next to me at the railings. 'Like spies now, are we?' he said before launching into a cod French accent. 'Leesen verry ker-foolly. I shall say zis only once.'

'What?'

'Never mind. You had to be there, ay. What about giving ourselves a time limit?' he suggested. I could sense he was looking at his watch. He said something about lunchtime. My eye was on a pigeon that I could see was careering into a Londoner making his way to work. The man shooed it away with his briefcase and I began to feel uneasy. A bus went past, blocking my view; even so, I kept my eyes fixed to my right in the direction of Coventry Street. I got to my toes and craned my neck past a delivery van. Something wasn't quite right. I waited for the bus to pass and looked again.

'I mean, shall we say three, three thirty?' I heard Maldwyn say, followed by a gentle nudge.

I remained steely. He persisted.

'Mostyn?' I could just about hear him say. 'Mostyn, answer me now, ay!' But his voice faded beneath the heavy traffic when it dawned on me who I was staring at.

It was him, I was sure. I started as if bolted by a jolt of electricity. Standing on one of the world's busiest junctions, I felt my life grinding to a halt. My hands went cold, my face grew hot, burning and swelling almost, closing in on my eyes. Everything was slowing down as if the earth had been thrown off its axis, stopping just in time for me to direct my focus, drawing me in so that I could see for myself. I couldn't quite make out what Maldwyn was mouthing at me at the far corner of my line of vision. All had gone quiet in my world. On the corner of Windmill and Coventry Street, a green man sign was flashing '*Over Here!*' in a slow throbbing glow, pinpointing my attention in a downward direction to the crowd beneath. They had been given a signal; it was time to disperse and make way – *make way, so the poor boy can see!* Slowly they parted, allowing the gradual emergence of a lone, smartly dressed figure waving slowly. It was him, all right. The world stopped.

It was Dad, hailing a cab.

I think I made out Maldwyn asking me what it was that had taken my attention. I don't quite know if I'd answered or not. The ghost-like appearance of my father had made my blood run cold. I had always hoped I could prove Mrs Levald's theory right, however crackpot it might have sounded, but not, never, never in a million years did I think it might apply to my dad. In my search for Mister Lloyd, I had found the man I'd not heard from since the day he left home, the man who was now getting into the back of a London cab. I felt a hand fall on my shoulder and shrugged it off.

'Dad!' I shouted, the cab pulling away with the change of lights. I scarpered in the same direction, abandoning bag, posters, everything. I ran through the crowds as fast as I could, cutting through huddled groups and weaving myself in and out of foreign folk, giving my country a bad name, no doubt, by jostling some of the more unsuspecting ones whose eyes were looking everywhere other than where they were going. I kept mine on the black cab and began waving frantically as it crossed the junction before making its way down The Haymarket, picking up speed. I ran faster, letting the cagoule, now loose, slip from my waist, and knocking over the 'Two for One' board outside the Criterion. Struggling to keep up I ran into another party of visitors, watching an Elvis impersonator. I left them no choice; they were quickly out of the way. I ran under the statue of the rearing horses on the corner of The Haymarket, the crowds thinner there, making it easier for me to catch sight of the lonely figure sat in the back of the cab, now slowing down at a pedestrian crossing.

Still waving I caught up with it, finally attracting the attention of its passenger before it pulled off once more. On my life it was him. The man looked back and cast me a faint smile through the rear window. On my life – *we have the same smile!* – yet he turned his back and the cab picked up speed, making its way to Trafalgar Square, where I lost him again.

He did not stop. He did not get out, let alone stand there with open arms. Did he recognise me? He vanished.

I lowered my arms and saw Maldwyn was standing right next to me. He must have followed me there, not shouting, not stopping me, just hovering in the background, waiting in the wings and ready to catch me should I fall, I suppose. I turned to him and, even though my throat hurt, I managed a smile. 'So, what do you think of Mrs Levald now?'

'Mostyn,' he began nervously, 'some people just want to stay lost.' Later he would tell me how hurtful it was when people did things we would never dream of doing ourselves, when no matter how hard we try, we cannot put ourselves in those people's heads, see their point of view, or even try to understand and make sense of it all. Later he would tell me that some people will not, others *cannot*, let us in to their worlds. Here on The Haymarket he worried he might be crossing a line and instead held out my cagoule. 'Come on, let's go home.'

'Sweet,' I said flatly, my very reason for being there in the first place now slipped from memory. I looked around to get my bearings and saw the Elvis impersonator was getting a cheer. 'We can get the 24 from Leicester Square.'

Maldwyn calmly put the bag over his shoulder and the two of us set off up The Haymarket in silence, me half-hoping for an arm on my shoulder.

When he had said home, I thought of home, home. It was the only place I could think of where I could imagine feeling better, my interest in London and its pigeons – the hope each one offered – now gone, burst like a bubble. In all the plotting and planning, the hoping and the wishing, it had never crossed my mind that I would be led all that way for this. I sat next to Maldwyn on the lower deck of the 24, my spirit and upper-deck ambitions dashed. I would have sat in silence all the way to Bangor if it was going that way, because in my head that's where I was: at home, hurrying the healing process along so that the pain, that horrible pain would go away.

It took Maldwyn's gentle prod to announce our arrival at the end of the line, the bus stop at South End Green. The walk back to Pilgrims Way seemed a harder slog than wading through the floodwater of the previous night. I passed the tree bearing my poster on the corner of Downshire Hill with the same lack of interest as most passers by. Whilst I yearned to see Mam, my heart was not brimming with delight as I contemplated our reunion. Nor was Maldwyn best pleased when he saw what faced him as we turned into Pilgrims Way: his precious mustard-yellow Mid-Life Crisis being towed away on the back of a lorry.

'Oh no!' he shouted. 'Forgot the Resident's Permit, ay!'

The comical sight of the yellow car bobbing up and down above the roofs of other parked cars snapped me out of my anguish, if only for a moment. 'You'd better run after them, Maldwyn.'

'OK, see you back at the ranch!' he said sprinting on
ahead, his pyjama bottoms flapping under the hem of his
jeans.

I stood on the pavement and lingered by the overhanging
camellia bush, not quite knowing how I would enter the
house. Here was the gate, here was the door, but I didn't
know *how* I should open that gate or how I should open the
door. Was I angry? Should I open it with some force? Was
I regretful? Should I be sheepish? Maldwyn was shouting
'*Oi!*' at the other end of the road and through a tiny gap in
the leaves I saw Mam at the kitchen window, holding the
kettle under the tap, her hair shorter, ushering in the
excitement of a new beginning. Something had come to an
end for me, however. I had abandoned all hope, wanted to
go home, and the groan of the rusty hinge as I opened the
gate said as much. The groan that brought Mam to the door.

We both stood either side of the stone step, the two of
us hesitant, knowing it could go one way or another. Mam
had been so cross and upset with me that morning that a
part of her, I'm sure, wanted to give me a slap and a good
shake in full view of the street. Yet on encountering my
pitiful figure between the gate and the door, she took a step
forward to meet me with her arms open wide.

'No luck?' she asked, pressing me tightly, her gingham
bosom telling me of a day filled with hairspray, new
garments and testers.

'Mam, I want to go home,' I said, the words muffled by
her embrace, their meaning never quite reaching their
destination.

'Where's Maldwyn?' she asked. We were meant to

261

arrive together.

I broke away. 'He's chasing his Mid-Life Crisis.'

'*Damia*, did they tow it away? I saw it had been clamped when I came back from the hairdresser's.' Whether she was cheering me up, making light, she walked to the gate to pop her head round for a better look. She didn't mean it like how I took it. I didn't wait. 'I forgot to put the resident's permit on the dashboard. Oh well, I did send him a text. Did he mention it?'

When she turned back towards the front door, I had gone, clunking feet on the stairs my only reply.

'Where are you going?' she shouted from the bottom of the stairs.

'I told you, I'm going home!'

'Oh, come on. You don't mean that.'

'I do.'

'And what about Mister Lloyd?' Her words were travelling through two floors now. 'I mean, we've got a few more days to go. And besides, good Lord, Maldwyn only arrived yesterday!'

No answer, just the sound of heavy stomping. I was packing.

'So you've just given up?'

'You were right. Nothing but pie in the sky, Mam.' I paced from basin to suitcase, bedside table to wardrobe, back to suitcase. 'And now I want to go home.'

I can only imagine what Mam was thinking. 'Oh my goodness, he's feeling sorry for himself, give me strength.' Possibly. All muttered quietly to the floral wallpaper, I imagine, before she embarked on her hollering ascent to the attic. 'Look here!' she shouted. I heard the creaking of the

262

handrail as she hauled herself up. 'Don't be so ridiculous! I only said it was "pie in the sky" because I didn't want your expectations crushed. I'm no Mystic Meg, but look where we are now. I thought you were mad and I went along with it because you were determined to find him and I didn't want to stand in your way! I've done everything I could to help you find Mister Lloyd and now you've changed your mind, you've given up, you want to spoil the rest of the holidays for all of us?' She got to the top of the stairs and saw the open suitcase on the bed. Now, leaning on the doorframe, she folded her arms. 'Just because it doesn't suit you to be here in London any more, it doesn't mean we have to do as you say at the drop of a hat.'

I appeared from behind the door, where I had been emptying the wardrobe. 'Don't then,' I said calmly. 'I can get the train on my own.'

We both heard the front door slam.

'Oh no you won't. You've just scuppered your chances of that by what you did this morning. Well, I'm not having it!' she shouted.

'Hello?' Maldwyn was calling from downstairs. If he was after a reply, he was wasting his time.

'Iesu, it's like treading on eggshells with you. I've just about had enough of your selfish, self absorbed, obsessive behaviour. I won't allow you to make us all suffer like this. This is the only bloody holiday I get, my only break in the year and you want to ruin it for me, just because you've given up on your search. Why choose to repay me like this? I mean, how do you think I felt this morning when I found you gone?'

'Well, now you know how I felt when Mister Lloyd left.'

'If you knew how it felt, why do it?' She was shouting at the top of her voice.

'I left a note,' I ventured feebly and went to sit next to Mister Lloyd's basket.

Mam cleared her throat and tried to regain her poise. 'I didn't see a note.' Her now quiet, yet still emphatic voice had begun to quiver.

'It was on the mantelpiece,' I protested, as if this was the one place she should have looked.

'Well, there was no note on the mantelpiece, Mostyn. You vanished from the house and I was worried sick that something had happened to you.' She walked over to the end of the bed and sat down next to the open suitcase, its contents thrown together like a jumble sale. She turned to the picture window and looked out on London. 'I mean, anything could have happened to you.'

'Mam—'

The house phone began to ring. It being the Rathbones', no one bothered usually, letting it go straight through to the answer machine; a message for Clement and Joy inviting them to an 'at home', generally, but in this instance the ringing seemed more persistent, as if the automated message had been switched off. I looked at the receiver on the bedside table. Would it never stop? It had cut across me as I was about to confess.

'Something did happen, Mam.'

She turned quickly away from the window to scan my face. Seeing my expression she clutched my hands. 'What? Tell me, what?'

'I saw Dad.'

She looked uncomprehending.

'He was getting into a taxi on Piccadilly Circus. I know he saw me. He still went.'

My mother turned to the London skyline again. Her sobbing was hard to sense at first, drowned as it was by the telephone ring. She wept for herself, for her boy. 'Oh God, Oh God, Oh God,' she said to the window.

I pushed the open suitcase that separated us out of the way and shifted myself next to her. I wondered whether I should put my arm around her shoulder. When I did, the ringing telephone instantly hushed. 'Why did you let him go?'

She started to compose herself and began to talk. In spurts. As she could.

'I did not make him leave. He. Shut down on me. He. Pushed me away. Not physically. No. Other reason. Than. He told me he was up and down with his moods. That it was nothing to worry about. I don't know if that had anything to do with it. But. He. Urm. Well, said he was scared of being close to anyone. It wasn't me. It. He said. Certainly wasn't. Or you. It's what we represented. In *his* head. Trust. He couldn't deal with it. Love. Commitment. The responsibility that comes with. Relationships made him ill and I don't think I will ever understand it more than that, Mostyn bach. I had to let go. Believe me. If he'd have wanted to come back, he would have.' She let out an ironic laugh. 'Terrible thing to say, I know, but I almost think it would have been easier if he'd died.'

I lowered my hand from her shoulder onto the bed. 'It might have made more sense,' I said, staring blankly at the room.

Mam leaned in. 'There was no one else, no other

Mostyn, not even another Paloma.'

'And no birthday card,' I said. Back in Graceland I'd be looking to Elvis for advice, the imagined one, the one who never let me down. He would sing 'Always On My Mind'. Here, as we sat on the edge of the bed, I thought of what Maldwyn might say. 'Maybe,' he would tell me one day, 'if we knew, ay, how people's brains worked, yeah, we wouldn't be in this ruddy mess in the first place, no.'

There was a knock on the landing handrail. It was Maldwyn. Standing halfway up the attic stairs and framed by the balustrades like Mister Lloyd once was behind the dowels of his sputnik trap. He gave out a small cough. 'Not sure to disturb you or not,' he said, ever the diplomat.

'Here's your second chance, Mam,' I whispered with a smile. She wiped the corner of her eye.

'Sorry an' all that. It's the professor on the phone. He's fine,' Maldwyn stressed, 'not to worry, but says it's urgent.'

I looked to Mam. She got to her feet, no doubt thinking that if that was the case, it must be some microwave problems, either that or where she kept the Hoover these days. It was neither.

'No, he wants to speak to you, Mostyn,' Maldwyn said, handing me the receiver he had brought all the way up, not knowing we already had a phone in the room. Maybe he'd known we weren't in the mood. I went over to grab it. 'Hello, Taid?'

'Everything all right?' said the older voice on the other side. Formalities.

'Yes, thanks Taid,' said the younger, struggling to sound normal.

'Where have you been, Mostyn bach?' Taid's second

question was always straight to the point. 'I've been trying to get hold of you all day.' It was no criticism as such, but certainly disappointment.

'Oh, the battery, sorry Taid.' I didn't want to divulge anymore than that.

'And your mother's not been answering hers, for some reason,' he went on, which by the tone of his voice *was* criticism.

I didn't say anything.

'Well, good news, Mostyn.'

I felt my skin tighten.

'They've found Mister Lloyd. He's in Pimlico, would you believe?'

CHAPTER THIRTY-FIVE

Hampstead, London

Funny things, families. Only a few hours earlier there had been an almighty row, Mam and I practically at each other's throats. But since Taid's life-changing call the stress had given way to a non-stop flurry of activity, messages and arrangements, including getting Gwil to look after the loft for the day; oh, and also the small matter of Maldwyn's Mid-Life Crisis still being stuck in the pound. And so here we were, happily arranging to pick Taid up at the Melton Street exit of Euston station the following morning. As well as all the pigeon medication and rescue paraphernalia, he was charged with the task of bringing all Maldwyn's owner and vehicle documentation. His blessed car could not be released without them. Funny it should happen to 'The Liberator', I thought as Mam and I listened to Maldwyn guiding Taid around his bachelor pad via telephone. We were sat at the drop-down breakfast bar in the London kitchen, looking on in amusement.

'Bear right as you walk out of the scullery, Professor. Through the kitchen, ay, and across the hall. The chest of drawers is in the lounge ahead. You with me, Professor?'

The birdman that sets things free, I remembered.

'Are we in a hotel, here?' I heard Taid ask. 'Lounges are only to be found in hotels or airports.'

Maldwyn pulled the receiver from his ear and stared at it with a quizzical eyebrow. 'Does it matter?' he mouthed.

'James Bond and Q this isn't,' I whispered across to my mother, who was trying to suppress a laugh.

'Are you in the lounge or not, Professor? The chest of the drawers is in the *lounge*,' said Maldwyn. 'Jeez, what a palaver.'

'Aha,' we could hear Taid shouting from the other end. 'That is indeed a tallboy, Maldwyn, not a chest of drawers. If you'd have said tallboy...'

Maldwyn put his hand over the mouthpiece. 'Is he always like this?'

Our eager nod welcomed him into our world.

He took a deep breath and spoke again. 'Just tell me, ay. Are they there, Professor?'

We all waited as Taid rummaged.

'Yes!' Maldwyn exclaimed when he was told they'd been found. 'Baby's coming back!'

Mam turned to me and covered her mouth. 'Pity.'

'Oi! I heard that,' said Maldwyn, pointing his finger at the two of us before making his way out to the hallway. 'Nice one, Professor. Now, about that other thing I mentioned earlier, ay?'

As his voice trailed off, I leant across the breakfast bar. 'This is happening, isn't it?' I didn't just make this up. You heard it too, didn't you?'

'I did!' she said in cahoots. 'I almost feel I want to ask him again. Like I want to pinch myself, make sure I'm awake, you know. Pimlico of all places! I thought that kind of feeling only happened when you're young. Shall we call him back when Mal's done? Just to be sure,' she added quickly. 'Or are we just being silly?'

We both laughed. Finding Mister Lloyd was like switching the light back on. Here I was, sitting in front of her, the son she thought she'd lost.

'You were right,' I said when I finally caught her eye.

'About what?'

'Whatever's round the corner isn't always bad.'

She smiled her sweet, soft smile.

Maldwyn walked back into the kitchen, receiver in hand. 'Right, well, all done.'

'Pass us the phone, Mal,' I said casually, attempting a wink at Mam. 'We want to speak to Taid. Again.'

Misterlloydfanclub: Ur joking me!
[I laughed out loud. It made me think of Lowri. Just the thing she would say.]
TheWingedAthlete: I know! Can't believe it!
Misterlloydfanclub: I can. Oh my god. I knew u'd do it.
TheWingedAthlete: 10X!!! 4 bein there. GD 2 know, whoever u r.
Misterlloydfanclub: Sumtimes we just need little signs.
[It made me think he was right. Maybe I didn't need to know who this Elvis was. Maybe this was all I needed. Faith.]
Misterlloydfanclub: So what happens now?
TheWingedAthlete: Taid arrivs tomoz. Then we take MLL home.

> **Misterlloydfanclub:** Wow. Jus like that?
> EZ as that?
> **TheWingedAthlete:** I guess. Cya
> **Misterlloydfanclub** has quit chat.

It was an abrupt goodbye but I supposed Elvis and I had agreed to keep a safe distance. I thought nothing more of it, my faith in human nature definitely on the mend. I had delved into the depths of despair and dragged everyone with me, but my torment was now turned inside out and shot through with a rapture of euphoria. At first, when I'd heard Taid's momentous news – 'day 16 an' all!' – I'd had an overwhelming desire to jump on the 24 bus, knock on every single Pimlico door until I had found the people who had looked after Mister Lloyd, and thank them for their kindness. I was persuaded otherwise. Taid had said they were away for the day and, besides, he wanted to come up to London and assess Mister Lloyd's condition for himself. So, of course, I came to my senses and agreed to wait till the following day. I was still knocking on those doors when I eventually got to sleep.

The general benevolence extended even to Bonnie La Brea, who was about to come into her own as the undisputed London navigator. Taid was to catch the six twenty from Bangor, due in London Euston at nine thirty-eight. According to her calculations, and allowing a four minute walk for Taid from platform to the exit, we needed to depart from Pilgrims Way at nine am *sharp* so as not to leave him waiting. One did not keep Taid waiting.

We had been up early, allowing enough time for Paloma and Maldwyn to prepare sandwiches in case of some hitch at Pimlico and for me to prepare Mister Lloyd's basket. Then, just as she was collecting a round of take-out coffees at the deli, Paloma announced she did not particularly relish the prospect of driving through central London – secretly I think she just wanted to enjoy her skinny latte – and so, with one hand on the steering wheel and the other on his Americano, Maldwyn took charge, holding on to Bonnie's every word. Good green-light karma rushed us through Haverstock Hill, Chalk Farm and Camden like a car full of paramedics swerving left, bearing right, this left, right! We got to Melton Street. Only yesterday I had pictured Taid waiting for me at Bangor station; today here he was waiting for me at Euston. We were two minutes late.

'How could that be?' Maldwyn asked as the Seat pulled in to the kerb.

'Well, I enlisted the help of one of the station porters, you see,' said Taid as they opened the tailgate. 'Nice chap. Got me a trolley. Said they'd had a steady season, lots of visitors and that the Credit Crunch hadn't really affected rail travel. Personally I just think they've shaved a carriage off each journey. It was packed.'

'Really,' said the car in unison. With such an inquisitive mind, Taid always asked people what sort of a season they'd had, and it always made us chuckle. It was good to see him again, I thought, as we settled into the back of the Seat for the second leg of our Pimlico adventure.

'What's the postcode, Professor?' shouted Maldwyn from the front.

'Hang on,' said Taid, reaching into his brown leatherette briefcase. 'Read this for me, Mostyn, will you?'

I took the printed email and read out the address for

Bonnie La Brea.

'You brought the documentation, ay, Professor?' asked Maldwyn, typing in. 'And the umm...'

'Yes, don't you worry,' said Taid, pulling out a pair of binoculars which he slid discreetly across the seat. 'Amazing what you can get on the high street,' he whispered.

My heart leapt. They were identical! I caught Maldwyn's eye in the rear view mirror and thumbed him a Big. Thank. You.

'Well, who'd have thought, eh?' piped Taid jubilantly as the car pulled out onto the Euston Road. 'Glad you came?'

Families. Funny things.

'Certainly am, Taid,' I said, contemplating the mixed bag it had actually turned out to be. 'To be honest, Taid, it's been a bit buy one get one free.'

'London can be incredibly good value, at times,' he agreed, sounding quite innocent and squeezing my hand firmly like only Taid could.

'Who'd have thought, eh, Taid?' said Mam, safely hidden behind her headrest. She turned in my direction and caught a glimpse of the binoculars lying on the backseat. 'Uh, those need to be put back where they belong, young man. No longer required!'

I smiled. Such secrets and lies, I reflected, and in such a small car. 'So,' I said, eager to get on to more pressing things, 'tell me again, Taid, how did they get in touch?'

'Well,' he began patiently, 'I was checking my morning emails and saw that there was an automated message from "those folks", as they like to call themselves, at Report Strays Online – I mean, why try and be friendly on an automated message? Anyway it read "please get in touch with regards to reference number GB07J43777", signed "From The Team", whoever they might be. Here it is.'

Taid pulled a copy from his briefcase and handed it to me. 'Don't bend it,' he warned, his automated response to anyone who handled any of his letters.

'As if,' I said as we made our way through the traffic. I read it dog-hungry. It was the note I had waited for and little did 'those folks' know how much their automated message meant to me. 'Then what happened?'

'So I went to the website and logged on, then clicked on Strays and looked for Mister Lloyd's page to check its status. Anyway, a new post was flashing beneath it and so I clicked on that. A message.' Taid pulled another printed copy out of his briefcase.

Of course, I knew what it said, but to read it for myself was further proof. A girl called Minnie had found Mister Lloyd on a ledge outside her bedroom window. She and her dad live in a basement flat and her bedroom looks out onto a small yard. Minnie spotted Mister Lloyd as she stood in the window looking at the rainfall and saw how he struggled to stay out of the rain. Feeling sorry for him she went over to the door that linked her room to the storage vault and the small yard and opened it so that Mister Lloyd could seek shelter if he wanted to. He did. It was then that she noticed he was ringed. Dad, or Richard as he signed the message, said, what with the poster, it was nothing short of divine providence. So they got in touch.

'I wonder what he means by "what with the poster", Taid?'

'We'll soon find out,' he said rather ominously.

We turned onto Edgware Road, heading in the direction of Park Lane. I had been so engrossed in reading the printout I failed to notice that Maldwyn was driving through London's Congestion Charge Zone. Bonnie, although guiding us with great charm, had no clue about these London ways and when I leaned over to break the bad news, I caught Maldwyn at the tail end of some strange, silent conversation that was taking place in between him and Taid through the rear view mirror. 'What was that?' I asked suspiciously.

'Nothing,' said Maldwyn, pleading innocence and handing the empty coffee cup to his girlfriend in the passenger seat, she looking equally guilty. Then Bonnie butted in and abruptly changed the subject by announcing we were about to reach our final destination – to reunite boy and bird, I added mentally. We pulled into the pavement of West Warwick Place. Oh, garlanded West Warwick Place! I shall never forget you. At least not as soon as I forgot the adults' suspicious mutterings.

We recognised them straight away when they opened the heavy black door. Like 10 Downing Street, I thought, though narrower and not as glossy.

'Didn't I tell you?' said Mam with a smug smile. 'Didn't I tell you it would make people stop and take notice?'

Father and daughter. Richard and Minnie were the very father and daughter who had found my vandalised poster so amusing on Hampstead Heath. On that day I had wanted to have it out with them but here I was having to resist throwing myself at them, going down on bended knees even, such was my gratitude. Aware all eyes were on me, I stood there on the threshold facing the rescuers, Mister Lloyd's basket in hand and too overwhelmed to speak.

'Don't suppose you've got a visitor permit, have you?' asked Maldwyn, breaking the awkward moment.

'Yes, of course. Come through,' said Richard, a QC whose job, I later found out, was to send people to prison. 'Minnie and I had our usual outing to the Heath on Sunday,' he continued as he walked us through the grandly furnished but small apartment. 'Anyway, we'd chanced upon your poster opposite the ice cream van. Charming it was. Minnie loves reading them, and this one in particular caught our eye as someone had written a comment alleging to be from Mister Lloyd and, moreover, expressing his joy of being free. It amused us a great deal, didn't it, darling?'

Minnie nodded shyly.

'Yes, we saw,' said Mam pointedly, her hand on my shoulder, the ribbing remark lost on Richard.

'Well, whoever did the so-called deed failed to put the protective sheeting the right way up. When the rain began to fall on our way home, we ran for cover by the tree and saw that the poster needed saving. So we took it.'

Maldwyn and I looked at each other. 'Bloody cheek, ay,' he mouthed.

'Then when we found the very same pigeon taking shelter in the front yard—'

'Divine providence indeed, Your Honour,' blurted Maldwyn. 'Tell you what, we'll let you off for nicking the poster. Now where is the poor bugger?'

Richard looked amused.

'—And what sort of a season have you had, Richard?' asked Taid hurriedly.

'We tend to be recession-proof, Professor Jenkins,' he

replied, directing us to the top of the stairs that led to the basement, letting Minnie and the rest of us go ahead. 'Circuit judges see the Credit Crunch's effect on society. It'll be riots soon,' he added portentously.

The voices faded as I walked on, my heart racing. I was here, little old me, *here* and bewildered, about to see Mister Lloyd again. Minnie – *if she only knew* – hurried on, me clumsily behind with the oversized basket. I could hear Mam saying what a wonderful coincidence it all was. How funny, she went on, couldn't get over it, and did they usually take the No 24 bus up to the Heath of a Sunday? Marvellous route, didn't they think?

'By the way, what's his first name?' asked Minnie as she led me through the basement bedroom to another door, leading to the vault, I presumed. I didn't answer. I was too nervous about seeing Mister Lloyd, wondering whether he was the same Mister Lloyd who had been borne away on Maldwyn's truck that day. Little did I know. And if I'd known before what I knew now, would I have entered him for the race? I still couldn't tell you. Fate had brought us to this basement flat and here was Minnie opening the door onto the front yard.

I couldn't see him at first. At the furthest point there was a box, a temporary home made out of a couple of Richard's wine cases, cobbled together so they could leave him some feed. The small water feature in the centre of the basement yard rather obscured my view but I knew then what must have attracted him here. I looked at Mam. Giving me an encouraging smile, she took it upon herself to hush the chit-chat. I made my way over the concreted yard as if it was a bed of burning coal, more nervous now than I had been walking on stage for the school debate. I got to the box. The moment had come, the moment Mister Lloyd and I finally got to see each other again. I turned back to the onlookers once more, huddled at the doorway, Mam clenching both hands to her mouth and nodding me to go on. Then we all heard it: the timid coo and the small shuffling of bird feet treading cardboard. Taid broke into a smile, as I must have done. Gently I crouched down, squatting next to the box, and pulled the opening towards me, catching a glimpse of a blu-barred wing as it made an about-turn. I edged my face further into the darkness as he edged his beak out of the shadows, his white wattle sneaking in to view before the rest of him waddled out. My eyes began to well up. I tried to stay still. I don't know whether it was my squat position or the intensity of the moment but I felt my body beginning to rock gently.

I looked over to Maldwyn and suddenly Mister Lloyd fluttered his wings and took flight, hovering all around me in the basement yard of West Warwick Place. There he was. It was him! I stood up. The clap of his wings sang with my heart and, overcome by joy, Mister Lloyd landed on my head, his claws combing my hair as he padded around up above. The familiar sensation rippled through every nerve-ending of my body. With acrobatic zeal we both turned around and beamed at our audience. I held out my hands and, as if no time had been lost, Mister Lloyd flew into the welcoming palms, to the rapture of the audience by the narrow door. I held him like a trophy, the ultimate prize for believing in Mister Lloyd.

'I've found him!'

Taid handed Mam one of his handkerchiefs. Maldwyn's

arm landed on her shoulder and her head fell gently against his.

'He must have a first name,' insisted Minnie.

'You name him,' I said, unable to take my eyes off Mister Lloyd.

'OK,' she said. 'Let's call him Percy. Mister *Percival* Lloyd.'

Mister Lloyd had a full name and I felt strangely complete, blissfully unaware of what was to be asked of me next, let alone the dilemma I faced.

CHAPTER THIRTY-SIX

Hampstead, London

'Shut up.' 'No WAY.' 'You are JOKING me.' Text messages kept flooding in from all over the world: The Algarve, Florida and the last from Lowri in Bangor. She was yet to go on her hols. I was on the back seat, peering at Mister Lloyd through the wicker basket whilst also reading Lowri's euphoric message aloud. That same enthusiasm wasn't forthcoming in the car. In fact, the atmosphere had been somewhat anticlimactic in the Pimlico basement after Mr Lloyd's initial emergence, and so too now as we made our way back to Pilgrims Way via the pound where the other stray, Maldwyn's Mid-Life Crisis, lay waiting.

'Most definitely a falcon,' Taid had said as he conducted a brief examination in the yard. The rest of us looked on, sipping celebratory refreshments with Richard and Minnie.

'The poor blighter.' At that point I was still holding him, the outcome I had wanted all along. 'How he must have suffered.'

'How he ended up settling in a basement flat in Pimlico is what I'd like to know.' Taid glided his bifocals up the ridge of his nose as Richard sniggered into his beaker.

'And via a stint in Trafalgar Square,' said Mam with a casual laugh. 'Will we ever know what any of us have really been through?'

Richard smiled, resting his arm on Minnie.

'So,' Maldwyn piped, 'initial impressions, Professor?'

'Further tests are in order when we get back to Pilgrims Way.'

A bit abrupt, I thought. 'He's healed rather well,' I protested, feeling all eyes were upon me.

'He has,' Taid added, his face hidden behind those bifocals. 'But we're going to have to do some pretty rigorous tests. Can you open the basket for me, dear boy? It's time to go.'

'Right you are,' said Maldwyn, a little too quickly. 'We'll keep you posted, Your Honour.'

'Thank you again.' It sounded so feeble when I said it, stepping out rather hurriedly as we had onto the pavement and piling into the car to make our way through central London. Looking back I can see why I didn't kick up a fuss at this point. I had found Mister Lloyd; he was in my hands, the one thing no one could or, I thought, *should* take away from me. Even if I swore I had seen Dad, I had no proof. Mister Lloyd, on the other hand, was here with me on the back seat, evidence against all those who had ridiculed me.

Still, it was an odd homecoming.

In the long bouts of silence, I began to text everyone. North-bound at Hyde Park I remember Taid pointing out the Animals in War memorial to his right: three carved rock doves leading the charge. I had been too absorbed to notice in time and my view of it was blocked by a tourist bus overtaking. 'Well, you'd never have thought it, would you,' Mam enthused. At Marble Arch we stopped at the lights and I watched as dozens crossed the road. My thoughts went to Dad, looking so dapper in his suit and much better than

I ever remembered him. Maybe freedom suited him. It didn't Mister Lloyd. I turned my head towards the basket wedged between Taid and me. True, his appearance was a little ruffled, his gaze somewhat lost, and, yes, he had put on a little weight, but surely there were a host of medicines and treatments that could be laced into his water. He would make a full recovery. Right? The red light turned green and the London traffic moved on. A welcome distraction from the subdued car interior.

At the pound in Kentish Town we spotted the yellow Mid-Life Crisis lurking behind the chicken wire fence. It was agreed that Taid would set up a makeshift hospital in the garage behind the house at Pilgrims Way before catching the last straight-through train from Euston at 19.10 while Maldwyn would be left to retrieve his prized possession on his own.

'Sustenance, Maldwyn bach,' said Mam, holding out a sandwich.

'For the ordeal?'

'Give over,' she said, nudging him hard before passing the rest to us in the back. Taid declined, his attention taken by the list of diseases he was jotting down. I too refused.

'God, she looks so pitiful over there, ay,' said Maldwyn resignedly, vacating the driver's seat. He pulled out the document folder. 'It's as if she's been waiting for me.'

Mam got out and the two met in front. I watched them talking, framed by the windscreen, in earnest it seemed, until Maldwyn waved to us in the car, kissed Mam farewell and ran off to the pound.

'What were you two talking about?' I asked when Mam got back in.

'Nothing much.' She readjusted the driver's seat and was reversing the car back onto the road.

'Oh, ay.'

'He was asking if he could do any shopping for me on the way back, that's all.'

'As if. He hardly knows the area.'

Looking in the rear view mirror, I saw Mam's eye catch Taid's.

'Right,' I cut in. 'What's going on?'

Taid folded the list into his breast pocket and rested his elbow on the window ledge. 'Look, as you know, we need to do a few tests. Check for a few diseases. I'm sure it's nothing to worry about.'

'Some reassurance, Ta—'

'But we do need to establish a few things first,' he cut across, massaging his forehead. 'It might be a little more complicated than it seems.'

My head slumped against the side window, startling Mister Lloyd into a flutter and bringing back the voice of the heckling visitor to Graceland.

Kill all diseased!

Taid may have had a way with words but, when it came down to sick pigeons, there was no skirting around it. It haunted me. He professed to explore other means, and yet, as we circled the Heath back to Hampstead, I wondered whether these 'other means' had been mostly for my benefit, to spare my sensitive nature. It mattered very little now. In Taid's club, at least, culling was the most effective method and he certainly wasn't going to bring any disease back to Graceland.

'Of course, cures are increasingly effective,' he would add as

283

he guided his visitors through the isolation cage. *'But time spent on cures could spread diseases. Why risk an epidemic in the loft?'* And – how could I forget – as a venerable fellow fancier once told me, *'a year's feeding a doubtful bird is an expensive luxury.'*

After all I'd been through would he make me have Mister Lloyd put down? We pulled up to the lane behind the house.

'Nothing is ever simple, is it, Taid?'

'Let's just get Mister Lloyd checked out first, shall we?'

Through the back way, Taid's equipment could be offloaded directly into the garage, where the hospital was to be set up. Mam was sent upstairs to fetch some of her beauty accoutrements while Taid and I – *keep busy!* – cleared the trestle table against the back wall of all its contents: pots of paints and oil, tyre gauges, carafes of marbles, spanners, washing powder, Allen keys; in their place we lined its surface with a clean towel.

Taid laid out syringes, a stethoscope, bottles of antibiotics, tweezers, ophthalmoscope, probiotics and now Mam's cotton wool pads, Mam's cotton buds, her hairdryer and a glass of cold water, vitamins and food boosts. 'Oh, and a bowl of warm soapy water too, please, Paloma,' he shouted through a side door that led to the back patio and the sitting room beyond.

I opened the basket and gently unwrapped Mister Lloyd from his blanket. Whether he knew what was up, I couldn't tell, and I tried not to let my worry show. I put my hands around the patient, wedging his feet securely in between my fingers. I'd done this countless times at Darwin HQ but when Mam brought in the bowl my heart pounded, spreading its pulsating urgency to my palms as I unwittingly rocked Mister Lloyd. I sensed he would now feel my fear. I turned to the improvised surgical table and all the equipment.

'Right,' Taid announced, his makeshift theatre ready. 'First thing we need to do is bathe Mister Lloyd. We must make sure that what accounts for the dullness of his feathers is dirt rather than ill-health.'

Was he just being kind?

Standing by, Paloma dipped one of her cotton wool balls in the warm water. Wringing it ever so slightly she handed it to Taid, who picked it up with a pair of tweezers. How Mister Lloyd must have struggled to keep up appearances in the metropolis! Lifting his glasses to see through the lower lens of his bifocals, Taid dabbed the feathered coat, brandishing each soiled piece of cotton wool for the benefit of his assistants. Gradually he cleaned off a layer of London scum, revealing a glossier, waxy Mister Lloyd.

'Now what we need is some skilful application of the hairdryer.'

'Over to you, Paloma,' I said wryly.

When Mister Lloyd heard the sound of the high-pitched, whirling fan, he began to wiggle excitedly in the confines of my hands and, as the fronds of his feathers danced in the wind, Mam's deft skills brought further improvements in his appearance.

'Next I'm going to clean his wattle. Cotton bud, please, Paloma.'

Mister Lloyd didn't flinch; in fact he looked rather hypnotised by all the attention. A few gentle strokes revealed a powdery-white beak. Another good sign, I noted with relief. Then Taid leaned in closer, face scrunched up, tongue latched to the top of his lip, bifocals moving in on Mister Lloyd's nostrils. He had been vaccinated against Paramyxovirus and so, in theory, there shouldn't be any danger of respiratory problems; Going Light, another worrisome disease and a sure sign of worms, was also ruled out because Mister Lloyd was distinctly plumper. But there were other horrors to look out for, and each medical term became a hammer blow as I recalled the long list: Coryza, Roup, The One Eye Cold, Pigeon Pox, Coccidiosis, Aspergillus...

Sweat began to dot Taid's chin. 'I'm afraid the nostrils are blocked. It could be Roup. Another cotton bud, please, Paloma.'

My eyes darted about the garage, looking for quarantine corners and wondering if the Rathbones would have me here for the rest of the summer, till half term at the latest. Somehow I doubted it. 'Could it not be just a simple cold?'

'Let's just see if we can get him to blow his nose,' replied Taid with a reassuring smile. 'Tissues and buds at the ready, please, Paloma.'

Mam had already anticipated the request. 'Years of watching *Holby City*,' she whispered in my ear.

Taid teased a cotton bud in front of Mister Lloyd's nostrils and he duly sneezed into the tissue. Not quite as many times as Taid would have done but a sneeze all the same.

'That's the bit of *Holby City* I couldn't be doing with,' Mam muttered under her breath. 'Ych a fi.'

'Well, it's not a case of Roup, at least,' he announced, still inspecting the lingering mucus deposit.

'So, are we in the clear?'

Taid remained non-committal. He hurried through some more tests, lifting the bird's small beak with the spring of Mam's tweezers, peering into the mouth and down the throat. The pharmacist, namely Mam, was required to crush some antibiotic and add it to his drink. General precaution, Taid said, and another encouraging sign. But still the atmosphere was downbeat. Surely they must know how I'd be feeling? Could they not pretend to be happy? Not getting my hopes up, I understood, but the lack of enthusiasm was troubling and not a little ridiculous.

'You can put him in his basket now, Mostyn,' said Taid coldly as he washed his hands. 'Let's leave him to drink his medicine in peace.'

'I feel I never want to let go of him,' I said nervously.

Taid grunted, thinking I couldn't hear.

Reluctantly I put Mister Lloyd in his pound. I was reaching for the lid when my growing high hopes were dashed. His droppings were dotted with patches of hairy fungus. Without looking at the others, I began to pull the lid down, but Taid's hand grabbed mine and forced it back open.

'Aspergillus,' I asked, feeling pitiful and trying not to show it.

''Fraid so.'

I gave a faint smile and nodded. 'So, what's the verdict?'

'I don't think we need worry much over that. But—'

'Really?' Was I home and dry?

Taid sighed. 'Look, there's some iodine in my box of tricks. A dose of that and a quick check of his breath for NSRD. But there's—'

'What's NSRD?' I didn't remember that being on the list.

'Look, Mostyn, there's something I have to—' The front door slammed shut, making me jump: Maldwyn.

'Quick, Taid. What's NSRD?'

Taid looked to the door then back to Mam. 'It stands for Non Specific Respiratory Disease.'

'I see,' although I didn't. 'Why do they call it Non Specific?'

'Means they haven't got a clue,' Maldwyn butted in, walking into the garage and throwing his documents onto the examination table. 'And I'll tell you who else hasn't got a clue,' he added with his puffed-up chest, 'those jobsworths down at the pound!'

We gathered around, glad of the distraction.

'For a start they wanted two hundred to release her. Then for every hour after midnight last night they wanted to charge me forty quid. Forty quid, I ask you! It was going to cost seven hundred squids just to get the bleeding thing back on the road, ay? Can you believe it, Paloma? I only paid Gwil four hundred for her in the first place. I thought, stuff 'em, gave them sixty to scrap the beautiful thing and got a taxi back. The Mid-Life Crisis, boys and girls, is no more!'

The three of us stood stock still.

'Handsome is as handsome does,' said Taid, grinning and making his way back to the table.

Maldwyn was indeed a man of action.

'I know you two wanted to see the back of her, don't lie to me, no.'

Catching my mother's eye I wondered whether she

wasn't stifling a smile. As for myself, I had grown quite attached to the car in the past couple of days and I was strangely sad I'd never again see it in all its gaudy yellow glory, nor its brown, faded sticker still advertising Max's family's garage. Worse, I would never be able to make that connection with him – never be able to seek him out and tell him whether the garage was still there, to tell his mother … To tell his mother what? What would I tell his mother?

I had never really wanted the car gone. It had just been a joke. I looked at Maldwyn in a new light, astonished by his ability to let go of a cherished possession.

'We'll miss it,' said Paloma, putting a hand on Maldwyn's arm.

He smiled briefly before he caught sight of the glass of water she was holding in her other hand. 'Rargol! Me and my big gob.' He glanced at the trestle table and Mister Lloyd's basket. 'Sorry. Upset over here. Me mind's all over the place. Trust me to burst in on you all like this,' he said, abashed. 'Why didn't you tell me to shut up, Professor, ay?'

Taid was packing one or two items off the table into his bag.

'So, hey, how's it occurin'?'

'That's exactly what I'd like to know,' I answered. 'Please, Taid! Is Mister Lloyd OK to come home or not?'

He leant back against the table and folded his arms. 'Well, there's that little matter of the breath test I need to carry out before I catch the train, as I said, but I think it's safe to say—'

I too took in a deep breath.

'—We'll only have to quarantine him for two weeks. If that's what we decide to do.'

'Brilliant news!' I began jumping up and down. I no longer faced the prospect of having to put Mister Lloyd down and – joy! – we were going home. I had done it, defied everything and everyone. I looked to the others, wanting to share this joyous moment and saw that, even in triumph, I was alone. I stopped and turned to the basket resolutely. 'Oh well. At least someone's glad to see you. Only two weeks quarantine, eh, Mister Lloyd, that's what the maestro said, "if that's what we decide to"...'

'Let's talk about this inside,' said Mam, coaxing me to the sitting-room through the open patio doors. 'Come along, Mostyn. Leave Mister Lloyd in peace to take his medicine. Cuppa? Anyone? Maldwyn? Yes? No?'

'Good idea.' Maldwyn emerged from the garage and sauntered towards the kitchen, Taid following. 'Never a dull moment,' I heard him say. 'Hey, why the long faces?'

I broke free from my mother's embrace and grabbed hold of Taid as he entered the sitting room. 'This is good news about Mister Lloyd, right?'

He looked to Mam. 'Well, yes, of course it's good, but I suppose we can't keep it from you any longer—'

I had not heard his voice sound this weak. True, his confident air and gait had been struggling all day. By now it was gone.

'Keep what from me?' I was trying to remain co-operative, get it out of them. I felt my cheeks quiver.

'There's, well – Mostyn, listen. I've never done what you've done. Found a racing pigeon against all odds. True, I've had some fly home weeks later. Diseased, some of them, but at least they found home. And then, for the sick ones, the only right thing to do was to – anyway.' He paused. 'If Mister Lloyd had been really sick, this would have been an upsetting, but straightforward thing to persuade you to do, the right thing, I mean. Now he's healthy enough to be quarantined. There is, however – well, I've never had to do what I'm about to ask you to. It's a risk.' He looked to the others. 'Help me here, someone!'

'No, get on with it, Taid! I need to hear it from you!'

'Yes, right. Well.' He brought out a handkerchief and nervously rubbed his nose. Gift from Nain. 'Right, in my opinion, there's a risk that Mister Lloyd is broken.'

'Broken?' This didn't make sense. 'But you've checked him. I've seen you check him. His legs and feet are fine, his wound is healed, you said. There's nothing broken, so what are you saying?'

'I'm using "broken" in another sense, my boy.'

'What sense? You've never mentioned this to me before. Unless you think I never needed to know—'

'I'm saying' – he cut in – 'there's a strong possibility that Mister Lloyd has broken himself into new surroundings. It's something I must have forgotten to tell you when we were training. Didn't mean to; it's just that I never expected us to find him, or ourselves even, in this situation, that's all. It happens to all the quitters.'

'What do you mean? Apart from expecting me to fail?'

'Oh, Mostyn, he didn't say that,' interjected Mam, looking imploringly at Maldwyn.

Taid took off his glasses and, dabbing his face in the handkerchief, went to sit on the sofa. 'Mister Lloyd's been here a couple of weeks now and, if we get him home to Graceland, the chances are he'll probably fly back to London.'

'To London? Oh, as if!' I laughed but my throat contracted, cutting it short. I felt the blood drain away from my face. How could this be?

Taid had his hand over his eyes so I turned to Maldwyn, who looked to be holding onto the doorframe for support. 'Sorry, mate.' He mouthed.

It was Mam who broke the awful silence.

'Cariad,' she began. 'I think what Taid is saying is that we have to face the strong possibility that Graceland might not be home for Mister Lloyd anymore.' She was standing beside me and tentatively hovering her fingers near my hair as she spoke. Taid let his hand drop and his eyes met mine again. They glistened like I'd not seen before, not even in the glowing light of the Darwin HQ stove. Mam continued. 'If I'm right' – Taid nodded – 'he'll need to find his way home. Of his own accord.'

I recoiled abruptly from my mother's hand and collapsed on a small stool by the fireplace. 'What are you actually suggesting?'

'Well,' said Taid, sounding croaky, 'your best bet, I'd say, is to take Mister Lloyd to a neutral place, say, twenty or thirty miles away from here, and release him. When he flies into the sky, he'll need to feel which is the stronger pull. London or Graceland. It's the only way to restore his homing instinct. Get him back home properly.'

'Let go, basically, isn't it, Professor?' said Maldwyn, his back now leaning against the wall of tapestry.

'I've only just got him back!' I shouted, staring hard at each of them in turn. 'I knew you lot were up to something!'

'I know!' Maybe it was guilt, maybe it was frustration, but Taid snapped and, in a voice I'd not heard for a long time, he got to his feet and said, 'All I know is Mister Lloyd didn't come home, did he? I mean, why is he still here, eh? Up till now, he has chosen London! Is this what you want?'

I couldn't answer.

'Can I chip in here, Professor?' piped Maldwyn, stepping towards me, chancing his outsider status was, for once, an advantage. 'The thing is, ay, your Mister Lloyd has got a little bit lost.'

Dad was smiling at me from the taxi. It didn't work.

'Oh, you don't say, Maldwyn! Where've you been? He's in that basket in the garage, you dumbo! I've found him!'

'Yes, *you* found him,' he shouted, grabbing me by the arms. 'Mister Lloyd didn't find you. He's lost in the head, man!'

'You're lost in the head you mean, man!'

Maldwyn gave out a loud sigh. I heard something fall from the mantelpiece behind. A photograph, I think. Mam rushed over to retrieve whatever it was while an embroidered pigeon stared at me from the Persian rug beneath.

'Listen now, ay,' Maldwyn continued, casting a quick glance to Mam above me and one to Taid behind him. 'I'm sorry we couldn't tell you in Pimlico or on the way here, ay. Just when you got him back, an' all. It's tough. Look, I'm going to spell it out to you. Mister Lloyd's homing instinct has got a bit fuddled and, if he's going to be the Mister Lloyd you know and love, the Mister Lloyd who's going to win races and bag prizes, he needs to find his own way home.' Maldwyn glanced in Mam's direction.

Dad, please get out of the taxi. Please say hello.

'That is, if you want things to be back to normal. It will

be a risk but is it not better to let him go?' Maldwyn winced by way of an apology. 'Let him go, ay?'

The whole room contemplated his question: the Prices, the Jenkinses and generation upon generation of the Rathbones. An aeroplane could be heard up above coming in to land. With its sound I ran back into the garage and picked up the basket, carrying it back across the patio, through into the sitting room and past the silent company. 'I don't want to let him go again! Not ever!'

Up in the attic I kicked the door shut, placed the basket on my bed and rushed to the basin, retching. I threw up. I threw up and turned both taps full on, swished the water all around and rinsed my swollen face, red and dotted. Mopping myself up with the towel, I took a hard look in the mirror. What to do? My eyes darted around and rested on the basket and the sleeping convalescent bird within. For weeks I had thought of little else other than finding that sweet creature, distraught that I had lost him and now distraught that I had found him. I had not expected this: having cradled him, safe at last, in my hands, I was being asked, *told* almost, to let him go. What rubbish! How dare they? What if Mister Lloyd chose the wrong path – couldn't help it – poor thing? Didn't they know what that bird meant to me?

I moved across to the bed and lay down next to the basket, my head to the side, sinking into the duvet. 'I never want to let you out of my sight. D'you understand?' I whispered through the wicker bars. 'I shan't mind if you never race again for me. I just want you to be there. D'you understand? I mean, who cares? You could be a lame, ex-racing pigeon, useless but lovable. That would be ok, wouldn't it?'

Mister Lloyd stirred. There was a knock on the door.

'Can I come in?' It was Taid's voice, out of breath after two flights and somewhat muffled through the layers of dressing gowns hanging from the door.

I looked at Mister Lloyd, padding around in good health thanks to the man who waited to be let in. I wrenched myself off the bed and walked to the mirror to dab my eyes. From there, I turned the handle slowly and part-opened the door.

'Look, my dear boy, I haven't come to persuade you one way or the other. Whatever you decide, it will be fine by me.'

I nodded.

'Am I at least allowed to see the patient?' Both expert and grandfather. I motioned him in.

'Ah! Good,' he said, stepping forward and inclining his head sideways over the basket. 'You're looking better, Mister Lloyd. And in need of some nourishment.' He turned to me and straightened his back. 'Bring him down shortly, Mostyn, and I'll make one or two final tests – minor ones, don't worry. And then we'll try and entice him with some of the old Graceland diet, eh?'

I made an effort to smile, before turning my head to the window.

'Fine view of the London skyline, that,' said Taid seeing me reflected.

'Mister Lloyd's new haunts,' I said quietly.

We both heard laughter from below.

'I think I'll start making my way down those interminable stairs now, Mostyn. Quite a challenge for the bifocals. What about yourself? Are you getting hungry?'

I shrugged.

'May I divulge that your mother and Maldwyn are preparing a feast? They've been studying Joy Rathbone's recipe books and decided on a rather swish pasta dish. Not my thing, obviously, but it's her holiday. She's even sending Mal to Maison Whatsitcalled for a pudding. With a hand-drawn map, I might add. After that, I dare say it'll be time for me to depart.'

I followed him as far as the door. 'Thank you for all you've done, Taid.'

He grabbed the banisters and looked back. '*Audaces fortuna juvat.*'

I smiled. 'Oh, you and your old show-off Latin.'

'How about trying to construe?' he suggested, peering over his glasses.

'You mean "translate"? Well, *fortuna*'s easy-peasy at any rate.' I hesitated, then I remembered what Mrs Petrovsky had told me. 'Fortune favours the brave.'

Taid nodded and began his descent.

'Someone said that to me yesterday,' I called out. 'In Trafalgar Square.'

Taid stopped and turned halfway.

'Has Mam told you about yesterday?'

'A little.'

'Taid, I'm ever so—'

'—tell me all about it when we're on our own in Darwin HQ. We'll send those two lovebirds out and get a Chinese. You and me. By the way, have I introduced you to Handel?' He gave a wry smile and turned to go.

I closed the bedroom door with my backside and leant against it, dressing gowns for comfort. I looked out onto

London, worried its lure was greater than Graceland, and began to pace up and down.

'Haven't I been brave enough already?' I fumed, addressing Mister Lloyd for want of an audience. 'Brave? I've told everyone I was going to find you, risked everything! I mean, I've driven people up the wall – driven myself up the wall, made enemies and nearly ruined Mam's life. And now here's Taid suggesting I let you go. Was it all for nothing?'

Mister Lloyd stirred, not gently. Was this his London?

To his side, my mobile phone. I picked it up and scrolled through those happy messages I had received earlier. I smiled. Lowri knew nothing of this setback. I thought about ringing her and yet I knew it was to be my decision and mine only. Whatever it was, she'd be rooting for me. I got to the window and looked out onto the London view. Rooting for me. I thought of Elvis. I didn't expect our conversation to take this turn.

TheWingedAthlete: U r rooting 4 me, rn't u?
Misterlloydfanclub: I am.
TheWingedAthlete: No comprende.
Misterlloydfanclub: Wot r u goin 2 do?
TheWingedAthlete: *Shrugs shoulders.* I mean, how do I explain 2 friends if MLL chooses London not Graceland? No one's gonna believe me I found him. Makes me look like a liar & a failure. Lynton wud have a field day.
Misterlloydfanclub: Is that all u care

> **Misterlloydfanclub:** wot about MLL? Wot
> dus he want?
> **TheWingedAthlete:** DUH! LOL. EZ! 2 cum
> home wid me!
> **Misterlloydfanclub:** Really?

about? Wot ur frinds think?
[It was a sharp blow, not even strictly true,
but I felt wounded. He went on.]
Misterlloydfanclub: wot about MLL? Wot
dus he want?
TheWingedAthlete: DUH! LOL. EZ! 2 cum
home wid me!
Misterlloydfanclub: Really?

I couldn't be sure what to say next. I sat at the desk,
must have done so for a while, staring at the chat room
window.

Misterlloydfanclub: U still there? It says u
r. NE Way. Not sure ur goin 2 like wot I say,
but I'll say it.
TheWingedAthlete: Go on then
Misterlloydfanclub: The birdman! He sets
things free, right? Iznt that wot they wnt 2 b?
They r 2 choose. This is not yr decision. It's
MLLs'. Y don't u let MLL find way home?
[I said goodbye and began to shut down.]
Misterlloydfanclub: Fine. Good luck. I'll be
rooting 4 U.
Misterlloydfanclub has quit chat.

I copied all my correspondence with Elvis and sent it to
myself in an email. I knew this was the last I was to hear of
him, most likely.

Mister Lloyd stirred, restless, behind me, unaware how
I was closing in on the end of one chapter and hoping he

298

would be part of the next. I sat down beside him to make a more confidential appeal.

'Have my efforts been worth it, I ask you, only to end up letting you go? Giving you a chance to make your own choice and setting you free somewhere else?'

I opened the basket and cupped him in my hands.

'So, tell me. Do we need to say goodbye, my Winged Athlete?'

I felt Mister Lloyd's wings pushing against my hands.

'Where shall we take you, eh?' I asked, putting him back in the basket. Not that I expected an answer. I closed the lid and went to scour Clement's bookshelves for a map.

There were occasional voices, the clanking of pots and pans and the pouring of wine to be heard, in between periods of silence behind the closed kitchen door. I slowly lugged the basket downstairs and passed the kitchen on my way to the sitting room. It was empty and I was glad. The room looked welcoming with its portraits. By late afternoon, it tended to be sunless but someone, Mam, I imagined, had switched on the reading lamps dotted around the place, giving a mellow orange light. I cleared a space for Mister Lloyd on the low table in front of the sofa and looked around the room. There was a pear flan on the sideboard, and the dark, polished dining table was laid ready. With their steel Fifties knobs, the double doors were still firmly closed. Lowri would have felt it a fitting place for an announcement, as did the Rathbone family portraits that were looking on and seeming to yell at me to hurry. I tiptoed towards it, placing a hand on each handle and dramatically opened both doors.

'Oh, hi there,' I said, somewhat surprised by my own

bravura. 'Anyone in?'

'Mostyn! Cariad, you're down.' Mam's face was wreathed in a smile.

I cleared my throat. 'I've had this idea.'

CHAPTER THIRTY-SEVEN

The car, Oxfordshire

No one objected this time when Bonnie suggested the Port-a-loo entrance. The car pulled in, without drama, to the disused runway at Windrush. Neither Mam nor I ever thought we would see this place again, let alone so soon.

She had been taken aback by my announcement a few days earlier.

'Windrush?' Taid had asked.

'You know. The racing pigeon liberation site?'

'Of course I know but you don't need to take him as far as that!'

'I know! But I reckon if he's found his way home from there before—'

'He may do it again?' Maldwyn nodded. 'I like it.'

'I thank you, Mal,' I replied triumphantly.

'It makes one think we were meant to go there in the first place,' my mother said happily, until the thought of it sank in. She took a large sip of her wine.

It went by quickly. The wait to get here. That evening Taid had fired instructions at me all the way down to Euston and, in his absence over the next few days, I kept my bird safe and resting with plenty of water, while the three of us that remained amused ourselves in the metropolis as I waited for Mister Lloyd's antibiotics to kick in.

'So, where shall we go today then?' asked Maldwyn. 'London Eye?'

'Ay, ay?' I said cheekily.

We crammed the lot in: the Natural History Museum and its new Darwin Centre, the British Museum and a takeaway supper, a boat ride to Greenwich and a last meal out. Mister Lloyd had had his earlier. Not through neglect, you understand; it was quite deliberate. The idea was to work up his appetite so that when he flew off the next day he'd be hungry enough to find home. Ours, I hoped.

My last night in London and I was up in the attic room, the binoculars left to rest on the window shelf. My myopic view was over. I had found what I had come to look for. It was time to set Mister Lloyd free.

And so the car came to a stop at what was once Windrush airfield. Bonnie La Brea had lost her signal, but we all knew where we were this time. Maldwyn switched off the ignition. The car was just as full as when we were here last, and even though I had dreamed I would have my pigeon back, I never believed I'd be back here, squashed among the holiday trinkets with Mister Lloyd in a basket on my lap. There were no sighs this time, no harrumphing, huffing or puffing, just the sound of the whistling wind breaking the silence: the soundtrack to a moment.

'Conditions are good,' I ventured after a while.

'Ay,' said Maldwyn, looking into the rear view mirror. 'So, what's it going to be? Single up method?'

I nodded abstractedly before turning to his reflection. 'As opposed to what?'

'Oh. Ay. Good point.'

We both burst out laughing. I opened the door.

'Urm, just one sec,' said Mam. She turned to Maldwyn and put her hand on his arm. 'Do you mind?'

Maldwyn stepped out of the car.

'I just wanted to say, Mostyn bach, that no matter what happens now, you did what you set out to do.' She cocked her head round the headrest. 'You found Mister Lloyd and now you can hold your head up high knowing that you were right. Yes, we fell out – Lordy Lord, you drove me up the wall with worry – but you were right and I'm proud of you.'

'Thank you,' I said. 'Have you taken some sorority vow, because you're beginning to sound like Bonnie La Brea.'

'Oh, give over,' she said with a laugh. 'Right, Mostyn bach, I suppose this is it.'

I nodded and opened the door, catching my mother's eye in the passenger mirror. 'No, this isn't just it. Something else good has happened. To you, Mam: Maldwyn.'

She smiled. 'You know, when I was at school, little bit older than you, maybe, Maldwyn was my first boyfriend. He used to walk me home every day but *never* by the top road.'

'But it's the quickest way home.'

'I know.' She turned to face me. 'I always thought it was because he was petrified of Taid, then he told me the other day he always preferred the long way home.'

'Why?'

'More time with me, he said.' She looked back into the mirror. 'Funny how life turns out.'

'Maybe sometimes you have to go the long way home,' I suggested.

'Could be,' she said, nodding, deep in thought.

'Bring your phone,' I said and stepped out of the car.

Maldwyn stood waiting by the boot. I took in the whole vista. Conditions were indeed perfect. If Mister Lloyd chose the right direction, he would be able to take advantage of the tail wind and reach home more or less unscathed.

'Right, let's go,' I said and gently put the basket down on the concreted runway.

'Don't you want to… urm, gather your thoughts?' asked Maldwyn.

'No thanks, Mal – done plenty of that.' I looked at the two of them and secretly pooled all my inner strength. I got down into a squat position and unfastened the buckles, slowly, so as not to alarm Mister Lloyd. 'Can you phone Taid, please, Mam?'

I cupped my hands, drawing my fingers together into a wedge, and began lifting the lid. I slid my hand in and rummaged around for Mister Lloyd, almost blindly, feeling the head and the fantail and taking him into my grasp.

'Taid,' said Mam. She had got through. 'Yes, we're ok. What's the weather like there? Champion, yes, it's lovely here too. Look Taid – what's that? The Rathbones are just about to set off? Ok, well we're just about to release Mister Lloyd and thought you'd like to know. Hello, are you there?' She put her hand over the mouthpiece. 'He's just saying goodbye to The Rathbones now. 'Oh, you're back?'

I pulled out Mister Lloyd and stood up straight.

'He's just getting to his feet,' said Mam into the mouthpiece. 'Mister Lloyd in both hands.'

Maldwyn tapped her on the shoulder. 'Paloma, he doesn't need a running commentary, just the time of liberation.'

Mam elbowed him. Back I went to Mister Lloyd. I closed my eyes. Yes, I knew the risk; yes, he could go one way or another; and, yes, Anne of Grey Gables was spoken for; but we would find him another mate in Graceland if he was to choose there. I tightened my grip on the bird, thinking if I held him for just five seconds longer, it would trigger happy memories. The will is crucial, Taid had said. In my head I was running down the Haymarket again, unsure if it was rage or sorrow I felt – maybe both. If Dad had stopped, what would I have done? If I could go back to one different moment by those railings, the outcome might not have been so brutal. Then, when I felt the calm bird stir in the grip of my hand, I realised, cruel as it was, that this here – now – and that there – then – is what had to happen. It was my fate. I lowered my arms and prepared to launch.

'Wait! Wait! Wait!' shouted Mam, quickly pressing buttons on her handset.

'What now, Paloma?' Maldwyn's hand was still poised at his wristwatch.

'A picture. We need a picture!' She put the phone to her ear. 'Dad? I'm putting you on hold. Maldwyn, stand over there!'

We both obliged and I held Mister Lloyd proudly to the camera with Maldwyn squaring himself up by my side.

The shutter clicked. 'Lovely! Both so handsome.'

'Right, ready?' enquired Maldwyn, back to his watch. 'Paloma, bring Taid back on.'

I kissed my bird on the top of its head, a small peck for the biggest risk of my life. 'Well, goodbye, Mister Percy Lloyd,' I said. 'Hope to see you on the other side.' And with a heavy heart I threw him up into the Windrush air.

'Remember me!'

I heard Mam convey the time of departure but my eyes were fixed on Mister Lloyd. Fantail out, legs in, he flapped around, chaotically at first, darting in all directions before coming down to land on my head. A few days ago I would have cheered, knowing he chose to cling on to me like this, but to bring him home via basket and car was an ending I did not want. With my hands over my head I took hold of the bird like a king giving up his crown and threw him back in the air. 'Please remember!' I shouted, watching him fly away, climbing higher until he got to an altitude where, I was hoping, his homing instinct would kick in. 'Where's the sun,' I mouthed as he hovered in the sky above, seeming to make a decision I could not read. He vanished behind his own dot in the sky.

'Come on,' said Maldwyn from behind. 'We'd better go, ay. If he flies back, he might see we're still here and not bother either way.'

I nodded. There was nothing to see.

'By the way, what day is this in your search?'

I'd stopped counting when we had found Mister Lloyd, thinking the search was over. I made the calculation in my head and delivered my result. 'Twenty-one.'

'Bang on,' he said, resting his hand on my shoulder and giving it a squeeze. 'Let's get in the car.'

On day one I had made a leap of faith. It had kept me going throughout my search for Mister Lloyd. But now, on our way home, that faith was wavering. Up there somewhere was the Mister Lloyd I knew and the Mister Lloyd I didn't know. On distance alone I was already defeated; Bangor was two hundred miles from Windrush and London only eighty. Hands down, London was the easier option but which one would he take, or had already taken, for that matter? As I stared through the window in the back of the car, I realised that, for me, this was going to be the longest of journeys.

Taid, still on the line as we set off from the runway, confirmed what I remembered. Mister Lloyd's last recorded flight from Windrush to Graceland had taken four hours and thirty-three minutes, making it an average of forty six miles an hour. 'Allowing for general rustiness,' he said, 'I'd hazard five and a half hours should do it, all being well.'

Yes, all being well, I thought, peering fixedly at the sky.

Bonnie guided us onto the M5 via Burford and Cheltenham, her sense of where she was going never faltering. Mam was regaling Maldwyn with recollections of the journey up, as and when we passed certain points on the way. She did her best to include me in the conversation with a 'do you remember' and a 'tell Maldwyn', but I wasn't much good, too attuned to a sense of movement all about me: the flow and contra-flow of cars on the motorway; the high-speed train running parallel to the carriageway, racing over and under bridges; birds shooting across the six lane highway (Mister Lloyd amongst them, I wondered) and darting helicopters across the Birmingham sky; aeroplanes taking off and landing; meetings and partings.

'Oh, there they are!' shouted Mam when we joined the A5 at Telford, startling me from my reverie.

'Who?' Maldwyn and I both asked.

'The Rathbones, of course,' Mam replied all excited. She opened the window to show a hand. 'Flash your lights, Maldwyn. Go on! Coo-eee!'

As if they could see her, I scoffed to myself, and yet when I wedged my head between the front seat, I saw an oncoming estate car flashing its headlamps and, just like Sir Bedivere's Lady of the Lake, Joy raising an arm for a lingering wave before disappearing around the roundabout behind us.

'Just the one wave,' said Mam with a satisfied push of the electric window button. 'That's all we wanted under the special circumstances. They're also rooting for you, by the way. Anyway, she and I are lunching in the West End when I'm next up in town. Time we had a catch-up.'

Her voice slowly dissolved into the rhythm of passing traffic. Supposing, I reasoned with myself, just supposing, Mister Lloyd's homing instinct had kicked in and he had made it confidently to Graceland in four hours and thirty-three minutes, I could not guarantee I would be there waiting. Road users were not as forgiving as open sky and we had already lost time getting back to the motorway through zig-zagging country lanes. After that there had been two hold-ups, followed by my queasy stomach forcing an unscheduled but urgent service-station stop. Of course, Taid would have called if there was any news but that didn't stop me from checking my signal and battery level obsessively, even texting Maldwyn – 'is that you again, Mostyn?' – just to make sure my phone was *definitely* working. With two hours still to go I looked out for familiar landmarks to track our progress, and with each notch of the journey another dose of adrenaline would pour forth, until at last we turned into our road and approached number 13. We were home.

The car was still rolling into its place in front of the garage when I unfastened my seatbelt and, before the engine was switched off, I was out and running into the backyard, scrambling up the garden path, ducking low branches and following the crazy, uneven steps to the Graceland gate.

Taid was in the doorway of Darwin HQ shaking his head.

For five and a half hours I had been yearning to get to this point, picturing the scene so differently, but here I was standing in front of Taid with the same grief-coloured cloud hanging over me. Back in Windrush the conditions had been perfect. Also here, back in Bangor. It was sure to be a glorious sunset over the Menai that evening, but what did it matter? Mister Lloyd wasn't home; I had lost him forever.

Mam and Maldwyn were getting out of the car. I looked all around me: at the shipping container, at the loft above and the aviary attached. I ran up the steps and entered the loft, just in case Taid had missed his arrival. No. Nothing. It had not worked. Lost, forever.

'Patience, Mostyn,' said Taid from down below.

'Patience?' I hurried my way towards him, bellowing. 'Patience? How much more patient can I be? I've been so patient they need to invent a new word for it! And look, I've nothing to show for it. No reward. Nothing!'

Taid rummaged uneasily in his holster.

'You told me I should let him go. I could have had him back right here, now, but I listened to you and I set him free. You tricked me, just because he was no more use to you as a racing pigeon.'

'Now steady on, my boy. That's not true!'

'Yes it is! You couldn't face telling me he should be put down and so you convinced me to let him go. Trying to be kind, was it? You knew he would find his way back to

309

London. I had him in my hands,' I was shouting, 'and now I've lost him forever! How could you do that to me?' I began to sob uncontrollably. I kicked at the shipping container, kicked at it with all my strength, kicked a loud hollow racket that pierced the whole of Graceland.

'Mostyn!' Taid called out, trying to pull me away. 'Will you please stop it? You'll frighten all the others.'

I turned to Taid and stopped, breathing hard. What did I think I was doing, upsetting the peace of Graceland, of all places? Borne away, Mister Lloyd had chosen elsewhere. It was over and I had to let it go. I heard Mam and Maldwyn's footsteps, rushing up the garden and calling to me. I turned to face the glorious sunset and, leaning against the warm corrugated metal of Darwin HQ, I let my back slide me down the red wall and collapsed in a heap on the ground.

'Mostyn.' Maldwyn squatted down next to me and pointed towards the sky. 'Look up!'

That evening I was alerted to a text message. We had been celebrating on the lawn overlooking the fine view when I heard the phone going. I saw it was Lowri and so I left the adults to their chatting and went to sit at the bottom of the stairs to read her message.

'So. Wot did he choose?'

What did she mean, 'What did he choose'? I hadn't told her anything about this afternoon, about Windrush or Mr Lloyd's big decision. Then it struck me. Of course. It made perfect sense. She was Elvis all along. I took in a deep breath and wrote back. 'He chose home!'

'Nice 1. Knew he wud. Soz. Wos only way I cud get thru to u. I <3 U! Can u 4giveme?'

EPILOGUE

It's morning, a few years later. We are running up to Graceland. I am holding Lowri's hand as we're in a bit of a rush. The glare of the sun sparkles through the trees. We are making our way to the top. I am wearing one of Taid's Savile Row suits that we have had altered for the big day – I look quite the dandy in it, even if I say so myself. Lowri is in one of Nain's vintage summer dresses that Mam had kept wrapped in the attic. 'Waiting for you,' Mam had said as we'd rummaged for it. We walk in to Graceland and the whole loft coos and flutters in rapture. It is a pity Taid isn't here to see us but I think he would approve and he will be with us in spirit, I know. Not that it is our big day, you understand, well... not yet. You see, Mam's getting married to Maldwyn and she has asked me to give her away. I was thrilled. My little sister, Blodwen, who is now six, is to be bridesmaid. Lowri will be on hand as well, of course.

She is laughing now. Lloyd Junior is messing up my newly combed hair, but I am too busy looking through Taid's old holster on the back of the door to care that much. It is where he kept them. The car is waiting.

'Here,' I said, handing Lowri one of Taid's pigeon print handkerchiefs. 'I think we're going to need these.'

Also available from Candy Jar Books

TOMMY PARKER: DESTINY WILL FIND YOU
by Anthony Ormond

When Tommy Parker packs his bag and goes to his grandpa's house for the summer he has no idea that his life is about to change forever.

But that's exactly what happens when his grandpa lets him in on a fantastic secret. He has a pen that lets him travel through his own memories and alter the past. Imagine that! Being able to travel into your own past and re-write your future.

Tommy Parker: Destiny Will Find You! is an exhilarating adventure that redefines the time travel genre.

You'll never look at your memories in quite the same way again...

ISBN: 978-0-9928607-1-4

Also available from Candy Jar Books

SPACE, TIME, MACHINE, MONSTER
by Mark Brake

Of the fifty biggest-selling movies of all time, most are sci-fi films. Ten million viewers tune in each week to watch Doctor Who. And in the ever-expanding world of computer games, sci-fi titles rule.

Yet our futuristic world was imagined long ago. Dreamt up in the minds of movie directors and classic sci-fi stories. And now it's the world we live in. How did THAT happen?! As space tourism becomes a reality and the first human to live to 1000 has already been born, it's about time you found out!

Jam-packed with aliens and time machines, spaceships and cyborgs and the end of time. *Space, Time, Machine, Monster* tells you how sci-fi helped build the world in which we live.

ISBN: 978-0-9928607-7-6